I0611900

Kaine's Retribution

Shattered Empire, Volume 2

D.M. Pruden

Published by D.M. Pruden, 2020.

ISBN: 978-1-989341-01-8

Print ISBN: 9781989341209

Free ebook offer

FREE EBOOK OFFER!

As a way of saying thank you for purchasing this novel, I want to offer you a free ebook.

To claim your free story please join my reader list by going to **https://www.prudenauthor.com/Kaine1-free-offer**

Exile

HAYDEN KAINE STARED at the blinking console lights and wondered how long he would live if the atmosphere vented.

Basic survival skills were taught at the academy, but aside from a few emergency evacuation drills, most of what he knew was anecdotal and theoretical. And over a decade old.

After all, how could someone know what to expect when a living body is exposed to the vacuum of space? Physics told him that his blood would boil, and if he held his breath, his lungs would explode, but had anyone tested it?

Academy drill sergeants spun gruesome tales to scare cadets with how horrible their deaths would be if they did not follow safety protocols. Though he acknowledged the wisdom of the teaching, he had no concept of what it would feel like to vent his air and end it all.

A perimeter alarm sounded, jerking him from his morbid thoughts. The tempting voice in the back of his head retreated like a coward when his mind was presented with a more immediate concern. He wondered if the time might come when it would not.

"Talk to me, Ship. What is going on?"

"Our angle of approach needs adjustment, Boss, if we don't want to bounce off the atmosphere."

He leaned forward to examine the readout. "Decrease by seven degrees."

"Your wish is my command."

Hayden pushed back into the pilot seat and tightened his restraints. For some reason, he never gave the AI a name. Not doing so was rude, but then the idea likely only bothered him.

Too many crazy ideas. Corralling them and keeping them under control was difficult. What he needed was a good stiff drink to settle down.

The tempting thought was quickly dismissed.

1

Remaining dry for twelve weeks and four days was a personal record; an accomplishment he realized he should feel proud of. Instead, he wondered why he still bothered with the effort.

Another, more urgent alarm sounded, accompanied by the smell of burning circuitry. The ship shuddered, setting off additional warnings.

"Piece of shit," he mumbled as he unbuckled. The salvage vessel had been old in his grandfather's time. Every major safety system was bypassed at least three different ways, and that was just by him. There was no way to tell how many other offspec repairs the previous owners had made just to keep the old bird flying. It was impossible simply to order new replacement parts anymore. People had to make do with what was at hand, or go without, and Hayden couldn't afford to lose his ship.

As he pushed himself to float toward the smoking panel in the back of the cockpit, he grabbed a fire extinguisher. After lowering the visor of his helmet, he opened the door and put out the flames.

"What failed this time?" he asked the AI.

"Fuel transfer control valve on the starboard side."

"That's kind of important. Bring up the specs on my HUD."

"Not to be alarmist or anything, Boss, but that little bump knocked us out of our approach window. We've got about two minutes to correct our course or be bounced into space. There's bingo fuel, so that could be a serious setback."

Hayden stuck his head inside the open panel to assess the damage. "It's the transfer relay again. Reroute the control signal through the manoeuvring thruster module, just like last time. I can put it back to normal as soon as we break atmosphere."

"You like dangerous living, don't you?"

"You didn't hide a spare FTCV in the hold that I'm not aware of?"

"Sorry, Boss, we're out of just about everything—unless you found something useful on that last wreck we visited?"

"Nope," he said as he strapped himself back into the pilot chair. "That sucker was picked clean by Derry and his crew."

"They do tend to make things more of a challenge these days."

The AI didn't appreciate how challenging. Since Derry's arrival, his merry band had already stripped every derelict Kaine found. Making enough to feed himself was becoming a concern.

"Tomorrow is another day," he said, more to himself.

After one last paranoid check of their entry vector, he settled back in his seat for the bumpy ride home.

At once, every alarm went haywire, and the panel covering his repair work exploded open in a spray of sparks. The ship jerked sharply to the left, and Hayden suddenly found himself pressed with more than his own weight against the restraining harness. He became dizzy and wanted to vomit.

The restraints dug into his shoulders. Out of the front window, the blue and tawny surface of Ricote spun dizzily across his field of vision.

"Ship..." Speaking was a struggle. He couldn't inhale a full breath. "What's going on?"

Shit!

Whatever happened took the AI out with it.

Outside, he saw flames lick off the hull. Sweat flowed freely from every pore of his body. His closed visor prevented him from wiping the stinging perspiration from his eyes. The rapidly rising cabin temperature would soon cook him in his spacesuit like a foil-wrapped potato.

In about one minute, maybe less—he'd lost track of time—the burning vessel would break up, and he wouldn't need to wonder what it felt like to die in the vacuum; he was about to be cremated.

There was only one bat-shit crazy thing he could think of, but he had to reach the thruster fuel control to make it happen.

Hayden reached his left arm back and looped what little slack there was in the restraining harness strap around it. Better to break that one, he thought.

As secure as he would ever be, he hit the buckle release.

Like a rat shaken by a dog, his legs shot out from under him toward the ceiling. Agony tore through his shoulder and elbow as the seat belt jerked.

Fighting the G-force, he grabbed the harness with his unrestrained hand. The torment to his injury was excruciating. He felt himself starting to pass out. Reflexively, he held his breath and squeezed his stomach, trying to force the blood back to his head.

As his vision cleared, he remembered his training and began the Hook Manoeuvre while he pulled himself down to the controls.

He anchored his feet under the console to relieve the stress on his injured arm. With his free hand, he tore off the panel access cover.

He was going to need a drink when this was over.

Surviving

THE LANDING THRUSTERS kicked up a cloud of fine dust around Hayden's ship.

While the whine of the engines spun down, he sat shivering in the pilot's seat and allowed his emotions to catch up to his body. He yanked off his vomit-baptized helmet and cast it aside. The soaked garment under his spacesuit stuck to his skin, and he was pretty sure he smelled of piss, too.

Never, in all his years of spacing, had he been so scared. Even when the Malliac almost destroyed *Scimitar*, the shared experience with his crew mates—with Stella—made it more endurable. With others sharing terror, it was as if hope was passed from one to another, so it was never entirely lost.

But this time he thought he would die alone, and it had frightened him to the bone. It was the most isolated he could recall ever feeling since Stella left.

Ten minutes later, he worked up the courage to try his shaky legs. After the first tentative steps to the rear of the cockpit, he studied the descent ladder with trepidation.

Getting down to the ground was the first challenge. The pain in his shoulder suggested it was dislocated, and he could barely bend his elbow. He considered jumping down, as he had done often in attempts to impress Stella. He could still hear her laugh.

"Don't come running to me when you break your foolish neck doing that," she'd say.

They both knew it was never a risk. Ricote's gravity was one-third of Earth's. Now, however, with his injured wing and jelly legs, he thought it might be a real possibility.

With a resigned sigh, he grasped the ladder railing with his good hand and descended from the ship.

He checked the barren landscape, concerned someone might see him kiss the dirt as he was tempted. In the end, he chose to hang on to the landing undercarriage until the quaking of his limbs stopped.

Inspecting the damage now was not what he wanted to do, but if he retreated to his house to immerse in some liquid courage, he might never again find the strength to approach the vessel.

Face your fear. Look it in the eye and tell it you cannot be beaten.

It was a hard-learned lesson, pounded into him as a child. His father and Iris, his surrogate mother, did not agree on many things about raising him. They were, however, united in not permitting him to indulge the temptation to accept failure and move on to easier things.

Kaines were made of sterner stuff.

Now, he was half a galaxy away from the destiny they intended for him. The empire he was groomed to lead was no more. Now, the only advantage to be gleaned from those lessons was the seed of courage to keep his ship running so he wouldn't starve to death.

Wincing, he forced his injured elbow to bend to access the data pad embedded in his sleeve. The postflight protocol came up, and he reviewed each item. As he inspected every listed component, the balm of routine settled his nerves.

When his first pass was completed and the damage tallied, he repeated the operation, locating several more problems. He couldn't recall ever being so focused on this task, but his lesson was learned. Taking things for granted had almost killed him.

Why did it take a disaster for him to learn anything?

His entire life was a series of calamities of his own making, culminating in his arrival in the Mu Arae system aboard the doomed ship, *Scimitar*. Human weakness and bad choices were the reasons for the loss of the women he loved.

Back on Earth, what seemed like a lifetime ago, he had betrayed Katie out of spite with a meaningless tryst. A different failing of his character drove Stella away.

"Hayden," she once told him, "your presumption that the end of civilization is your fault is...well, I can't live with someone who assumes the burden that should be carried only by a god. You're better than that vanity."

Although his drinking was the catalyst for her leaving, remorse had built the true barrier between them. She grew up fearing the Malliac would capture her. For her, crippling a civilization in the process of destroying the monsters was an inconvenient side effect. For Hayden—for trillions of others—the cure was worse than the disease.

There had been no real choice. Closing the FTL network was the only way to prevent the empire from being overrun. Limbs had to be amputated to save the patient.

He kept telling himself that during his intermittent attempts at sobriety. It didn't help.

The inspection completed, he retreated to his house for something to eat. Standing before the door, his heart pounded, as it did every time he came home; the naïve hope that this time, when he opened it, he would find Stella enjoying a cup of tea as if nothing had happened.

The dark, empty interior smelled like dust and rotting food. The power was out again. A hint of a smile crept across his face. Yet one more thing to repair; a new distraction. Between the aging battery unit and the repairs to his ship, he would be preoccupied for some time.

Over a can of cold beans, he sat at the table and reviewed the damage to his vessel. As each item came up, he referenced the listing of the stash of salvaged parts collected for just such a purpose. Calm returned as he realized he could repair most of the damage—with one notable exception.

The faulty FTCV that almost killed him was something for which he couldn't kluge a fix. He would need to find one, and they were as rare as a virginal conception.

The easiest solution was to buy one from Derry, but the son-of-a-whore wouldn't part with it for a fair price if word got out that Hayden was desperate to acquire it.

There was little chance that the fireball of his return that streaked across the sky went unnoticed in Katox. Any crash would draw Derry's scavengers out of the settlement to pick at the corpse of a downed ship. They would be disappointed when they made their way to where they believed he crashed. The sighting would be attributed to a meteorite that burned up.

If nobody suspected that had been his contrail, he might be able to fool Derry that his interest was casual. If so, there was a chance—a minuscule one—that he could purchase a few drinks and sweet-talk the man into a deal. All he needed was some hard currency.

Mu Arae was isolated long before the FTL network collapse made the condition permanent. Most commerce was done through barter. Since the destruction of the Malliac, people had abandoned their nomadic lives and settled in habitable environments around the system. Consequently, money was making a comeback. The new regional government didn't like to receive its tax revenue in the form of chickens and produce. Derry would only deal in currency. His warehouses were too full for him to be interested in trading for anything.

Hayden had burned through the last of his cash two months earlier. He considered tearing the place apart to see if he found loose change. If he did, it would only be enough to buy a bottle of barely drinkable hooch. Besides, he went through that exercise last week and didn't find anything, hence his current attempt at sobriety.

His only chance was to collect what was owed him by a few acquaintances. They would be at their usual watering hole. Putting the press on people that shared his situation was not his first choice, but that was the reason he made loans to them. He figured he could not buy booze on a whim if it was in other people's pockets.

Grabbing his coat, he started for the door before he remembered his ship was grounded. It was too late in the day to begin the long trek into Katox. He would leave early in the morning. The walk would do him good.

Rolling his shoulder, he hoped it was not dislocated. There had to be something in his old medical kit that would speed the healing process. A good night's sleep and some exercise wouldn't hurt either.

Time for a Drink

THE FLIMSY METAL DOOR clanked shut behind him. Even as his eyes adjusted to the dim lighting, the reek of vomit, piss, and spilled booze assaulted Hayden's nose. At another time, in another life, he would not risk being found dead in an establishment like this—if that was even the word for the place.

Shithole was the more accurate term for Molly's bar.

The only redeeming feature was that it was within stumbling distance of home—and the fact that they accepted his credit most of the time.

Moira, the proprietor, was the first to notice his entry. "Well, ain't you a sight? We all thought you was dead."

Hayden glanced at the familiar faces that interrupted their drinking to acknowledge him. They were the ones who didn't owe him money. The few who kept their heads down told him everything about the likelihood of getting paid today.

He removed his goggles and pulled the habiq from his head in a cascade of dust and sand. The burnoose-like hood was caked with the fine, wind-blown clay that coated everything on the godforsaken moon.

With a big grin, he sidled up to the bar. "You know how it is. Wherever I go, I bring joy. I've just been sharing it with other people lately."

"Kaine," she said, "you're so full of shit, your eyes should be brown."

They shared a laugh before he ordered his favourite drink. Returning, she placed it in front of him and fixed him with a no-nonsense gaze.

"So, where've you been? We heard rumours that some strange things are going on out there in the void. Ships and crews disappearing again..." she lowered her voice, "...like in the old days."

Ten years on, and people couldn't shake their fear.

"Are those stories circulating again? I didn't see a thing, and I spend more time out there than most of the clowns spreading rumours."

He punctuated his reply with a disarming smile. How could he tell her, or anyone, that he knew for a fact the invaders were all dead? It would mean admitting he was there when everything went to shit. They might even piece together that he was responsible for their isolation.

"I didn't hear anything. Been too busy scavenging wrecks."

She leaned forward; her grip still tight on his glass. "When will you be able to pay your tab?"

He offered up his best boyish grin. "After I find something worth selling."

Moira's expression remained hard.

"Soon," he said more soberly.

With an unconvinced grunt, she released her grasp and went to intervene in an argument before it devolved into a fight.

Sighing, he picked up his drink and downed half of it in one gulp. He couldn't blame her for her surliness. The locals were already living hand-to-mouth since before they had to hide from Malliac hunting parties.

A heavy-handed slap on the back roused him from his musings. "Hayden, my good man, can you spot a friend for a libation?"

A large, scruffy man sat down. His few remaining teeth were ochre, and his halitosis was almost overwhelming. Accumulated grime was ground in the skin of his huge hands. Judging by his stench, the man had not bathed in months.

"Malcolm," said Kaine, barely concealing his disgust. "I'm tapped out until you pay me for that last load of deck plating I delivered."

"Uh, yeah, about that..." Malcolm's ugly face contorted grotesquely in an unfamiliar attempt to appear contrite. "The bailiff confiscated everything. Told me some bullshit story about back taxes being owed..."

"He cleaned you out?"

"The entire warehouse."

"What about your cash?"

He shook his head. "They got everything."

"Can't you give me at least a portion? I need parts for my ship, or I'm grounded."

"Sorry, man."

Shaking his head, he looked about the bar at the other patrons. It was an all too familiar story. Since the collapse of the net and Mu Arae's isolation from the Confederacy, local attempts to reestablish governance had cropped up all over. Petty dictators vied to carve fiefdoms out of their former administrative districts. Most people circumvented taxation by resorting to barter. It had been an effective tactic. He took another sip and wondered what the situation was like in systems that had military assets when the network went down.

Ricote was one of three habitable moons and the remains of the former colony. With the planet Dulcinea destroyed, survivors had to choose between living under the dictates of petty local administrators or hiding amidst the wrecked starships and asteroids that littered the system.

Upon realizing he was not going to benefit from Hayden's charitable nature, Malcolm wandered off to try his luck elsewhere.

Hayden cursed under his breath. The only reason he was broke was because he spent too much money in places like this. Until recently, business had been good. With a little self-discipline over the past ten years, he would now be rich, or at least significantly better off.

He was not wired like that. The closest brush he ever came to being a responsible adult happened after graduation from the academy—and that had landed him here.

Maybe if Stella was still with him...

Scowling, he downed the last of his drink. The offensive hooch scorched a path down his throat.

Hayden fished in his pocket in search of something to pay for a refill. Moira's generosity went only so far. Finding nothing but sand, he smiled wryly.

Staying sober would not be a challenge; it would just make starving to death less bearable.

He needed to find cash. It was the only thing that would acquire the part to make his salvage ship space worthy again, not that it ever truly was.

His wandering eye caught sight of Derry getting drunk in the corner with his entourage. Indisputably the wealthiest scavenger in the sector, the man had a warehouse filled with enough parts to build two new ships, and he wouldn't deal with anyone whom he deemed competition. There was a finite number of wrecks left by the Malliac, most of which had already been located and stripped bare.

Hayden had proven himself an exceptional scavenger. With his intimate knowledge of starships, he was able to locate valuable small parts overlooked by others. His time helping Cora, the engineer aboard *Scimitar*, had taught him how to make the most out of every bit of hardware. Her preternatural skills had kept the out-of-date starship operational when other engineers would give up on it.

He lifted his empty glass to his mouth as he thought of her. There was no reason to believe she, Pavlovich, or any of the crew had survived the final battle with the aliens. Even if they had, *Scimitar* plunged into a black hole to disappear forever.

They were gone, and he was trapped in the asshole system of the empire. At least he was alive, a condition that would be under threat if he could not resume his new livelihood.

Waving his farewell to Moira, he strode toward the door.

"Oy, Kaine."

Wincing, he stopped and turned. "Hey, Derry, I see business is good."

"Me and my lads are celebrating. We found a pristine, excelsior-class courier ship hidden in the asteroid field; untouched. I'm feeling generous. Let me buy you a drink."

As Derry's booming laughter echoed about the bar, it was apparent that even inebriated, the man's generosity would not extend beyond an offer of cheap booze.

Even hammered, he would never be persuaded to make a deal for the needed part, no matter how onerous the terms Hayden might agree to. Another, more imaginative way was required. He joined the partying group and gratefully accepted the cup of grog presented to him.

As the evening wore on and his nemesis slurred his stories to drunken companions, an idea formed. And the beauty of it was that Derry would never realize how generous he was about to become.

How Low Can You Go?

HE DIDN'T NEED TO DO much. Just refrain from drinking.

Mustering all his self-discipline, Hayden accepted one drink then nursed it late into the night. The temptation to down it and grab another, and then several more, was almost overpowering. It felt like another person inside of him was trying to hijack his mind. Having listened to that voice far too often in his past, he was determined to stay the course.

For five hours, he pretended to listen to bawdy stories and insulting jibes from Derry and his entire crew. He was not the only one they treated poorly. Everyone who wished to be in their orbit endured it as the price of inclusion. Normally, his host didn't give Hayden the time of day; they had a visceral dislike for each other that went beyond being competitors. Today was different. He wanted to rub Hayden's nose in his success. Given the choice between scavenging for what he needed versus dealing with Derry, his preference would be the former.

But that option was unavailable.

Besides, if everything went according to plan, he wouldn't need to deal with the man at all.

As the group became heavily inebriated with the passage of time, he reflected on his own situation. There was a time that his honour meant something to him—when following a code of conduct came naturally. Yes, he got into a lot of trouble in his youth, but it had been harmless, immature fun, for the most part. He only ever broke rules; never laws.

What he planned tonight would disappoint Iris and enrage his father. His circumstances were different now. She was dead, and Walden Kaine was thousands of light years away.

He was on his own and desperate enough that he resisted the liquid temptation in his cup.

The party wound down as midnight approached. Derry and most of the others were passed out and snoring quietly. Only half a dozen remained on their feet.

Hayden slipped out unnoticed, and once outside, he checked his chronometer. He had a little more than an hour before Moira would rouse the sleeping drunks so she could close.

Setting off at a jog, he made his way to the warehouse. It was easy to find in the dark, being the most brightly lit structure on the outskirts of town.

Derry had acted carefree this evening, but he was no fool. One of his men did not attend the celebration, so Hayden had a good idea who was on guard duty.

His suspicions were proven correct when, lurking in the shadows, he spotted the fellow on his circuit. Observing for a few minutes told Hayden how long he had.

When all was clear, he dashed to the perimeter fence. His cutting laser took care of the simple lock and chain that held the gate closed. With one eye on the spot he expected the guard to approach, he scurried to the building. He wondered why Derry made things so easy. Perhaps it was because anyone who had interest in the contents of Derry's warehouse was known to him.

He realized how flawed his plan was—if it could even be called that. He was making things up as he went. It was crazy and stupid to be doing this. The frontier justice he faced if caught was understood. There was no constable in town, and no gaol, but the new graves of two would-be thieves made clear the potential consequences if he was discovered. Everything rode on his ability to quietly abscond with the part, repair his ship, and be off on a salvage mission before anyone suspected what was missing. It would take weeks to search for one specific item without knowing what to look for.

As he repeated the plan to himself, it sounded stupid, but he was already inside the door, so there was little point to backing out.

Perhaps he might come up with a less risky course of action if he was drunk. Inebriated and lazy, he would probably make an offer to Derry and hope he was intoxicated enough to accept a reasonable deal. But if Hayden revealed that he was grounded, the terms might not be anything he could live with, no matter how much booze the other man consumed. As things stood, nobody was aware of his need, so he hoped no one would suspect him of thievery.

He pulled out a small penlight and shone it around. The interior of the warehouse was enormous. Rows of neatly arranged shelves rose twenty metres to the ceiling.

He'd been in the building before and observed how Derry ran things. He was an organized businessman who knew the value of ensuring his inventory was easily located when someone wished to buy.

After a furtive check of the door, Hayden crept through the dark to where he knew his prize was kept.

A large, disorganized pile of salvaged components lay in the far corner—the recovered booty that had inspired Derry's generosity. It had been hurriedly dumped there so the rare opportunity to drink on their boss's coin could be enjoyed to the fullest. Nothing had been cleaned, and the stench of volatile fluids leaking to the floor filled Hayden's nostrils. If he had the time, he could try to find the required part in that mess. Derry would never realize it was missing, but it would take too long to locate, if one was even there.

Finding the FTCV on Derry's ordered shelves took little time. As he held his prize, Hayden found it difficult to believe that something so small could cause so much grief for him.

The squeaking hinges of the door stopped his blood cold.

Extinguishing his torch, he squatted and pressed against the shelf to listen. Furtive footfalls made their way toward him, and a beam of light pierced the darkness. For the moment, the shelving concealed him, but for how long, he didn't know.

His foolish plan was unravelling. He could make a dash for the door when the man went around a corner, but he would likely be seen. Even if his face was not identified, he was known well enough that it wouldn't take much speculation to put him on the list of suspects.

Hayden crept toward the door, staying pressed close to the shelves. Risking a peek, he saw the guard unlock an office door, and the enormity of his folly struck him like a blow to the head.

Derry had security cameras! There was no need for an elaborate alarm system. Anyone could be identified the minute they entered the door.

Shit!

Something clicked in his mind, and he brought his breathing under control. This was like one of the military exercises he'd participated in at the academy. The objective was clear. He needed to get into that office and destroy the security record before anyone had a chance to review it.

He shoved his contraband in a pocket and dashed across the open space. His only advantage now was his military training.

He peeked through the partially opened doorway. The watchman sat at a terminal, his back exposed.

Hayden wrapped his habiq around his head to conceal his face. Striking while his resolve was still strong, he burst through the door and charged. Before the man could turn, he was in a chokehold. The injury to Hayden's left elbow screamed, but he was running on adrenaline and pushed the pain back. Adjusting his grip to compensate for his damaged tendons, he applied pressure until the struggling man fell limp.

Searching the fellow, he found his belt and used it to bind his arms behind his back. He tied the habiq over the man's face in case he regained consciousness, then gently laid him on the floor.

Sitting at the terminal, he quickly determined the guard had not yet logged in. Hayden could tell at a glance that he was not going to be able to hack his way in.

Panic twisted his gut as he realized everything was going to hell. The only way he was going to prevent the security AI from identifying him was to destroy it. That was easier said than done. He was familiar with the computer system. Derry had salvaged it from a military wreck. The biocircuitry was protected by an impervious, carbon-fibre composite casing intended to withstand the vacuum of space. The design was an old one but effective enough to deny him access to the memory wafers.

He wracked his mind, trying to recall something about these computers he had learned in his military history classes. They had only been deployed for five years before a fatal flaw was discovered. While the casing could survive anything short of a nuclear explosion, the organically based circuitry was vulnerable to temperatures that fell far below that of atomics. All he had to do was heat the box to around six hundred degrees and the bio-gel inside and whatever was stored on it would be destroyed.

Hayden lifted the guard from the floor and hoisted him over his shoulder in a rescue carry. Outside the building, he laid the man on the ground then returned to the office.

Not wishing to waste precious time, he ripped the processing module out of its cradle, further aggravating his injured arm. After hauling the unit into the warehouse, he tossed it on the pile of salvaged parts.

Searching, he found the source of the previously discovered offensive smell. A viscous red gel dripped from one of the recovered engine components and had formed a two-metre-wide puddle. In a hurry to dump their prize and go drinking, Derry's men had left a convenient solution to Hayden's problem.

His laser cutting tool in hand, he knelt beside the pool. Extending his arm, he triggered it, and the red liquid exploded into a pillar of flame. Kaine staggered back, shielding his face from the intense heat that seemed to emerge from the depths of hell. Everything close ignited, and the blaze quickly spread. Within less than a minute, the inferno would engulf the rest of the structure.

On reaching the door, he risked a quick look back to watch a column of flames rise and lick at the ceiling.

He dragged the unconscious guard past the perimeter fence until the heat of the fire was no longer intense. After checking that the man still breathed, he removed the belt from his wrists and retrieved his habiq.

He wanted to try to wake him, to give him a chance to escape and call for help. Looking back at the conflagration, he decided it would soon draw a crowd and firefighters from the town. The guard would not be alone for long.

He fled into the night. The burning building would provide light for most of his way home.

An Offer You Can't Refuse

"SHIT!"

Warm blood trickled between his fingers as he applied pressure to staunch the flow from the reopened wound.

Hayden crawled out from under the belly of his ship. He squinted in the brilliant sunshine until his vision adjusted. It was already noon, and his repairs were no further along, despite rising before dawn.

His time was running out. Before long, Derry would put things together and conclude what Hayden had done.

His thoughts turned to that evening. He recalled looking back for an avenging angel on his heels as he ran home. Instead, all he saw was the glowing sky from the fire, like a giant flare pointing to his crime.

Normally, he only went to town as a lost measure to continue his miserable existence. Now, that was impossible. He had no choice but to flee and try to build a new life elsewhere. The alternative, remaining, only made it a matter of time before his guilt was discovered and Derry's men exacted revenge before putting him into a shallow grave.

He gingerly probed the injury. The cut was deep and would require more than a dirty bandage.

Shaking his head at his clumsiness and annoyed by yet another obstacle preventing his escape, he trudged through the blowing dust toward his hovel. An accident was inevitable, given the little sleep he'd gotten the previous seventy-two hours. The wind-driven grit stung as it clawed at his exposed face. The stinging sand seemed appropriate admonishment for his carelessness.

After wrapping a towel tightly around the wound, he hunted for his old medical kit, eventually locating it beneath a pile of neglected laundry. Without looking inside, he already knew he had no more synth-skin to dress it. He would need to go old-school and use staples.

He opened the battered metal box and surveyed his almost depleted supplies. The antiseptic was nearly gone, and he had nothing left to freeze his arm before beginning self-surgery.

Disappointed, he cast his eyes about the kitchen area. This was going to hurt like hell, and there was nothing available to dull the pain.

It was just as well. He needed to remain sober so he could quickly finish his repairs and get off-planet. Every minute he remained grounded was more time for Derry to finger him as a suspect.

He removed the bandage and cleaned the laceration as best he could, picking out sand grains that seemed to get everywhere on this damned moon. After applying the last of his antiseptic, he gritted his teeth and reached for the staple gun. The cure would hurt far worse than the injury.

Three staples later, he tossed the device back into the medical kit and packed it up.

He looked out through the abraded kitchen window at his grounded ship, and a sigh escaped. The replacement part was not an optimal substitute for his ship's damaged FTCV. Too many models removed from the defective one, he was forced to spend three days adapting his fuel flow system to accommodate the pilfered component.

Hayden's heart stopped when someone emerged from behind his ship.

The hooded figure stared back at him.

An improperly tied habiq, worn to protect from the elements, obscured the man's features. The abrasive, sand-laden wind whipped at the fabric covering his head and rattled off the windowpane.

A desperate glance at his useless ship confirmed that he was trapped.

Sighing, he reached into a storage compartment and pulled out his mauler pistol. A quick check of the outdated firearm reminded him that it was not recharged. It only had two bolts remaining. If the stranger had any companions, Hayden wouldn't be able to put up much of a fight.

He strapped the holster to his right thigh and looked out once more to reconsider his options. Upon deciding that none existed that didn't postpone the inevitable, or make matters considerably worse, he walked to the door.

The stranger's arms hung relaxed at his sides, but Hayden did not drop his guard. After donning sand goggles, he emerged slowly, hand resting loosely on his holstered mauler.

As the space between them closed, he realized how large the fellow was. He estimated the man was over two metres tall. The billowing garment he wore failed to obscure a well-muscled physique but revealed no weapon.

Grip tightened on the pistol, he continued until he stood a short distance from the man.

They stared at each other.

"State your business," Hayden called above the wind.

"You gonna use that thing?" the muffled voice said.

"Not unless you give me a reason."

In response, the stranger raised his empty hands. "I'm not armed. I'm just here to talk."

Hayden's hand remained on his still holstered gun. He shrugged. "So, say what you came to."

"Any chance we can get out of this wind?"

"You can start by telling me your name."

"You'll just forget it in a minute. Miles Derry sent me."

His heart jumped, and he squeezed the pistol grip tighter, resisting the urge to pull it out.

"What does he want?"

The man shook his head. "He didn't say, and I didn't ask. He asked me to bring you back to Katox."

Hayden tried to swallow past the dry lump in his throat. He followed the man's gaze to his left to see two men about thirty metres away, standing near a ground skimmer. None of them appeared armed, but the desert protection they all wore could easily conceal a weapon or two. Hayden's mind raced, and panic grew when he realized there was no way he could fight his way out of this.

"Who are your friends?"

"Just some mates I brought to check out a crash site."

"Did someone go down? I didn't hear anything."

"Somebody thought they saw a ship come in hot a couple of days ago, but we didn't find anything. Must've been a meteor."

"Yeah, probably."

The wind filled the silence that fell between them.

"So, what should I tell him?" the man asked.

"Who?"

"Derry. Are you going to come with me to see him?"

Confused about whether his paranoia was making decisions for him, he decided to test the opening the man just gave him.

"I'm sort of busy right now. Can I come in later to see him?"

The stranger shrugged and glanced back at Hayden's ship. The access hatch was open, and tools lay scattered about the ground. "That doesn't look like it can make it to town. I'll bring you back here when you're done."

Hayden studied the fellow. His posture was relaxed, hardly how he expected an enforcer's to be. A quick check of his companions suggested that they were bored and perhaps annoyed at having to stand out being sandblasted under the sun.

Even if they were a gang of goons with concealed weapons, Hayden's depleted mauler would be of little use against them all.

He released his grip on the pistol. "Lead the way."

A Lucky Break

AS HAYDEN ENTERED MOLLY'S, he spotted a familiar figure loitering at a table in the back. His pulse quickened when he recognized Derry. He seemed pensive, jaw clenched, and hands balled into fists on the table. They had not seen each other since the fire. His last memory of the man was of him passed out on a couch.

Did he guess? Hayden doubted the wisdom of coming. Before he could turn to walk away, he was spotted.

"Kaine, I'm glad you came. I hope I didn't take you from anything important?"

Caught off-guard by the casual manner, he hesitated. "Your man said you wanted to see me."

Derry's smile was awkward, as if it was something unfamiliar, and gestured for him to sit. "Um, you know I had a big fire at my warehouse?"

Hayden swallowed and tried to remain cool. "Yes, I heard about that. Sorry it happened to you."

"Oh, thanks..."

"Was anyone hurt?" Hayden's stomach tied itself into knots. He had not waited around to see if someone helped the security guard.

"My man was on duty, but somebody pulled him out of the building."

Hayden released his held breath. "Did he say what happened?"

"No, he took a bump to the head and can't remember much of anything."

He allowed himself to relax a little. "What is it you wanted to speak with me about?"

"I'm in a pickle, Kaine, and there aren't many I can turn to. I don't easily make friends, you included, I suppose..."

Hayden didn't drop his guard, and he remained alert to any surprise as he coaxed Derry to continue.

"Here's my situation...everything I owned went up in that fire. Not too many people are privy to this."

"Why are you telling me? Aren't you afraid I'm gonna blab about it?"

Derry chuckled. "Everyone thinks you're a decent guy."

The words hit him like a blow to the face. The man had no clue what Hayden had done to him. Derry interpreted his silence as modesty, because he continued.

"Kaine, I owe people. They're not very nice people either..."

He shook his head. "I'm sorry, Miles, I'm broke, otherwise I'd lend you the money." The lie came to his lips far too easily.

"No, no, you don't understand. I don't want that. I want to hire you."

"What?"

"Yeah, you see not only did my inventory go, but all the cash that I had on hand too. I can't pay any of my boys, and none of them are too keen on working on commission. I hoped I could persuade you to help me out?"

"What kind of arrangement are you thinking about?"

"Nothing too complicated. I just want you to, maybe, enter into a contract with me. We can agree to partner up for the next few weeks. You're a damn good salvage monkey, Kaine. One of the best around here...well, aside from me." He chuckled.

"I'm listening."

"My ship is grounded because my fuel cells went up in the fire. I need a helping hand here, and I'm hoping you can give a buddy some help."

Never in his wildest imaginings had he considered that term to describe their relationship. If anything, Derry always treated Hayden with contempt, always making any tightwad offer sound generous beyond reason.

For years, he'd fantasized about putting this man in his place. He was too full of himself and always extracted the last possible drop of profit from anyone he dealt with.

Yet here he was, small and humbled, practically begging for help from the man who had put him in his predicament. He honestly believed that his magnanimous nature was motivation enough for Hayden to jump at the opportunity rather than laugh and walk away.

All he could think of were flames reaching like a beacon to the sky. He swallowed hard. "What kind of arrangement are you talking about?"

"Well, if you could go out to salvage on my behalf, I'll split the profit on everything you bring in, 50-50."

"How is that good for me? Right now, anything I find is 100% mine."

"Yeah, that's not the whole deal. Let me finish?"

Hayden nodded.

"I need to start over, and to do that I require inventory. My ships are grounded until I can replace the fuel cells I lost. If you give me a helping hand, I'll give you 50% of everything that I find once I'm back up and running, up to twice the amount of that you spot me."

Hayden studied him for any sign he was being played, unfortunately seeing a lot. For Derry, the terms were generous beyond precedent, which was a problem. They were unbelievable coming from a man who would lease his dead grandmother's grave.

His first inclination was to tell him to go to hell. The man had never given any slack to him when he went to him during his own bad times. Now, here he was, practically begging for a handout. He had balls.

Hayden did not give the consequences of the fire any serious consideration. Only now did he realize he had the only operating salvage ship in the region. It made perfect sense for Miles Derry to suspect him of having something to do with his misfortune. Instead, he was now offered an unprecedented opportunity.

Guilt gnawed at him. If not for what he did, Derry's people would still be collecting pay, and their families would still be able to eat. For the past few days, everyone had been scraping by, but there were no guarantees things would improve. In one breathtakingly selfish act, to keep his crime undetected, he had almost destroyed the economy of an entire town.

What would happen if he turned down the offer? How would things change? People could starve, and Katox would die. Only Hayden's pride would benefit from rejecting it.

Once again, because of him, everyone's life was worse.

Despite how much he disliked the man who sat across from him, this was a chance to right a wrong.

He couldn't repair the damage he had done to the empire. That was impossible. But here and now, he saw an opportunity to do something else to undo something he'd caused. How could he refuse?

After they shook hands over the arrangement, Hayden moved to the bar and ordered a drink.

He marvelled at his good fortune, first at not being suspected of starting the fire, and second for being the recipient of Derry's uncharacteristic generosity.

Good things simply did not happen. What was drilled in him since childhood and confirmed by experience was that the cosmos did not play favourites. Everyone was the author of their own destiny.

And yet...

His thoughts turned to his old ship, *Scimitar*. The crew had valiantly confronted insurmountable odds and were destroyed, the nobility of their cause not considered. He, however, singlehandedly set off the explosion that shut down the interstellar jump gate network, plunging civilization into a dark age. By some bizarre twist of fate, he had survived, despite the magnitude of his sin. It was all being repeated now on a smaller scale.

It seemed that there was no balance; no rhyme or reason to events, good or bad. It was all random. Despite the destruction he continually seemed to precipitate, Hayden Kaine battled on. Maybe living to see the damage he authored was the retribution demanded by the universe.

Maybe the only noble thing he could do was fix his ship and leave the system forever before he cost any more lives with his selfish decisions.

Maybe no matter what he did, shit would happen. Deep down, he hoped that might be the case.

For the moment, fortune appeared to favour him, negating the necessity of any guilt-driven temptation to cast himself into exile.

This place was where fate had conspired to place him, as part of his punishment.

He downed his drink.

It was best not to try to take on destiny. It was time for him to finish his repairs and take the path set before him.

Nothing Changes

TWO LOUSY DAYS WAS all it took for Derry to show his true colours.

Hayden stood before the table in the bar from which Miles ran his business.

"This isn't even a tenth of what that load is worth," he said, waving the credit voucher in Derry's face.

"My expenses won't pay for themselves, Kaine. You didn't expect me to eat those costs, did you?"

"You're going to do this?"

Derry put down his paperwork and stretched like an annoyed cat whose nap was disturbed. "Hayden, I truly appreciate your willingness to help me out," he said, an oily smile on his mug. "But after speaking to you, some of my creditors came to me, and we arrived at a mutually beneficial arrangement. I am solvent once again."

"So now that there is some cash in your pocket, you're going to back on our deal?"

"What are you talking about?" His attempt to appear surprised was unconvincing.

"We shook hands on it..."

"No, I can't recall anything like that happening between us. Can you show me the paperwork?"

"What?"

"I never go into a business arrangement without a written contract. Our discussion was a proposal. We agreed to consider terms, but we never entered into a binding agreement."

"You son of a bitch." He moved forward, intending to reach across the table. Two previously unnoticed burly associates sitting at adjacent tables stood, scowling. He raised his hands and stepped back.

Ignoring Hayden's intended assault, Derry said, "I included an extra few percent on the payment in consideration of your willingness to assist me in my time of need." A smug smile grew, exposing crooked yellow teeth.

Hayden glanced at the bodyguards, then back. Unable to think of anything to say that would adequately express his disgust, he exhaled, crumpled up the voucher, and threw it in Derry's face.

"I want it all back."

"What are you talking about?"

"The salvage I brought in. The deal is off, and I'm not selling to you. I want it all loaded back on my ship."

He raised an eyebrow. "All transactions are final, Kaine. If there is nothing else, I'm very busy."

His goons stepped forward.

"Next time I hope someone burns your business down with you in the building."

He regretted the words the moment he said them.

Derry frowned. "My investigators tell me that the fire was deliberate. You don't know anything about that, do you, Kaine?"

Hayden couldn't tell if he was bullshitting, but the air in the bar suddenly became thin.

"Until this moment, Miles, I had no motivation to wish you harm."

He let the threat hang and stormed from the tavern.

After marching a hundred metres, he turned to look back at the empty street. Prying open his hands; he saw where his nails had dug into the flesh.

He couldn't believe he had been so naïve. His guilt had blinded him to something experience tried to warn him about. All he wanted to do was storm back inside and bounce Derry's skull off the tabletop.

He wondered if it was a universal truth that no mistake could ever be rectified. If not, then under what conditions was it possible? Maybe his humiliation was justice; retribution for his past sin. Perhaps there would be a way to make it up to a more reasonable person. That word did not apply to Derry, nor did he dwell on his losses. He moved on, never missing a stride. Only fools like Hayden believed everyone bled the same way he did.

He looked at the dusty faces of the crumbling buildings; the dirt path that passed for a street. Most of the people in Katox dressed in worn rags.

The entire star system was cut off from its lifeblood. It had always been a colony, dependent on support from the Confederacy. When it became isolated, it began to die like a limb deprived of blood flow. It was only a matter of time before everything would descend into postapocalyptic chaos.

These people were abandoned and forgotten, with no means to rise above their condition. No supplies would ever arrive to replace the worn equipment. No expertise would come to build up industry or educate. This society would degenerate into minor fiefdoms ruled by petty lords like Miles Derry. People like him were the only ones who would find a way to prosper from the situation.

How many other places in the once vast empire faced the same thing, or worse?

Perhaps it was ill-spent effort attempting to make amends for the harm he'd caused, but that didn't mean it was wrong to try.

Derry's implied threat gnawed at him. Did he suspect? Was he biding his time, gathering enough evidence that there would be no outcry when one of his goons blew a hole in the back of Hayden's skull?

He did not intend to wait to find out.

There was no more debating. It was time to get off this dust bowl.

Escape

HAYDEN FIRED THE MANOEUVRING thrusters prematurely, sending his ship into an unintended spin.

Cursing, he halted his rotation and slowed the ship's drift before it could slam into the side of the derelict. He paused to collect himself. His thoughts drifted to what he recalled of the previous week. Shutting his eyes against the throbbing in his head, he reconsidered the wisdom of his plan. His hare-brained idea had seemed much simpler and brilliant under the influence of alcohol.

He'd decided he would build a relativistic drive and set off to the nearest inhabited star system. He didn't know what he might find, but it had to be better than here.

Some plan, he thought. It had sounded far more sensible when he was drunk.

Most still-operational ships were converted drop shuttles or short-range transit vessels. None of them had the drives to push a ship to near the speed of light. That was largely because there was nowhere to go within ten light years, but mostly because hardly anyone knew anything about maintaining them.

With his academy training, and more so from his time spent helping Cora repair *Scimitar*, Hayden was one of the few who could pass for an expert in the technology.

The result of it all was that nobody found much value in the components or nuclear fuel for the near light-speed engines, so they generally were ignored by salvagers.

This was the fourth ship visited since leaving Katox...or was it the fifth? Sixth?

The others were pretty much picked clean, yielding only a quarter of the parts to make his stupid idea work. The one he now floated in front of was his last chance to find anything. If it proved empty, his only recourse was to set out for deep space to look for undiscovered wrecks.

If he were honest with himself, he was still hung over and should be nowhere near the helm of a ship. But self-assessment was not his strength. He needed to work, even if it was toward a ridiculous goal. Besides, he found it far easier to face the morning-after than the demons that hounded him.

Closing his eyes, he sat back and inhaled. When he opened them, he held a nearly empty bottle of cheap rum. Incredulous, he couldn't recall retrieving it from his jacket. He shoved it back in his pocket. "Pull yourself together, Kaine."

For almost a standard year, he drank almost nothing but tea. Sure, he bought the odd drink at Moira's but always marshalled his will to keep his consumption to respectable social drinking. Two at the most; no getting blind drunk. It was not easy. The emergency stash always lurked in the back of his mind when things got tough.

Things always seemed that way since Stella left.

He stared stupidly at the burned-out hulk drifting in front of him. Without thinking, he pulled out the rum and drained the contents.

Immediately disgusted by his weakness, he hurled the emptied bottle to the back of his ship and heard it shatter against a bulkhead. Shards of broken glass drifted, weightless, about the cabin. They would remind him of his impulsive stupidity for days to come.

Perhaps it was a good thing he was out of booze. Drinking himself to oblivion out in the deep of space would not end well.

A flashing light on his console attracted his attention. A faint radiation signature registered from somewhere inside the wreck.

He smiled at his good fortune and played his searchlights across the scarred derelict in the hope he might locate an undamaged docking port.

Finding one, he manoeuvred his vessel into position and slowly approached until the hatches were aligned. Since the freighter had no power, it couldn't deploy locking clamps. Hayden activated his own magnetic seals and felt a brief shake as the two vessels came into contact.

Donning his EVA suit, he opened his hatch to reveal the carbon-scored exterior of his newly claimed salvage. Five minutes later, his cutting laser breached the door, and he stood inside its airlock.

Prying open the interior door, there was no indication of pressure on the other side. Entering the corridor, his magnetic boots snapped to the deck. He shone his light about to assess his situation.

Like every other ship scavenged over the previous ten years, this one was littered with floating debris. Occasionally, he came across the remains of a crewman who wasn't sucked out into the void when the hull was breached.

This time, some of the bodies wore pressure suits and showed clear damage from energy weapons. The poor bastards had tried to defend themselves. Hayden knew far too well how futile that effort was. In his experience, even seasoned rangers were no match for the Malliac.

Locating the engineering section took him little time. Within forty minutes, he retrieved his prize. As he herded the weightless canisters back, his earpiece crackled with static, and he froze in place.

"Ship, did you just try to contact me?" He shook his head, reminding himself he should give the AI a name.

"Negative, sir."

Sir? What the hell is going on?

"Check the proximity sensor logs. Is there anyone nearby?" It was the only reason he could think of for a random burst on a private channel.

"Yes."

"Is it Malliac?"

"No, but it docked with this wreck twenty minutes ago."

"What? Why didn't you alert me?"

A sickening silence was the response.

"Ship? Answer me. Are you still there?"

Cautiously, he magnetically secured his toolkit and reached for the mauler pistol at his thigh. His heart skipped a beat at the realization the gun was aboard his vessel.

Idiot!

He retrieved the cutting torch from the toolbox. It was a shitty substitute and would only be of use at close quarters but was better than nothing. It was not uncommon for pirates to leave salvagers stranded when they stole their ships; that was, of course, if they didn't kill them.

Switching off his mag-boots, he floated above the deck for a moment to orient himself. Hand over hand, he guided himself along the wall.

Halting at the last junction, he shut off his helmet lights. One by one, he deployed three marble-sized surveillance modules in the direction of the derelict's breached hull. Instantly, three separate views from around the corner came up on his HUD as the units floated past the only access to his ship.

The cutaway opening glowed faintly from the dim light of his ship's airlock. He switched to the infrared band and stared anxiously at the passing scene. None of the cameras showed anything. He had no idea how many pirates were aboard.

Hayden tried to swallow past his dry throat. His comm link dead, the rapid swish-bump of his pulse filled his ears. With no other choice available, he gripped the cutting torch and pushed himself forward. Gracefully bounding from the walls, he arrived at the opening.

After a moment to slow his breathing and bolster his flagging courage, he pulled himself in.

Now, he was faced with two risky courses of action. He could pressurize the airlock, making enough noise to alert whomever was inside. There was an incredibly small chance he might be able to strike a deal with them.

Or he could leave the outer door open and blow the inner one. Explosive decompression might do all the work for him.

If, as he suspected was the case, the pirates had kept their EVA suits on, the tactic might only buy him brief seconds of advantage.

Before he understood what happened, the decision was made for him. The panel on the wall lit up. Either they were on to him, or else they planned to leave and were in for a shock.

Eyes glued to the door, he raised the cutting torch and held his finger over the activator, prepared to charge the opening. Timing his rush, he pushed off toward it. Too late, he realized it had only opened a few centimetres before stopping. He rebounded off the door, and the cutter flew from his hand.

Twisting in the zero gravity, he contorted himself in a hopeless effort to recover his lost weapon.

His element of surprise spent; he was completely vulnerable. The hatch resumed opening, revealing the interior of the cabin. He only caught a glimpse of one of the pirates, a big man seated at the ship's control console.

A familiar voice came over his helmet speaker, sending a chill down his spine.

"Welcome aboard, Mister Kaine."

Ghosts

"PAVLOVICH?"

Hayden grabbed at the bulkhead to stop his weightless rotation.

He stared, incredulous, at the ghost in the pilot's chair.

Behind his helmet's visor smiled the weathered face of a man in his mid-fifties, with a wild, grey-flecked black beard. Deep brown eyes shone beneath bushy eyebrows.

Open-mouthed, Hayden could not take his eyes from the giant of a man. At two metres, Pavlovich's presence dominated the cramped ship.

"Holy shit, you're alive."

"Astute as always, Kaine." Pavlovich waited for Hayden to enter before he threw a switch on the console to close the door and begin pressurizing the cabin.

"Wha...what...how?"

"Take it easy, you're not going crazy."

Hayden's former captain released the seat harness and floated toward him; right hand extended in greeting.

Still stunned, he stared at it to assure himself his mind wasn't playing tricks on him. Then he pushed the arm aside and embraced the big man.

Pavlovich awkwardly patted him on the back. "Yeah, I'm here, and glad to see you too."

Assured he didn't hallucinate; he disengaged and removed his helmet. As his wits returned, he studied the face of a man he long believed dead.

"What are you doing here?"

"Looking for you, dummy. We tracked you here, but when you didn't answer, I drew the short straw to check out your ship to see if you were okay."

As Hayden shook off the last of his disorientation, the meaning of the words registered.

"We? You're not alone?"

"Hell, no. The others are scouring the wreck for you as we speak."

In an abrupt change of topic, Pavlovich pointed to the console. Half of it was torn apart, and components dangled from jerry-rigged wires like an unruly shrubbery. "I can't believe you risked your life in this poor excuse for a ship."

"What the hell did you do?"

"Your AI was not very helpful in telling me where to find you."

"That was you screwing around with it?"

"Yeah, I think it might be broken."

Hayden regarded the destroyed helm panel. He frowned at Pavlovich.

"It was an outdated model, anyway, Kaine. Cora would be seriously pissed at you for risking your life in this thing."

"She's alive? How is she?"

"There is a lot to explain. Why don't you come to *Scimitar* and find out for yourself?"

"It was destroyed. How...?"

Pavlovich chuckled. "What the hell do you think brought me here?"

"No idea. I'm not entirely sure I'm not crazy."

"Well, come to the ship and give me a chance to prove that you're as sane as I am."

Hayden smiled. "I always doubted that."

"Hardy-har." The big man retrieved his helmet from the console. "Are you coming or not?"

"What do you think?" Hayden said as he grabbed his own.

When the doors to the airlock opened, Hayden's mouth dropped open and his feet refused to move. He blinked and shook his head.

"Is that the *Scimitar*?" he asked, not taking his eyes off it.

Pavlovich puffed his chest and smiled proudly. "The one and only."

"How? She was derelict, gutted by fire, her reactor damaged beyond repair. She exploded! How is this possible?"

"Did you see her blow up, Kaine?"

Hayden tried to recall the details of the last seconds of the ship, recorded and watched by him a thousand times. He'd relived the memory twice as often, vividly recalling the scream of his ship's engines almost burning out to push him away from the black hole that had its grips on the wreck of *Scimitar*. His last glimpse of the doomed vessel was of it vanishing in a flash.

Pavlovich gently rested a hand on his shoulder. "It's a long story. Why don't you come inside? I promise to explain everything."

Kaine nodded and allowed himself to be led through the hatchway. From within the airlock, he peered into the interior of the battlecruiser but made no move to enter.

"What's the matter?" said Pavlovich. "There are no ghosts here."

Smiling at his own foolishness, Hayden stepped onto the deck. Pausing just inside, he surveyed the familiar corridors. "She doesn't smell any better," he said with a wink.

The captain sneered. "I'm having difficulty finding good cleaning staff."

Their trade in barbs was interrupted by a voice over the speakers. "Is that you, Lieutenant?"

"Cora? It's so good to hear you."

"I was so excited when the cap'n said we were coming to find you."

"Are you ready to see Kaine again?" asked Pavlovich.

"Umm, sure. That would be great."

"We'll meet you in the briefing room in a few minutes."

"Not using your quarters for meetings any longer?" said Hayden. "That's different."

"Yeah, well, some things didn't fit in my old cabin. C'mon, let's not keep her waiting."

He followed Pavlovich down the corridor. "Is something wrong with her? She didn't sound like herself."

"The last few years changed us a lot—some of us more than others. Cora's not quite the same girl you knew."

Kaine stopped walking. "What's happened?"

"I should let her explain."

"Why are you so evasive? Who else is on this ship?"

Pavlovich sighed. "Of the original crew, only me, Cora, and Gunney. The rest aboard are strays we picked up along the way."

"Only the three of you? Shit."

"Yeah, well, we all knew the risks when we joined the service." The captain extended his hand to indicate they should continue walking.

As they entered the next section, Hayden became confused about where they were going. "This part of the ship is different."

"Necessary modifications." Pavlovich directed him to an open doorway.

Skeptical, Hayden eyed him for a moment before proceeding inside.

The briefing room was a large chamber that encompassed three decks. A holographic star map floated above a circular conference table in the centre of the room. Embedded in its middle was a translucent white hemisphere, pulsing with energy from within.

He whistled and nodded approval. "This is very impressive, Captain."

Pavlovich smiled and invited him to sit. Placing his helmet and gloves on the table, Hayden took a seat.

"What's going on? None of this is standard tech."

The white semisphere pulsed with light as Cora's voice filled the room. "No, it isn't."

He searched about the room before his eyes settled on the object. "Cora?"

"Yes, it's me."

"What the...?" He stared, wide-eyed, at Pavlovich.

"She was injured in the battle. When our jump reactor overloaded as we fell across the black hole's event horizon, the ship jumped..." He shook his head. "Well, we're still not sure where we ended up, but we were lost. *Scimitar* was damaged beyond repair. Gravity was out, life support failing, and we had hull breaches on half the decks. Almost everyone was dead, and Cora was in bad shape when I found her in what was left of the engineering deck."

"What happened? How did...?" He gestured toward the sphere.

"The Glenatat robot was the only still functioning tech. She and it were quite close, as you know. I think the damned thing was actually in love with her—"

"My body couldn't be repaired," she said, sounding annoyed, "so Alcon came up with a plan to save me."

"I underestimated it. The Glenatat gave it to us to do more than help fight the Malliac. It modified our surviving systems to keep us alive. Then, somehow, it got us to a habitable planet—don't ask me where, because I still haven't figured that out. Anyway, the machine used the planet's resources to repair *Scimitar* and keep Cora from dying."

"Alcon constructed and transferred me into this." The half globe flashed briefly.

"What...what is it? What did it transfer? Your brain?"

"No, he melded my personality, my knowledge—my essence, you might say, with...I suppose it's best described as a bio-computer."

"It copied you into a machine?"

"No, Alcon modified himself to join with me—oh, Hayden, this is so hard to describe. After a decade, I still can't find the right words, but it is beyond anything human experience can appreciate."

"She exists throughout the ship," said Pavlovich. "She's a part of *Scimitar*."

Tears ran down Hayden's cheeks. "Oh, Cora, I did this to you. I'm so, so very sorry—"

"Oh, you did nothing of the kind. Stop that right now. I'm not here against my wishes. I chose this."

Hayden wiped his face and turned to his former captain. "What else?"

Pavlovich grinned. "The robot revealed a lot of Glenatat technology to us. We were forced to build everything from scratch, though. It took time, but between Cora and Alcon, we came up with a way to rebuild our engines. We are the only ship in human space with faster-than-light capability."

"You restored the network?"

"Hell, no, nothing that extensive. We got access to designs for discarded old Glenatat tech; one of their first prototypes for a literal FTL drive. It is their equivalent of the steam engine, but it works, Kaine. We used it to come back here."

Hayden reappraised the evidence of the alien technology around him and emitted a low whistle.

"We can restore interstellar travel to the human race and become richer than Croesus in the process," said Pavlovich, still grinning. "We've just a few little difficulties to overcome."

"Such as?"

"The journey back nearly exhausted our fuel. The stuff is kind of hard to find, and it took us most of the last ten years to gather enough for the trip."

"What is it?"

"The shit is refined from a rare mineral the Glenatat call erganium."

"How scarce are we talking?"

"They abandoned the technology for something better as soon as they could. We estimate it is only present in one percent of terrestrial bodies orbiting F3V class stars," said Cora.

"That's pretty specific."

"You don't appreciate the half of it," said the captain. "We've compiled a short list of prospective Confederation planets and moons that could contain it in their crusts."

"This is all very interesting," said Hayden, "but I don't understand why you're here. Is there erganium here at Mu Arae?"

"Unfortunately, no."

"Then I'm confused. If you could go anywhere, why did you return to this shit hole?"

A wry smile snuck out from beneath the big man's beard. He turned to the woman who emerged from the shadows.

"Stella?"

She smiled coyly. "Hello, Hayden."

His mouth suddenly went dry, and the small room seemed to contract. Part of him wanted to run from the ship, but he couldn't move. Realizing he held his breath; he inhaled and made a pathetic attempt to return her smile.

"I found her before I came looking for you," said Pavlovich. "I asked her to join our merry band, and she accepted."

Frowning, she said, "Conditionally."

Grateful for the distraction from the awkwardness, Hayden said, "What is this all about?"

"Well, it turns out there are more Malliac floating about the galaxy—a lot of them. We encountered a few scouts in our travels, and after a couple of harrowing escapes, we determined that an early warning system would be in order."

"So you need Stella to keep them off your ass?"

"Yes, but there are many ways an empath can come in handy."

"Like what?"

"Did I mention wealth? Do you realize what offering access to FTL tech can be worth? The planets of the Confederation are cut off from each other."

Hayden turned to her. "You agreed to this?"

"Look, Kaine, I think you figured out that one of Stella's conditions is that we bring you along."

She blushed when Hayden fixed her with his gaze.

"I understand that my reasons for coming to you seem shallow and selfish, but hear me out," said Pavlovich.

"I'm listening."

"I need this talented young woman to make this venture happen. It turns out, I now need you too—no offence intended."

"None taken."

"This can work out to your benefit in several ways. First, I know about you beating yourself up over the collapse of civilization."

Hayden glared at Stella as Pavlovich continued.

"Well, just imagine the possibility for this tech to restore the Confederacy; maybe reshape it into something better. Sure, you can elect to take it on the chin as the one who brought everything down but consider the opportunity to rebuild it all. You could go home to Earth a very wealthy man and herald in a new age for humanity."

Hayden's frown deepened, and his gaze darted between the two of them. Stella appeared uncomfortable.

Unable to find the words, he rose, grabbed his gloves and helmet, and stormed from the room.

Explanations

HAYDEN WAS ABOARD HIS ship and preparing to depart, to where, he had no idea. It had taken him three hours to repair the damage Pavlovich did to the console.

Pavlovich's voice came over the comm. "Kaine, let me in. There's more to explain!"

He stared at the closed hatch and considered his options. With a heavy sigh, he admitted the captain into the airlock and waited for it to pressurize.

The inner door opened, and Pavlovich stepped through, his helmet already removed.

"I am instructed to persuade you to stay."

"Instructed?"

He rolled his eyes. "All right, they threatened to all walk out on me unless you join the party."

"I don't believe you. Stella, maybe..."

"She and Cora are the ringleaders of this mutiny. They convinced most of the crew it is in their interest if you come along."

Wary, Hayden said, "Gunney too?"

"Yes, even that grumpy old cyborg is in on it. You made a deep impression on him. He mumbled something about you being the best XO he ever worked with. Don't tell him I told you that, by the way."

"I thought your crew was new?"

"Look, Kaine. Stella is out if you're out. Cora is threatening to pull out too, though I can't imagine how she can accomplish that trick. With them offline, everyone else is second-guessing things."

"Tell 'em the truth; I'm bad news. I'll get them killed."

Pavlovich stared at him intently, frowning. "Is that what this is about?"

Hayden tried to reply, but the captain raised a hand to silence him. "Yeah, your girl told us everything that's been going on; your attempt to pickle your liver for a decade out of some sense of guilt."

Hayden's face warmed.

"Kaine, if you don't join the party, all of their lives are as good as over. Stella will stay with you in this godforsaken system out of some misguided belief that she can save you from yourself another way. Cora will retreat into her little VR world and may never come out. Yeah, Gunney and the others will come along, but our chances of making this work, let alone survive while trying, are next to nil. Do you want all of that on your conscience too?"

"Don't do that—"

"Hayden, what we did saved trillions of lives. Don't you get it? You're a friggin' hero. Sure, if we had enough time, we might've found another way to shut out the Malliac without collapsing the transit net. What you don't realize is that the Confederation was on the brink of a civil war. We stopped that."

"What are you talking about?"

"Did you think that I was posted to the asshole of the empire for no reason? Believe it or not, at one time I was on the fast track to the admiralty. That was until I refused to join in on Admiral Thomas's little plan."

"Okay, you got my attention. Keep explaining."

"Thomas and a few of the members of the high command were quietly recruiting officers they believed were of like mind with them. They saw the system as politically flawed, with too much animosity being fostered between the colony worlds and Earth. In their minds, the whole thing was destined to collapse unless they took it over and ran it themselves."

"A coup? That's ridiculous. Thomas would never be involved in such a thing."

"He told me as much to my face when he tried to recruit me to the cause."

Hayden stared at him, mouth agape. While attending the academy, he heard many uncomplimentary rumours about the admiral, but treason had never been among them.

"When I told him where he could stuff it, he decided I needed to be removed. I guess having my throat slit was too extreme, so I was sent to the outer systems 'for disciplinary reasons.' He did everything he could to slander my reputation and ensure that nobody would listen to anything I said if I ratted him out. It was a smart plan, because it worked."

"I can't believe that. Word would spread—"

"Thomas is far more cunning than you give him credit for. He spent a long time vetting those he drew in. He obviously made a mistake with me, but I know of a lot of others who were cozy with him before he called on me. All of them turned their backs on me."

"You can't be the only one to turn him down."

"I'm sure there were other people. There is a good chance that most of the commanders in the less important postings were put there by Thomas for the same reason. I had no way to find out, because all my communications were channelled through high command. I was cut off, and anyone who shared my point of view likely was as well."

Hayden rubbed his temples. "Was there a timeline?"

"A vague one when he approached me. I set that back by a few years. I'm pretty sure he was more careful who he tried recruiting after me. Whether you want to believe me or not, Kaine, you saved the confederation from the likes of Thomas by breaking the jump network."

"By killing the patient. Sure."

"Think about it. Whoever was in on the coup is either isolated in the Sol system or trapped elsewhere. There is no way for them to coordinate or redeploy resources to pull it off. Their plans are dead."

"But so is the Confederacy."

"Not if we can bring back FTL travel. Don't you see? If someone other than Thomas and his gang controls the tech, the empire can be reconstructed without them being involved; they will be impotent while we root them out. We can make the government stronger and safer."

"And all of this will be under your benevolent rule while you grow rich?"

"Don't be an idiot. I pretty much proved my political ineptitude when I got myself exiled. But you, on the other hand..."

"Me?"

"Didn't your influential father plan your career? Stella told me you were being groomed to run for the presidency one day. You still can, Kaine. You can campaign as the man who saved us from the Malliac and helped rebuild a better version of the Confederacy. I think that might make your father proud, don't you?"

"I never wanted any of that."

"You're a shitty liar. You should work on that before you put your name on the ballot."

"So, your initial story about taking me along to appease Stella...?"

"Oh, that was entirely true. Recent events since you walked out forced me to consider things more globally. As much as I hate to admit it, I didn't see the bigger picture. Your value is greater than I first imagined—not for my fortunes, but for those of the entire Confederation."

Hayden tracked a shard of broken glass floating past his face. He plucked it out of the air and examined it.

"Come on, Kaine! How much more do I need to sell it? If you don't want to do it for the greater good, or for the wealth, at least do it to get Stella out of this shit hole system."

"Okay, Pavlovich, your point is taken."

"And?"

"I'm in."

Reunions

HAYDEN THOUGHT HIS small ship seemed at home docked in *Scimitar*'s hangar. The aging salvage vessel, in desperate need of a refit, reminded him of *Scimitar* when he first came aboard her. Then, he was a wet-behind-the-ears graduate cadet, unbelievably arrogant and so determined to be anywhere else but here.

Standing again on the familiar deck, he felt at ease for the first time in a decade, and he thought that strange. In the brief time he had served as Pavlovich's first officer, he never believed himself accepted. He didn't take the time to settle into life aboard this ship. Of course, beginning his tenure with one crisis followed by another was not conducive to becoming comfortable.

And yet he realized how much he missed the old wreck. Watching her vanish; believing her destroyed, had created a cavity in his soul that was impossible to fill. At the time, he believed his greatest loss was the life he'd intended to resume on his return to Earth. Now, as he walked the corridors, he understood that part of him had mourned the new life he had begun to build with the people.

Almost all of them were now dead. Though he only knew most of them in passing, their deaths affected him deeply. Nothing assuaged the crippling guilt he carried. If not for him, they might still live.

"Hayden?"

The familiar voice startled him.

"Stella! I didn't see you there. I was lost in thought."

Her smile was shy. "Yeah, I sort of felt that."

"I suppose I could never hide much from an empath. I guess that had something to do with our problem."

She frowned. "Hayden, I..."

"No, no! I didn't mean to imply it was your fault. It was all me, I..."

She smiled and held up a hand to stop him. "I just wanted to say I'm glad you agreed to come along."

"Oh? Pavlovich gave me the distinct impression you wouldn't go with him unless I came."

Her eyebrows rose. "Really?"

"You mean, you didn't tell him that?"

"Yegor sometimes reads too much into what I say or don't say."

His shoulders slumped. "Oh, okay."

"It's not that I'm not delighted you're here..."

"I get it. I was foolish to believe the problems between us could be so easily solved."

"They can only be fixed if we're together, right?"

He smiled. "Right."

They stared at each other. He was unsure if he should try to hug her.

"I, er, suppose a lot happened since Pavlovich found you," he finally said. "I'm surprised..."

"Go on. What surprised you?"

"Well, you often spoke of how much you missed your father. I thought part of agreeing to work with him might be to see your dad again on the Glenatat home world."

Her face fell. "We tried, but the wormhole didn't open, and the location of their Dyson sphere was purged from Cora's database."

"Oh, I'm so sorry."

She wiped a tear away and put her arms around his neck. "Thanks. He's in a place he always dreamed of. I'm sure he's happy, studying their culture. I just miss him."

He pulled her close and decided to shut up, lest he ruin the moment. A crewman rounded the corner. They disengaged and shyly acknowledged the man.

"Hayden, this is Adam Parker. Adam's our navigator."

Parker's dusky face lit up with a broad, toothy grin, and he extended his right hand. "I'm very pleased to meet you, sir. Stella and the captain told me a lot about you. Cora too...oh, and Gunney..."

Hayden shook the young man's hand. "I hope they said nice things." He smiled, hoping his joke was interpreted as one.

"The way they spoke of you, well, I'm just so proud to shake the hand of the man who saved humanity from the Malliac. Are you returning as XO?"

"I, er, I'm not sure. My role here hasn't been finalized."

"Well, I'm looking forward to working with you."

He grinned and nodded to Stella before continuing down the corridor. Hayden watched him disappear around the corner.

"He seems like an unlikely fellow for Pavlovich to recruit. Where did he find him?"

"Most of the crew are former raiders."

"Really? I never would guess that about him."

"The ones you encountered for the last decade are system scavengers, little more than pirates. Parker and the others were picked up in deep space, transiting between systems."

"How did Pavlovich manage that trick?"

"In Parker's case, their ship was in pretty bad shape. *Scimitar* rescued them, and the captain retained those who wanted to remain."

"And the rest?"

"They were dropped off at the first raider outpost they came across. What did you think Yegor did with them?"

"I, er, well...I didn't know what to think, to be honest."

"He is a bit unconventional and rough around the edges, but he's not a barbarian. Did you forget how he talks a tough line, but doesn't mean much of it? If he did, I wouldn't be here."

"I'm not really sure what to make of Pavlovich—" Hayden didn't know why he cut off his comment. He intended to add that he never really trusted his former captain, something he had expressed to Stella many times after they were marooned. "I suppose I should take him at his word, until he gives me reason not to."

They stared at each other.

"Well, I must go," she said. "Lots of things to prep before we depart."

"Yeah, right. I should find out what I'm supposed to be doing."

"Come by to visit me, when you get a chance." She smiled.

"Right...of course. We have a lot to talk about."

She kissed him on the cheek and turned to leave.

Hayden watched her disappear around the same corner as Parker.

He replayed their farewell in his mind; each time, it sounded lamer to him.

'We've a lot to talk about...?'

"You're an idiot, Kaine," he muttered, realizing how poorly he'd handled that encounter. They'd not spoken in almost a year, and he grew sick believing that he came off like an indifferent ass to her.

Maybe he just needed more time to adjust to this new situation; perhaps she was being cautious—or they both were.

Though he told himself that his acceptance of Pavlovich's proposal was a means to fix the disaster he caused, the prospect of reuniting with Stella was even more appealing. A week before, neither opportunity was imaginable to him. Now, he believed there might be a chance to achieve at least one of them.

Kaine pulled his upper body out of the access panel and shook his head. "How is this thing supposed to work?"

"I sent you the specs last night," said Cora through the ear jack he wore. He wished he still had an active cerebral LINK to communicate with her, but it became defective long ago and there was no way to replace it.

"I tried to read them, but the stuff amounted to gobbledegook."

"Seriously?"

"I don't mean any offence, Cora. I'm just not current on supraluminal physics."

"Well, as XO, the cap'n expects you to be familiar with every system of the ship."

"That was a lot easier before you installed all of these new Glenatat upgrades."

"I'll send you some supplemental notes to study this evening."

He sat on the deck and took a long gulp from his water bottle. He was stripped down to his undershirt and his trim physique glistened with perspiration.

"Why is it so friggin' hot down here?" he asked.

"A side effect of having to improvise with some of the materials we were forced to use. Ng is installing a heat sink for this part of engineering, but it's taking him some time."

"He's another one of the raiders Pavlovich recruited?"

"Yes, and he's not inexperienced, but..."

"What is it, Cora?"

"I sometimes miss having a body. There's nothing like doing the work myself, feeling the ship's operation through the floor plating. Now, even though I can access all her systems, it just isn't the same."

Hayden frowned and stared at his drink. "I regret this happened to you."

"For the last time, it isn't your fault. Please don't do that to yourself, or to me."

"Sorry."

Despite her words, he knew better. If not for his plan that doomed not only the confederation, but also *Scimitar*, she might still be the sweet girl he met ten years before.

"It's not as bad as you think being linked to the ship. You should pay me a visit in here some time."

"Is that possible?"

"Sure, using a simple VR interlink."

"I would like that."

"It's a date, then. I'll set it up and let you know when everything is ready," she said. After a pause, she added, "You're sure Stella won't mind you visiting me?"

The question caught him off guard. He had no idea how she would interpret him spending time with Cora in her reality, or if she would even care.

"I'm sure she'll be fine with it," he said.

"Okay, but just to be sure, I'll chat with her about it—girl to girl."

He smiled and was about to respond when the alert klaxon sounded.

"What's happening?"

"Long-range sensors picked up a group of ships approaching," she said. "You should get to the bridge."

Grabbing his shirt, he dashed to the engineering hatch then bolted through the corridors toward the command centre.

• • • •

Kaine's arrival on the bridge resurrected a host of emotions he thought were behind him. The familiar adrenaline rush and flurry of focused activity brought it all back. It was something he'd missed.

"Kaine!" said Pavlovich from his command chair. "We're a bit light on crew. Man the tactical station."

"Aye, sir," he replied as he advanced to the console. He was relieved to see its basic interface had not been modified. After taking a few seconds to digest the readings, he announced, "Three—no, four ships bearing down on our position. Distance, five hundred thousand kilometres."

Pavlovich nodded then addressed the air around him. "Okay, Cora, there's been enough down time to fix things. Get us moving."

"They've caught us with our pants down, Cap'n. Ng is bringing our fusion reactors online."

"How long?"

"We need twelve minutes."

"Shit!" Pavlovich turned to scowl in Hayden's direction but continued speaking with Cora. "Do what you can. Those bogies will be on us in...?" He raised his eyebrows to Kaine in expectation.

"Twenty minutes," he replied.

"Cora? Ten minutes before they lock weapons on us. Move your virtual ass."

"Excuse me, Captain, but who do you expect to be targeting us?" asked Hayden.

"Goddamn raiders, that's who."

"With that kind of ordnance? Since when?"

"You were isolated for too long. A lot can happen in ten years. These guys aren't based in this system. They're from Hip 84051."

"That still doesn't explain how they got their hands on missiles."

"Look, Kaine, I would love to give you a history lesson of what's gone on for the past decade, but we're a bit busy. Get your ass down to engineering and help Cora and Ng heat up the engines."

Hayden swallowed his other questions and headed for the hatchway. As he opened the door, Pavlovich called back to him. "While you're at it, see what the hell is keeping Gunney. I need him up here, pronto, in case that isn't obvious."

Kaine closed the door behind him and ran down the corridor. The armoury was on the way, and that was where he expected to find the cyborg.

Halfway there, he encountered him, clanking his way toward the bridge.

"The captain needs you, ASAP."

"Of course, he does, but I won't be of much use. Our rail gun ordnance is depleted, and our X-ray lasers are offline."

"What about the Glenatat weapons?"

He raised one eyebrow. "Same story."

"Right. Get to your tactical alcove. By the time you arrive, the guns should be hot."

Hayden turned and continued toward engineering.

On arrival, he found a small man hovering over the primary monitoring console. Ng looked up, desperation on his face. "One of the plasma injectors on engine two is malfunctioning."

"Get the other engines online," shouted Hayden.

"I can't, the magnetic coupler is down on one and four."

"What about three?"

"She's running, but most of her power is being used to maintain the artificial gravity and reinforce the hull plating."

"When did that change?"

Cora's voice answered in his ear jack. "It was a necessary compromise to get the new superluminal drive online."

"Well, at the moment we've got four hostiles bearing down on us, and Pavlovich believes they're about to fire nukes."

"I warned him it might come down to this," she said.

"Cora, we need to get this tub moving, or at least get some power to Gunney's weapons. If we can fix the injector..."

"There are no spares, but we can maybe retrofit the secondary one from the old jump engine...or, you can."

"Me?"

"Ng's good, but he hasn't logged enough hours with these babies. You helped me pull them apart when the Glenatat refitted us."

"That was a long time ago, Cora."

"Well, I can't do it, so you get the job. I'll talk you through it."

"I thought you were coaching Ng?"

"I'm doing several simultaneous things. None of it makes up for not having a body, though."

"Okay, fine. How long will it take?"

"More than we have," she said.

Down the Rabbit Hole

VIOLENT SHAKING KNOCKED Hayden from his feet. He cursed as his supporting hand slipped and his head hit the access opening.

"The ship's taking a beating," he said as he repositioned himself and resumed his work.

"The Glenatat hull modifications are holding," said Cora. "We can take a lot more hits before the armour fails."

"How are the radiation readings?"

"Everything is normal. Pay attention! You don't want to bend the stabilizer when you remove it."

"I know, I know—"

Pavlovich's voice replaced Cora's in his ear jack. "What in the seven hells is going on down there?"

"Almost finished, Cap'n. The XO is doing a great job."

"Can he do it faster?"

"Got it!" announced Kaine as he gingerly extracted the injector from the access hatch.

"Give it to Ng. I can talk him through the next step. You should get back to the bridge."

Pavlovich was in his earpiece again. "How much longer, Engineer?"

"Two minutes, Cap'n. Then there will be plenty of power for the lasers."

"What about getting the ship moving?"

"That will take another ten, tops."

"Damn it, Cora!"

The abrupt silence over the ear jack told Kaine that Pavlovich had terminated the connection.

He was out of breath by the time he arrived at the command centre. He noted that Stella occupied one of the acceleration couches and was safely strapped in. Her jaw was set, and her attention locked on the tactical readout cluster. She seemed less vulnerable than he remembered her the last time they were aboard *Scimitar*. He wondered if her practise at shutting out the emotions around her was paying off.

"Gunney," said Pavlovich, "Cora tells me there is ten percent power to the forward X-ray laser battery."

"Bloody well about time," grumbled the cyborg, "but I need a hell of a lot more than that."

"Make use of what there is, Gunnery Officer." He turned to Hayden. "Good work, Kaine. Now take over on the sensors and give me some options."

The lights dimmed, and he felt a fluctuation in the gravity plating as power was drawn to fire *Scimitar*'s weapons. He relieved the crewman at the sensor station and took a moment to study the readout.

"Damage to the engineering section of the lead ship. They are breaking off. Two of the remaining vessels are altering course. I believe they want to flank us, Captain."

"Cora! Where are my engines? We're sitting ducks here. If they board us, we're screwed."

"Number two is now at eighty percent, Cap'n."

"At least we can manoeuvre," said Pavlovich. "Helm, take evasive action. Navigation, plot us a course out of here."

"I doubt that will do us much good, Captain," said Hayden. "Without more than one operational engine, we can't outrun these ships and defend ourselves at the same time."

"I'm open to suggestions, Kaine."

He clenched his jaw, grinding his teeth. The options were limited, and even their enhanced armour couldn't take an indefinite pounding. If the raiders didn't intend to destroy *Scimitar*, it was only a matter of time before their skiffs would attempt to dock. No Rangers were aboard, and there were not enough people to fight off boarding parties at all possible access points.

Pavlovich turned to Stella, but before he could ask her anything, she glared at him. "No! Absolutely not."

The captain turned up his lip and grumbled, "A fat lot of good having an empathic psychic aboard if she won't use her talent on the bad guys."

She ignored Pavlovich's provocation. Finally, when he seemed to realize she did not plan to change her mind, he hit the comm switch at his elbow.

"Cora, how much juice is left in the Super-L engine?"

"We consumed most of our fuel on the last jump. There isn't enough to get us all the way to Pictor Prime."

"Well, how far can it get us?"

"About a thousand AUs from the central planet."

"We'll make do. Fire it up."

There was a brief hesitation before she responded. "Aye, Cap'n. It'll take about ten minutes."

"I'll give you six." Pavlovich slammed his fist on the button.

The ship vibrated as a missile exploded on the hull.

"Maintain current heading, Helm. They don't have much of a bite anymore."

"They must've used up their big ones," said Kaine.

"They only want to herd us in a particular direction. If they wanted to hurt us, they would be firing up their rail guns."

"Which begs the question, why do raiders possess fleet technology? At least two of those ships are UEF corvettes."

"Former UEF. I told you; a lot happened."

Three more impacts in fast succession nearly knocked Hayden off his feet. He checked the readout. "They're focusing their fire on engineering. They are trying to exploit a weakened section of our armour."

Pavlovich snarled and hit the comm button. "Cora, the bad guys are starting to scratch the paint. Now would be a good time for us to leave."

"We're good to go, Cap'n, but I'm concerned about—"

"Noted, Engineer."

He addressed the helmsman. "You heard the lady; take us superluminal, NOW!"

The air around Hayden crackled with static electricity. His skin felt like ants crawled over every inch of him. Everything blurred, and the noise of the bridge dropped to a deep, low-frequency roar.

The gravity plating seemed to fail. Though he felt himself floating, a quick glance down assured him he was still firmly connected to the deck. The contents of his stomach insisted they wanted to exit, and he fought hard to keep from vomiting. An oppressive pressure pushed down on his brain. There was no pain, but reaching for his head, he discovered no sensation in his extremities.

Then a chaotic blast of colours enveloped everything, as if a rainbow had exploded around him. Like individual strips of cloth caught in a wind, countless coloured bands flapped aimlessly. Gathered by an invisible force, they were stretched into an ever-thinning ribbon extending off to infinity before him and behind him. He had no sense of acceleration or movement, but the ribbons of light rolled by at an unimaginable speed.

Then it all ended.

Pain erupted behind Hayden's eyeballs, and his stomach heaved. He doubled over and vomited onto the deck. His still ringing ears heard a couple of other people retching, but when he looked for who it was, he discovered his vision was still foggy.

"Oh, shit," said Pavlovich, "I don't think I will ever get used to that."

Hayden sought him out with his still clearing sight. "What the hell just happened?" he asked.

The captain leaned forward in his command chair as if he was going to be ill. He massaged his temples and said, "We went superluminal. No wonder the bloody Glenatat replaced this tech. This sucks."

"How far did we travel?"

Parker, the navigator, appeared to be in no condition to answer. Pavlovich struggled to his feet and leaned over the navigation station. "Twenty-three-point six light years."

"That's insane! We only travelled for a few seconds."

"It was a lot longer than that. All I know is that I want to puke every time we do this."

Hayden studied the front holograph, showing a small sun burning against a carpet of stars in the distance. "Where are we?"

"We are most of the way to Pictor Prime, or at least we should be. I think Cora said we could get to within a thousand AU of it, somewhere inside the Oort Cloud."

Hayden's eyes widened. "This is incredible! I didn't believe you when you described the potential of this technology. This could change everything."

"Yeah, except for one small detail: we're out of fuel, and if we don't find some more, this will be the last trip we ever make."

Taking Stock

FOR THE NEXT TWO HOURS, the crew repaired the damage from the attack. Hayden moved between stations, inspecting the work and offering advice where he could. He kept thinking about all the gaping holes in Pavlovich's story.

To him, it made no sense that raiders had the ability to acquire military hardware, or for them to gang up and attack *Scimitar* without provocation. Why was there no ammunition for the ships' primary weapon? Then there was the question of how they were found in the vastness of interplanetary space. The only conclusion he could arrive at was that the raiders—or whomever they really were—had been hunting *Scimitar*.

But why?

The answer, he believed, lay in the behaviour of the attacking fleet. They wanted to capture the ship. He could only conclude that somebody else knew of the FTL tech, and he doubted they were the only ones.

Pavlovich was right about one thing: Hayden had been living in seclusion for too long. He had no idea of the political situation between once connected star systems. What friends were now foes? He imagined that most had descended into an eat-or-be-eaten scenario, with multiple factions vying for dominance of the local resources.

As he walked toward the infirmary, Stella emerged. She returned his smile and waited for him.

"That was quite the adventure," he said. "How are you holding up after all that?"

"I practice my blocking techniques; I was mostly able to shut out the crew's emotions. It was challenging, but I'm getting better at it. The most difficult time was when we dropped back to normal space."

"That is something I won't look forward to again."

"Pavlovich described for me what it is like, but it didn't prepare me for the visceral nature of the experience."

"At least he warned you," said Hayden. "I had no idea what was coming."

They both laughed, and her hand brushed against his. His heart jumped into his throat for the instant before she pulled back.

Trying to regain his composure, he said, "What was that episode between you and Pavlovich about?"

A hint of a frown creased her forehead. "When he first recruited me, he tried to get me agree to make my reactive empathic abilities available to him."

"You mean your ability to disable people through their cerebral LINK."

"I told him emphatically that I would not do that, because I can't control it. People could die. I will read emotions during negotiations and such, but under no circumstances will I harm anyone for him."

"He must realize that you would disable most of his new crew too?"

She shook her head. "Removal of their LINKs was a condition of signing on. He wants to use me as a weapon. I won't do it."

"Even if it means our survival?"

"The raiders didn't intend to kill us. I sensed none of those kinds of emotions from them."

"You're evading my question, Stella. What if we are faced with a more deadly situation in the future?"

She swallowed and looked away. "I don't know."

He reached for her hand. "I don't need to be an empath to realize my comments upset you. I'm sorry."

She squeezed his fingers then reclaimed her hand. "I'll be fine. It is not the first time it has come up."

Realizing he was making a mess of the situation, he said, "Do you know why we were attacked?"

"No, but I suspect it's connected with how Pavlovich recruited the new crew."

"Why?"

"I don't know the details; it all took place before he found me. Just a sense I get from unguarded emotions and the odd comment from him."

"There is a staff meeting in thirty minutes. I'll add that question to my list."

Her hand gripped his wrist, and her worried face looked up at him. "Hayden, don't press him on too many things. He's hiding something, but I also sense something else—something dangerous. He is not the same man you knew ten years ago. Be careful."

"I'll keep that in mind."

She attempted a disarming smile and stood on her toes to kiss him on the cheek. "I must go. Will you come by to visit later? Just to talk."

He smiled. "Yes, of course."

As he watched her walk away, he realized that Pavlovich was not the only one keeping things from him.

Hayden entered the briefing room to find the captain, Gunney, and Stella present. Taking his seat, he almost asked if Cora was coming but managed to catch himself.

"Now that everyone is here, let's get to business," said Pavlovich. "Let's start with an engineering update."

"Most of our hurt from the attack is fixed," said Cora.

"The hull damage is repaired already?" said Hayden.

"The Glenatat armour is composed of a material enhanced with an advanced type of nanotechnology. It is essentially self-healing and can be modified for different threats, given enough time and data to do so."

"Thank you, Engineer. I'm sure Kaine will eventually make himself familiar with all of the ship's adaptations soon."

"I'm making it a priority, sir," he said.

Pavlovich grumbled something inaudible before he said, "Go on with the report."

"All four fusion drives are back online and operating at full capacity," she said.

"Good. Gunney will be grateful for weapons with some kick."

The cyborg's face remained impassive. "There is still the problem of the rail guns having no ammunition. I don't like being solely dependent on the lasers after our encounters with the Malliac."

"I don't sense their presence," said Stella.

"We are pretty far from Mu Arae, and they are restricted to travelling at sublight speeds," said Hayden. "Even if they'd made a beeline for here, they won't arrive for several years."

"That assumes some didn't already spread into this part of the galaxy before we encountered them," said Pavlovich. He looked directly at Stella.

"As I said before, I do not detect them."

"I'm prepared to accept that for the moment," said Gunney. "But I still want some tungsten for manufacturing the projectiles. Or some ready-made ones would be nice."

"The survey database indicates there are deposits in this system."

"There is also an arms cache on Cetus," pressed the cyborg.

"Yes, but if it is still stocked, I doubt they'll simply let us in to help ourselves."

"I'm just offering up options, Cap'n."

"We'll get you some projectiles, Gunney."

"Speaking of the armoury," said Hayden, "what do we know about the UEF detachments that might be stranded here?"

"That is another story," said the captain with a sigh. "Predisaster reports I was privy to suggest that the Thirtieth Fleet was due here for manoeuvres. I don't know if they arrived before the network went down, so we should anticipate they are here."

"Who was in command?"

"Admiral Kwong."

"Was he one of...?"

"One of the conspirators?" said Pavlovich. "Yes, which means our arrival here won't be greeted warmly."

"So why, exactly, are we here, as opposed to any other system?" asked Hayden.

"Erganium. There is a large surface deposit on one of the moons of Elgar, the innermost gas giant."

"I'm sorry, but how do you know that? Until a few days ago, I never knew the stuff existed, so it is hard for me to believe it would be listed in the database."

"It is associated with a specific ratio of other common minerals," said Cora. "There is a high probability we will find some at Elgar."

"But not a certainty?"

"No," said Pavlovich, "and if we can't locate any, we'll be screwed. We used up the last of our fuel to come here."

Silence hung over the room as that statement was digested.

"Well," said Hayden, breaking the gloom, "I suppose we should plan our moves carefully if we want to avoid encountering the fleet."

"Cora," said the captain, "what is the status of your upgrade to our sensor bugs?"

"The drone software is rewritten, but the hardware isn't updated. Once that is done, their spectral bandwidth will be extended, and we can deploy them out to a hundred thousand kilometres from the ship."

"That can be useful," said Hayden.

"Agreed," said Pavlovich. "Make that a priority. How long do you need, Cora?"

"I can use an extra set of hands. If the XO wouldn't mind helping? He did a wonderful job extracting that injector."

"See to it, Kaine. Once the bugs are up, we will head to Elgar and with some luck avoid encountering any UEF ships."

"What happens if we meet one?" asked Stella.

"Best scenario? We'll be welcomed as part of the family."

"And the worst case?"

"Gunney had better be prepared to make do with the energy weapons." He surveyed the faces across from him. "If there are no further questions, everyone knows what to do."

As the others dispersed, Hayden hung back. "Captain, can we talk?"

Pavlovich nodded. "Cora, would you give us the room, please?"

"Aye, Cap'n."

"All right, Kaine, what's on your mind? I could smell the wood burning during the meeting."

"Pardon?"

"An old expression, meaning, I could tell you were thinking of something."

"Oh, yes. Why did those raiders attack us? And why were they in UEF ships?"

Pavlovich grinned. "Still dwelling on the past, Kaine?"

Hayden's face remained stony, and Pavlovich's smile faded.

"To answer your first question, we may have made a few enemies before we picked you up."

"How?"

"After making our way to the edge of the Mu Arae system, we still needed some materials for repairs. We happened upon a raider transport finishing their journey from Hip 40307. We engaged them."

"You pirated the pirates?"

"Yeah. We took on anyone who wanted to serve with us and set the remainder of the crew adrift in lifeboats."

"You just make friends wherever you go. Why were the ones who attacked us in military ships?"

"Hip 40307 fell to the them seven years ago. Most, if not all of the fleet stationed there saw no benefit battling to save a shitty old base and joined with them."

"And because they are now using UEF vessels, you had a ready-made supply of replacement parts by taking one of their ships."

"It seemed like a good idea at the time," said Pavlovich.

Hayden frowned and examined the table, trying to gather his thoughts.

"What's on your mind, son?" asked the captain.

"What if every system in the Confederation is like that? What do we really gain by what we're doing?"

"Listen, Kaine, I'm pretty sure there are other systems where the same thing is happening. I'm also confident there are a number that maintain the status quo. Every situation will be different, depending upon the stability of the local governments at the time and who the detachment commanders were."

"That's my point. The federation may be so broken up that reintroducing FTL capability could be a bigger disaster than the collapse of the network. At best it will probably mean a century of restructuring. At worst, all-out war between colony worlds."

"So, you're suggesting it's better if we just find a quiet little corner here and live out our lives? How did that work out for you back where I found you?"

"I didn't ask you to come find me."

"If you regret your decision, your ship is still in the hangar. Feel free to use it."

Pavlovich stormed out of the briefing room, leaving Hayden with a lot to think about.

Reconsideration

HAYDEN PUSHED THE REPAIRED module back into position and wiped his brow. He checked his chronometer to discover he had worked through most of his rest shift. He thought he might be able to catch an hour's shuteye before Pavlovich expected him on the bridge.

Sitting on the deck of his small ship, he leaned back against the console and questioned what he was doing.

Ever since his disturbing conversation with the captain, Hayden's thoughts and emotions had been at odds. He closed his eyes and tried to still the storm in his head.

"Permission to come aboard?"

Stella's lyrical voice roused him from his funk.

"Granted." He smiled; aware she saw through his facade.

"My goodness, it's close in here. How can you stand this heat?" She sat on the floor beside him.

"It gets that way when none of the ship's systems are active."

"What are you up to?" She looked about the cabin. Scattered around the deck was the detritus from his repair work.

"I couldn't sleep, and my ship needed some maintenance."

"Are you planning a trip?"

He started to answer then shook his head and shrugged. "I don't really know what I'm doing."

"I waited for you to come by last night." There was no admonishment in her words.

He sighed. "I'm sorry. I was—am—an emotional mess. I didn't want to burden you with any more of my crap."

She smiled sympathetically and patted him on the thigh. "When we first met, you would never admit to such a thing. You've come a long way, Hayden."

"Living for a decade with an empath will do that."

Her expression changed to an earnest one. "Do you regret our time together?"

He tried to smile. "Never. Only the circumstances. You?"

She looked into his eyes, and her hand caressed his cheek. "Only that I couldn't do more to help heal your hurt and make it easier for you to forgive me."

He gently clasped her hand. "You don't need forgiveness for anything."

"Oh, Hayden, you're not a good liar. You never said it, but I know that somewhere inside, you resent me for my part in all this. If I had been more forthcoming about my ability, things might be different."

"I spent ten years reliving those moments, and every time, I came to the same conclusion. There was no other way. Even if I was aware you could wipe out the Malliac, I would never ask you to do it. When you used your power, it almost killed you."

"But it didn't."

"We didn't know that," he said. "Things worked out the only possible way they could."

"Then why do you continue to torture yourself if there was no other choice?"

He sighed. "Even though there was no other way, what I did destroyed a civilization. Maybe it was the best of a list of undesirable outcomes, but that still doesn't diminish the magnitude of my crime. All the lives that were affected—destroyed." He shook his head.

She hugged his arm and leaned into his shoulder. "You're being far too hard on yourself. I wish you saw that."

"I'm sorry I drove you away."

They sat together in silence for a long time.

"Are you going to leave?" she asked.

"I don't know. I'm not sure I want to be a part of something that can make things worse."

"Where would you go?"

"There is, or was, a large population in this system. I can find a place and blend in."

"But that isn't what you want to do, is it?"

"In my ideal fantasy, we put everything back together the way it was. Then you and I settle down on Earth and raise fat, happy babies."

"While you fulfill your family's plan for you? What about your dreams and aspirations, Hayden? Do you have none of your own?"

He regarded her but had no answer.

"Maybe the problem is not so much forgiving yourself as it is needing your father's forgiveness. Even now, ten years after the fact, you still live in some fantasy world where you restore your destiny and make him proud."

She stood and kissed him on the top of his head. "You need to decide who you are living your life for. Then, maybe, you can be satisfied with the one in front of you."

She smiled sadly then turned and departed.

He buried his face in his hands, letting the conversation swirl in his head. His fatigue only seemed to amplify his confusion. What he needed was a full night's sleep.

A klaxon sounded. Pulling himself together, he inserted his ear jack.

"Cora? What's going on?"

"Four ships are approaching at high velocity. We need you on the bridge."

He got up and gathered his tools. "ETA?"

"Two hours, forty-one minutes before we are in their weapons range."

"On my way. Is there anything else I should know?"

"Yes, I can't raise the cap'n."

Sprinting through the corridors, all kinds of questions raced through Hayden's mind, not the least important being the whereabouts of Pavlovich. Had it not been an emergency, he would have checked his quarters. The ship needed an experienced officer on the bridge, and as XO, the duty fell to him, regardless of how little sleep he'd grabbed.

He pushed open the hatch to find everyone at their stations. He didn't need Stella to tell him how tense things were. Relieving the watch commander, he sat in the command chair and ordered a complete status report. One, by one, in practised order, the crew manning key stations responded.

"Ten bogies converging on our position from multiple vectors," said the tactical officer.

"I was told four."

"Additional ships appeared on sensors just before you arrived, sir. They're approaching from the opposite direction to the others."

"Is there an updated intercept time?"

"One hour, eight minutes to weapons range."

"What the hell? Cora?"

"My original estimate was correct, but that was before these new ones in front of us showed up."

"Navigation, give me some evasion options."

Parker responded, "They are covering us from pretty much all key vectors, sir. We can't avoid them."

"Almost like they were expecting us," said Kaine.

"That's because they were," said Pavlovich, who had just entered the bridge.

"How is that possible?"

"I informed them where we are."

All eyes turned to the captain.

"I beg your pardon. You told them were to find us? *Why*?" asked Hayden.

Pavlovich's answer was to advance toward him. "You're in my seat."

He glared at the bearded man towering over him.

"The chair, Kaine?"

After hesitating, he decided to comply and got up.

"Thank you, XO. Helm, bring us to a full stop."

"Captain, I believe we are owed an explanation of what is happening," said Hayden.

The hatch opened and Stella entered the bridge with a look of grave concern.

"While you were up all night working on your ship," said Pavlovich, "I conducted a little research about what's going on in this system."

Hayden swallowed his surprise. "How did you do that?"

"I made some inquiries of some old buddies I knew to be stationed here."

"You can trust them?"

He chuckled. "About as far as I can throw them under five gees, but they did provide me with some useful intel regarding the present political situation."

Hayden ground his teeth and bit back a comment. A quick glance at Stella caught her shaking her head, warning him to be careful.

"What did you learn?" he asked.

"I heard differing accounts, but the one common thread is that there was a coup in this system. Admiral Kwong is dead, along with a third of the Thirtieth Fleet."

"What happened?"

"A faction of the military overthrew the government in a bloody conflict that lasted for almost five years. Kwong was on the losing side."

"Do you know anything about the victors? Are they pro-Confederacy or something else?"

"The story depends on who I spoke to and what side of the fight they were on. Ulysses Stromm is the new strongman here, but his grip on power is tenuous at best. From what I can gather, not long after their victory there was a schism. A portion of them broke away and are now in active military opposition to Stromm's regime."

"So which faction is en route to us?"

"Both of them."

"*What*?"

"It couldn't be helped. I had to divulge that we were in the system in order to get the lowdown from anyone I talked to. It didn't take long for either party to figure out where we are and send their ships."

"So, what is going to happen when they all arrive?"

"I expect there may be some exchange of fire."

"And what is going to prevent them from targeting us?"

"Well, I sort of led each to believe we are sympathetic to their cause. They are both rushing here to secure us before the other can. If I played this right, they'll shoot at one another and leave us alone."

"What on earth possessed you to do that?" asked a livid Stella.

"Honestly, the information I got was inconclusive as to which side holds the upper hand in this conflict. I want to make sure we choose the right allies."

"So you're letting them sort out who the stronger force is," said Hayden. "That makes tactical sense."

"Thank you, XO. I do know a thing or two about tactics."

Hayden frowned at Pavlovich. "Why is either side is so interested in us? Did you tell them about the FTL drive?"

"Hell, no, I don't trust any of them. I intimated we just made the sublight journey from Arcad V."

"But that is nowhere near Mu Arae. Surely they'll be aware of the fleet distribution at the time of the disaster?"

"Yeah, I had to talk like a Dutch uncle, but I convinced each party that we were on return jump sequence to Earth when the net went down and trapped us. Which reminds me, Cora, adjust our logs to make it look like that's what happened, as well as modify the crew manifest."

"I'm already on it, Cap'n."

"You didn't answer Hayden's question," said Stella. "Why are they so interested in us?"

"The war in this system has been long and costly. Both sides incurred heavy losses of personnel and ships. With no way to rebuild or secure more, any space-worthy vessel is valuable. Much more so in our case, because we are an operational warship."

"What is the plan, Captain?" asked Hayden.

"We sit back and watch the fireworks. When it becomes clear which side holds the upper hand, we join in and help finish the fight."

"And how will we explain our reluctance to engage in the beginning?"

"Gunney told you that earlier. We are out of ordnance for the rail gun. As far as the lasers go, we can fake a technical glitch responsible for the delay. Needless to say, we should obscure the Glenatat weapon emitters."

"How do we hide out adaptive hull modifications? Or Cora?"

"I don't know all the answers, Kaine. That's why you are here. You *are* staying, yes?"

Several sets of eyes focused on him. He glanced at Stella, who seemed frightened. He reflected on his almost automatic response to the emergency and how he had so easily assumed command until Pavlovich's arrival. Had the old man planned that as a test for him?

"My place is here, Captain."

"Excellent! When this situation is sorted out, we'll decide what to do with that ship of yours."

Cornered, all Hayden could do was bite back his comment and nod. He'd been played masterfully. Stella's warning had proven true. Pavlovich was not to be trusted. He wouldn't make the same mistake again.

What Game Are You Playing?

THE CREW OF *Scimitar* worked for the next hour to prepare and make it appear they were a UEF ship that had been in transit for almost a decade.

"Visitors need to be confined to the unmodified sections," said Hayden. "It will be difficult explaining the modifications in engineering."

"We won't be able to prevent access indefinitely," said Pavlovich. "Whomever wins the fight for our hand will want to inspect their prize at some point. Any ideas?"

Hayden regarded the sphere in the middle of the briefing room that housed Cora's essence. "This entire section is modified. We can't allow them to see any of it." He rubbed his chin as he pondered the impossible trick of concealing such a significant portion of *Scimitar* from curious eyes.

"Cora," he asked, "can the nanotech material that covers our hull be adapted to look like something else? A bulkhead, for instance?"

"Yes, what are you thinking?"

"This area is next to fusion reactor one. If we explained the wall as shielding against a radiation leak..."

"Ah-ha, it would discourage anyone from looking too closely near where the FTL drive is located. Brilliant idea, Kaine."

"Well, it would be temporary at best. I can't imagine whomever claims us not wanting to take us back to their base for a refit."

"What do you think, Cora? Can it be done?" said Pavlovich.

"Yes, but we will have to remove the material from the hull. There is no time for that before they arrive."

"Then we'll do what we can for now and work to that solution after things get sorted," said Pavlovich.

"Captain," said Hayden, "I understand that all of this is necessary for our immediate survival, but what is the long-term plan? Surely we can't reveal the existence of our advanced tech to anyone in this sector?"

"No, we won't be doing that. The goal is to secure the erganium from Elgar's moon. We'll need to find a way to send somebody there at the earliest opportunity."

"If we're even given such a chance."

Pavlovich smiled. "You worry too much. The right circumstances will present themselves. Let's just make sure we're ready to take advantage of them when they do."

Hayden shook his head. "I wish I shared your confidence."

"You don't know the two principal actors in this conflict like I do, Kaine."

"You know them both?"

"One of them far better than the other, but yes. On the one side is Ulysses Stromm. We went to the academy together."

"Were you on good terms?"

"Eh, that depends on your frame of reference. We were drinking buddies for a time."

"A time?"

"There was a girl."

"I see," said Hayden with a nod. "Which of you was the winner?"

"You sound like a misogynist, Kaine. We competed for her affections, but she chose somebody else. Still, my relationship with Stromm was never the same after that. We've not spoken since graduation."

"What about the other player?"

"Cesar Malkovich."

"And what do you know about him?"

"Quite a bit. He's my cousin."

Hayden stared at the captain for several seconds. "You don't seem to be too bothered that we might be going to battle against a member of your family."

"Actually, I'm worried we'll be forced to fight on his side. Cesar is an asshole; always was, even when we were kids. In a lot of ways, I prefer the idea of dealing with Stromm."

"It sounds like it may be a shit show no matter which way things go."

The captain shrugged. "Sorry about that. This situation is the best I could do."

Hayden suspected there was much that Pavlovich chose not to reveal. Had he the time, he would be inclined to push for more, but the announcement from Cora shut off all discussion.

The fleets were about to arrive.

Kaine and Pavlovich returned to the bridge, much to the visible relief of Gunney, the acting duty officer.

"Report," said the captain as he assumed his chair. Hayden proceeded to his station. Stella was nowhere to be seen, and he briefly wondered where she could have gone.

"The two fleets are within weapons range, sir. The grouping in front of us will arrive first."

"How far behind is the pursuing group?" asked Hayden.

"They began their deceleration and will be here five minutes later," said Cora over the speakers.

"Gunney, keep the lasers hot. Find some targets on both sides but don't lock on just yet," ordered Pavlovich.

"Aye, Cap'n, but I sure wish I had projectiles."

Hayden was inclined to agree with the gunnery officer. At close range, their available conventional energy weapon might do significant damage to the other ships, but a rail gun would be devastating. He was confident neither of the approaching fleets shared *Scimitar's* current disadvantage. If either side chose to unleash fire on them, the adaptive hull might protect them but also give away their secret. He couldn't imagine the fallout of that situation, but it wouldn't be good.

"Incoming communication, sir," said the communications officer.

The captain glanced at Hayden and raised crossed fingers. "Let's hear 'em."

"*Scimitar*, you are ordered to stand down. Power down your weapons and prepare for boarding."

"Kovacs, is that you?" The hint of a smile peeked out from under Pavlovich's beard.

"Pavlovich, you old bastard, is that really you? Torrence told me it was your ship, but I didn't believe him."

"In the flesh, you old pirate. Why so aggressive? I informed him whose side we are on."

"Sorry about this, but I have my orders. I need to secure your vessel before the rebels arrive. What is your defensive status?"

"We've got lasers, but the power buffers are glitchy. I'm glad you're here to save our ass."

"Hold your position. We are forming a perimeter around you."

"Sir! We are receiving another priority message on a different channel," announced the communications officer.

The captain shot the man a dirty look.

"What's going on over there, Yegor?"

"The ships pursuing us are trying to interfere with our comms." He waved to Kaine and indicated the communications station. "I think they want to jam our signal."

Suddenly realizing what Pavlovich wanted, Hayden dashed across the bridge and pushed the operator out of the way. His fingers flew over the interface, and a moment later, loud static filled the speakers.

The remainder of the message was lost in a hiss of noise.

"Thanks, Kaine. Now, put me through to the other fleet."

"...I repeat, this is the UEF *Callisto*. Identify yourself."

"We are the UEF *Scimitar*," said Pavlovich. "Hostile, unidentified vessels surround us and are threatening to board. We request assistance."

"Acknowledged, *Scimitar*. Can you defend yourself?"

"Negative. Our emitter coupling is damaged, and our rail gun ordnance is exhausted."

"Understood. Be prepared to take evasive action. We'll be there soon."

"Message received. Thank you, *Callisto*." Pavlovich made a slashing motion at his throat, and the connection was terminated.

"Cora, we're going to need full power to the weapons and maximum manoeuvring thrust in a few seconds."

"Everything is at your disposal, Cap'n. I sure hope you know what you're doing."

"You and me both, sweetie," said Pavlovich. He sat forward suddenly and searched the bridge. "Kaine, where's your girlfriend? I could really use her."

"I don't know, sir."

"Damn it. Cora, find her and persuade her to join us, if it isn't too much trouble."

"Rail gun fire!" shouted the tactical officer.

Hayden returned to his monitoring station. He watched in morbid fascination as high-energy projectiles from both fleets impacted their targets. The vessel closest to *Scimitar* split in half when it was struck midship by an incoming projectile.

Farther behind them, two of the closing ships bloomed into brilliant fireballs.

"Well, that's interesting," said Pavlovich, eyes riveted on the image.

Kaine hovered over the sensor station console. "It appears they are firing low-yield nuclear warheads."

"No shit. What about the rebels? That was no nuke that split that ship in two."

"No, sir, they used a kinetic mass projectile for maximum damage."

"Well, that's an interesting disparity in ordnance, isn't it?"

"Something else is going on as well. Only one of the ships surrounding us has been struck. I'm having difficulty pinning down coordinates for the remaining vessels."

"You think they are using some sort of stealth field?"

"That is the only thing I can think of, Captain. If they are emitting bogus signals, we may not be able to reliably target them."

"I want to see this for myself, Kaine."

A moment later, a Hawking class destroyer appeared on the holographic imager. At twice the mass of *Scimitar*, she was formidable. Yet the image was unstable. It flickered and popped in and out of focus.

"What the hell is the matter with the projector?"

"Our equipment is functioning perfectly," said Hayden. "Look at the background star field. It isn't affected, only the ship."

"I've never seen anything like that before, have you?"

"During my last year at the academy, we took a tour of the orbital assembly structure. At the time, the commanding officer of the facility made a sidebar comment about them incorporating a new classified defensive technology on some of the newest ships. Maybe this is it?"

"If it is..." Pavlovich studied the shifting image. "I'm becoming nauseous watching it. Gunney, can you get a lock on that ship?"

"The targeting computer says nothing is there. If you want me to hit it, I'll make a guess."

"No, don't."

The captain turned to Hayden. "I think I know what we need to do. Kaine?"

"I agree, sir. The incoming ships have the inferior technology."

"Mm-hmm. Gunney, pick out one and let 'em have it. It's time for us to declare ourselves."

"Aye, Cap'n."

A moment later, the gunnery officer shouted, "Sir, I've tracked the exchange of fire. There is more ordnance coming from the arriving rebel fleet than can be accounted for by the ships I am tracking."

"Kaine, confirm those readings."

Hayden studied the readout on his console then went to check another station.

"Well, XO?"

"There is definitely an anomaly. There are least four additional weapon sources that can't be accounted for."

"More stealth tech?"

"I think it is a form of refractive cloaking. When I increase the sensitivity of our enhanced graviton detectors, I see indications of mass at those locations."

Suddenly, a brilliant flare erupted on the screen as the Hawking class destroyer vaporized.

"And now it would seem that both sides possess nukes," said Pavlovich.

"Sir," said Hayden, "refractive cloaks will render our lasers useless."

"What will our Glenatat weapon do against either side?"

"Hypothetically, the dark energy cannon should not be affected by any of this technology, but are you sure you want to tip our hand?"

"No, I'm just weighing all the options. Have any more of the approaching ships been hit?"

"One visible ship remains on course, sir. All others are destroyed."

"And the cloaked ones? Have any of them been targeted?"

"No, sir," said Gunney, "not as far as I can tell."

Pavlovich's eyes remained glued to the tactical display. To Hayden, he seemed unsure for the first time since he'd known him.

Scimitar had not yet been fired on. It was conceivable that they could remain neutral for a while longer under the pretence of faulty equipment, but he feared they might soon be forced to pick a side. In his opinion, the appearance of the invisible vessels armed with nuclear projectiles had sealed the deal in favour of siding with them. Pavlovich's uncertainty, however, gave him pause. What did the captain see that he didn't?

"Kaine, can our Glenatat sensors give us better info about those cloaked ships?"

"I'm not sure." Hayden activated them and examined the output. "Better indications of size: each ship is 380 cubic metres."

"Only 380? That's awfully small."

"It's large enough for a single power plant and a small rail gun, not much else. No room for a crew."

"A drone?"

"Yeah, that sounds about right. It would have to be locally controlled from that remaining ship."

"That's your target, Gunney."

"Aye, Cap'n."

The ship's lights dimmed as the powerful X-ray laser fired. Hayden watched on his instruments as the bow of the targeted vessel glowed a brilliant crimson as repeated pulses of their weapon struck it.

Suddenly, it blew apart as a high-velocity projectile tore through its weakened superstructure.

"It has been destroyed by a rail gun volley," said Hayden.

"And the drones?"

"Maintaining their course but no longer firing. They are drifting under inertia and will pass our position in forty-two seconds."

"Any risk of collision?"

"You mean as in a last-ditch suicide type attack? No."

Pavlovich considered the empty star field on the monitor. "Is there any chance we can nab one of those? Having the details of that tech could come in handy."

Hayden shook his head. "Not without revealing that we can see them. If we didn't have an audience..." He shrugged.

"Sir," announced the communications officer, "there is an incoming transmission."

The captain nodded and sat back in his chair.

"I see you found your trigger finger, Pavlovich. Thanks for the help."

"Our pleasure, Kovacs. My engineer fixed our problem in time to lend a hand. What the hell was that all about? Cloaked ships? I've never seen tech like that before."

"A lot has happened here. I'll let Stromm explain the situation to you."

"You're not sure how much you can tell me, eh? I understand."

"How are your engines running? Can you follow us back to base, or do you need a tow?"

Pavlovich chuckled. "You're never going to let me forget that incident, are you? No, we've got plenty of power. Just tell us the coordinates."

"They're being transmitted now. Normally, I would send an officer over to assume control of your ship, but I think you've shown us whose side you're on. You can retain command of your vessel until Stromm decides what to do with you and your crew."

"Understood. Lead on, and I'll buy you a drink when I see you."

"You owe me several drinks. Kovacs out."

Pavlovich exhaled and stood. He approached Hayden and lowered his voice. "Out of the frying pan..."

"There is a problem, Captain. Sooner or later, they are going to find out about us. What happens then?"

"I want a meeting of all department heads in half an hour. Include your girlfriend. We need to come up with a plan, or we may never leave this system."

A New Plan

ALL THE "DEPARTMENT heads" Pavlovich had euphemistically referred to were assembled in the briefing room.

Gunney was present, representing the tactical team. In another time, a company of regimental Rangers had been at his disposal. As things stood, a small group of former pirates who knew how to operate weapons served as a poor replacement.

Cora represented the technical and engineering disciplines, while Stella stood in for the medical services. Hayden had no idea how she became saddled with that responsibility.

He was the command representative, though with the captain in attendance, he wondered how redundant his presence was.

"We need a plan," said Pavlovich.

"I presumed you had one when you got us into this situation," said Stella, making no attempt to conceal her anger. "Perhaps if you had shared your brilliant idea with us to begin with, we might have something to work with."

Hayden placed a hand on her arm. Annoyed, she shook him off.

"Okay, I'll concede that things didn't turn out as I envisioned, but we are in a far stronger position than if we had tried sneaking around the system."

"How do you figure that?" said Hayden.

Pavlovich frowned. "Had we not declared ourselves, we would have been fired upon by the first patrol ships that came across us."

"Now we'll only be shot at by one side," Stella said.

"That's right," said the captain, "and they are the weaker of the two forces. They employ exotic tech to make themselves appear more formidable than they really are."

"They destroyed two warships," said Gunney. "I wouldn't say that was the work of a weak opponent."

"I read your tactical assessment, and I agree with you. Despite their control of the inner system, the current government is probably unstable. Neither side could afford to lose those ships."

"Which begs the question," said Hayden, "why did they engage in a fight over us? Gaining an out-of-date battle cruiser at the expense of so many vessels, one of them a Hawking class destroyer, seems like a bad trade to me."

Stella stared down Pavlovich. "What aren't you telling us?"

The captain spread his hands. "I don't know any more than you. It makes no sense to me either."

Cora joined in. "How will we get the erganium we require without attracting attention? Now that we are under armed escort, I can't see how we can do it."

"And, as mentioned," said Hayden, "it is only a matter of time before our new friends want to take a closer look at *Scimitar*."

"You let me handle that," said Pavlovich.

All eyes turned to him. Realizing the scrutiny he was under, he shrugged and said, "I know Kovacs and Stromm, and, I'll bet, half of their upper command. I'm familiar with how these guys think. I can get inside their heads. Don't worry."

"You'll forgive us if we don't seem reassured," said Stella.

The room grew quiet as she and Pavlovich stared each other down. Hayden was sure she must be reading something from the captain. He could think of no other reason why she would push him so hard. She wasn't military, like the others in the room, and didn't realize how close she came to insubordination. He needed to find a way to defuse the situation before Pavlovich decided he'd put up with enough from her and confined her to quarters, or worse.

"I have an idea about the erganium," he said.

The tension in the room broke, and all eyes turned to him.

"Well? Don't keep it to yourself, Kaine. What is it?"

"Our present course takes us to within a couple of million kilometres of Elgar."

"Close enough to wave at the planet. So what?"

"Well, Kovacs suggested he thought we might be having engine trouble."

"He was needling me about an old embarrassment."

"I realize that, sir, but he wouldn't know if we really did have problems or not. We've already bullshitted him about our power to the lasers. What if we incur a navigational error as we near the planet's outer rings? If we were to drift inside them, we would be concealed from their sensors. We could launch my ship and hide it in the rings until the fleet passes out of sensor range, then proceed to the moon to look for the mineral."

Pavlovich regarded Hayden as if he noticed him for the first time. "Son of a bitch! That just might work, Kaine."

"We would still need a plan for how to reunite with *Scimitar*," said Cora.

"How about if we go one step more?" said the captain. "What kind of system failure would force us to park in orbit to make repairs?"

"The only thing I can think of would be a massive radiation leak. Protocol is for us to abandon ship pending repair."

"I don't like that idea," said Hayden. "Can you think of anything else?"

"No, no! I like it," said Pavlovich. "It addresses a lot of our problems. It would prevent Kovacs from sending anyone over to inspect us. They wouldn't be outfitted to address such a problem and would call a repair vessel from the inner system. It would give us the time we need to refuel the FTL."

"But we wouldn't have a crew," said Stella. "Wouldn't they evacuate everyone back to Pictor Prime with them?"

"He will take whomever is listed in our crew manifest," said Hayden. "If we were to omit certain skilled individuals from that registry, they wouldn't suspect we'd left anyone behind."

"That could work," said Cora. "They haven't requested to see it yet."

"What if they decide to do something we don't expect?" asked Stella.

"Like what?"

"I don't know; tow us, for instance?"

"I can use our drones to trick their sensors into thinking our containment leak exceeds their hull rating. They won't be able to take us under tow for fear of contamination."

"It sounds like we have the makings of a plan, people," said Pavlovich, beaming.

"To make this appear convincing, we'll need to look like we've all been exposed to radiation," said Stella.

"I can help with that too," said Cora. "Let's talk later about it."

"Then it's settled. You and Kaine come up with a list of personnel to omit from the manifest. Make sure it includes you, XO. We don't want to run the risk that any of the details of what happened at Mu Arae may have found their way here. You might not be welcome."

"What about Stella?" he said.

"I want her with me when I meet with Kovacs and Stromm."

A frown creased her forehead as she considered the captain's suggestion. Finally, after a long pause, she nodded.

Hayden could not conceal how much that arrangement disturbed him. He thought he caught a subtle appearance of satisfaction on Stella's face, and he suddenly wished he had psychic abilities of his own.

The door to Stella's cabin opened, and she greeted Hayden with a sly smile.

"You took long enough to find your way here," she said as she stepped aside to admit him.

"I've been occupied with all the preparations."

She tilted her head and raised a skeptical eyebrow.

He felt himself blush. "And, yes, I avoided coming to see you."

Unable to maintain eye contact, he searched about the cluttered room for a place to sit, eventually opting for the edge of the unmade bed. She approached and sat next to him.

"What made you finally decide to risk it?" she asked.

"I think there is an old expression about addressing the hippopotamus in the room..."

"Elephant."

"Really?"

She nodded. "You were saying?"

He wrung his hands and studied his feet while gathering his thoughts. "Back at Mu Arae, when you left me, I was relieved."

"You'd been holding back a lot. Guilt, anger, resentment."

"After your departure, I guess I went through a catharsis of sorts. I felt unrestrained. I drank far too much and retreated into myself, constantly replaying the event and looking for something I could have done differently."

"I sensed the conflict in you every day. Believe me, Hayden, it hurt me a great deal to leave, but after years of trying to reach you, I decided there was nothing I could do. You needed to forgive yourself before anyone could help you."

He kissed her on the cheek. "Are you sure you want to go with Pavlovich? It will be dangerous."

"No more so than if I remain here with you," she said, "and, besides, I'll be of more use going with him. It doesn't sound like this Stromm character is someone we can trust."

"Not if he was involved in the original coup in this system."

He studied her face. "Why are you here, Stella? The story of you wanting to make your fortune like the others doesn't wash with me."

"A girl can't want to buy a few nice things?"

"You know what I mean. You lived your entire life pretty much removed from all those trappings. Why the sudden interest in getting rich? There's something else."

"It isn't anything complicated, Hayden. I saw this as an opportunity for you to redeem yourself, and I knew you wouldn't want to go with Pavlovich without some motivation."

"You're doing it for me, then?" He shook his head. "This is some costly therapy."

She squeezed his hand. "I went as far as leaving you for your own good. Why can't you believe I would do this for you?"

"Because you should live your life for yourself—not for me, your father, or anyone else."

"I'm an empath, Hayden. As much as you try, you can never know what it is like. When I am around others, I experience everything they do. When I am alone, I am empty."

"It seems like a heavy price to pay for the ability. Sounds like a curse to me."

"When I'm with you, it is a true blessing."

She wrapped her arms around his neck and pulled him down onto the bed.

Parting Ways

THE LAST DROP SHIP waited in the hangar, prepped and ready. Most of the crew had already been ferried to Kovacs's vessel, the *Iliad*. Pavlovich rubbed his neck where the dermal masking had been applied.

"You're sure this makeup is going to fool their doctors, Cora?"

"It's a synthetic dressing layer that mimics the effects of radiation exposure. Unless they try to do a biopsy, it should work."

"And what do you suggest I do if somebody wants to cut a chunk out of it to look more closely?"

"Don't let them," she said. "The shots you and the others took should counteract the treatment you'll receive once you get over there. The mask is programmed to respond to the chemicals they give you and will react as if the therapy is working."

"So, no side effects, then?"

"I didn't say that. You'll puke your guts out for a while, like they'll expect."

"Great," said Pavlovich. "On the bright side, I'll drop some weight like I've been meaning to."

"That's the spirit, Cap'n."

"Kaine, once we're gone, you'll be on your own."

"As will you, sir," said Hayden.

"Yeah, well, what I meant to say is, we'll have to hope everything goes according to plan. If this works, I'll be returning with the crew aboard the repair ship."

"You're taking a huge risk that they will permit it."

"They'll need somebody who can walk them through all the modifications they think we made to keep the old girl running for a decade."

"I'm more concerned about our people. They're pirates, and I don't know them. I'm not sure they can all stick to the script."

"They will. I've made sure they're all motivated."

Pavlovich let the comment hang, leaving Hayden's imagination to fill in the blanks as to what that meant. Out of the corner of his eye, he spotted Stella approaching, a bag slung over her shoulder. The captain turned and winked at Kaine, and he worried that Pavlovich's mentioned motivation had something to do with her.

She sidled up to Hayden and kissed him on the lips before intertwining her fingers with his.

"Good, I see you two are cozy again. I like the family to get along with each other."

"Our relationship is none of your business, Captain," she said.

"Of course," he said, grinning.

After their final farewells, Pavlovich and Stella boarded the drop ship, and it carried them to the *Iliad*. Hayden made his way to the bridge.

The place was empty, most of the crew having transferred.

"How are you holding up, Cora?"

"Everything is under control. We're only in orbit, after all, the engines are offline, and life support is on minimal. The only thing for me to do is maintain the false radiation signals our drones are sending out."

"You're sure they can't see through that?"

"You worry too much."

He sat in the command chair. "How long until they are out of sensor range?"

"Forty-seven hours."

He sighed and shifted his position then rose and advanced to the science station. After inspecting the readout, he moved on to the tactical instruments.

"You're going to wear yourself out if you do that for the next two days," said Cora.

"I know," he said, leaning against the console. "Patience isn't one of my virtues. Did your scans of the moon find any erganium?"

"I confirmed significant associated mineral deposits in the right ratios. I'm fairly confident we will find what we need down there."

"Yeah, okay."

"Maybe now would be a good time for you to join me in VR? It'll give you something to do other than worry."

"Oh, er, thanks, Cora. I don't think..."

"Stella said it would be all right."

"I'm sorry?"

"She said you can come visit me if you want. "

Hayden's face grew warm. "I don't know; we finally got our shit together..."

"Yes, she told me all about it. I'm happy for you two."

"Then you must understand—"

"What do you think is going to happen, Hayden?"

"What? Er, nothing. Nothing at all. I just..."

Cora's melodious laugh filled the bridge. "Maybe some other time, then?"

Realizing how foolish he must seem, he smiled. "Sure, that sounds good."

"I'm detecting engine heat from the other ships. They're leaving."

"Oh, good," he said, glad for the change of topic.

"But there may be a problem. Only three are departing."

"What?" He hurried back to the science station to check for himself.

"It looks like they left a babysitter behind to keep an eye on us," said Cora.

"Well, that complicates things. Shit! Do you think they suspect something?"

"I'm not certain we are why they remained behind. They fired their engines to drop into a lower orbit."

"That's odd. Can you determine a reason?"

"I'll need some time."

"Sure." He returned to the command chair and watched the other ship on the holographic viewer as it grew smaller.

"My guess is that they are on an approach to one of the planet's moons."

Hayden's heart skipped a beat. "Is it the moon we're interested in?"

"No, I can confirm that much."

Hayden scratched his head. "Is there anything significant about the one they're going to?"

"There's not much in our database, but it doesn't really stand out in any way. Most of the twenty-three moons orbiting Elgar are small, many volcanically active due to tidal forces. Some have thin atmospheres; a few are covered in water ice."

"They sound a lot like those around Jupiter or Saturn back home. Any signs of habitation?"

"Records show that two of the outer ones had mining operations before the collapse. We're too far away right now to determine if they are still operating."

"What about the one we're interested in?"

"Pomp is a—"

"Pomp?"

"Yes. All of this planet's moons have names associated with the works of the composer, Edward Elgar. There is Pomp, Circumstance, Enigma, Hope, Glory—"

"Okay, I get it. I was never much into classical music. Out of curiosity, are the other planets in this system named after composers? John Lennon, perhaps?"

"Never heard of him, but the other gas giants are Bach, Brahms—"

"Thanks, Cora, I'll look them up later. What were you saying about the moon? Pomp, was it?"

"It is one of the inner moons, about the size of Earth's satellite, terrestrial with tidal-generated tectonism."

"And how about the one they went to?"

"It is called Harmony and is basically a small captured asteroid."

"Maybe they are searching for rebel activity, but I can't imagine why something that small would interest them."

The ship on the screen had all but vanished as it made its way around the curve of the planet.

"Keep an eye on them for a bit. I want a better idea of what they are up to before we launch to look for the erganium."

"Our bugs are small enough to avoid detection," said Cora. "I want to send them out to survey some of the other moons. We might be able to locate a source of the mineral that our long-range scans missed that is more accessible."

"That's a good idea. If we can make things easier on ourselves, I'm all for it. You're sure they won't be spotted?"

"Naw, that's covered. They'll never know."

He nodded his approval and returned his attention to the screen.

Hayden continued to stare at the point on the planet's horizon over which the other vessel had vanished. An uneasy feeling settled on him. A small scouting craft would be a more appropriate choice if they were sniffing out rebel bases, smaller and more difficult to detect. That ship behaved in a far more relaxed manner than one operating in enemy held territory had any right to.

Cora's idea was a wise one. It was best to learn as much as possible before they took any action. They'd had too many surprises.

"YOUR FRIEND KOVACS is a real jerk."

Pavlovich smiled beneath his bushy beard. "Did your empathic abilities tell you that, Stella?"

"I don't need to be an empath to see that he is a creep."

"How long did it take for him to make a pass at you?"

"You knew he might do that and never said anything? You're an even bigger asshole than he is."

Pavlovich glanced around the ship's mess to reassure himself they were alone. "You should keep your voice down. Yes, Jim is a misogynist; it's only one of the reasons women didn't serve under his command back in the day."

"I'm surprised he was permitted to have one, if he's that kind of person," she said, returning her attention to her meal.

"He is something of an analytical genius. When I knew him, he was a rising star in the Intelligence Corps."

"So, he's a spy?"

"God, no! You got a hint of how subtle he can be. No, Kovacs oversaw data analysis and interpretation. He had an uncanny knack for sussing out significant information from the most innocuous events."

"And we are sitting right under his nose. Brilliant planning, Captain."

"The fact that he's in command of this little task force suggests he's moved on. But we still need to be careful of what we say around him and his people."

"I'll keep that in mind when he next gropes my ass."

"He really did that? What happened?"

"I didn't slap him." She frowned. "I was so shocked; all I could manage was a dirty look. But next time..."

"Probably best if you don't. We can't afford to make enemies of these guys."

"Where does that leave me and the other women in the crew?"

"I'll issue an order that everyone is to buddy up. You shouldn't go anywhere on the ship without me to watch your ass."

She glared at him.

"Sorry, an unfortunate turn of phrase. I'll run interference for you."

"Thank you, but it shouldn't need to come to this..."

"I think we should expect some breakdown of societal norms. This system has been cut off and at war for a long time. This may be an indication of the attitudes of Stromm and the rest of his cronies who are running things."

"What's going to happen when we arrive at the central planet?"

"There's no point in bullshitting you, Stella. You can see right through me, anyway. The answer is I don't know any more. Originally, I hoped military discipline had remained intact, but I'm seeing signs that things have become more..."

"Barbaric?"

"Well, in a word, yes. Neither side in this conflict wants to abide by the accepted rules of war. Even the coup, from what I have gathered, was brutal and bloodier than necessary."

"Why would this happen? Hasn't humanity evolved beyond this kind of behaviour?"

He regarded her. "Didn't you grow up in a system that was cut off, like this one is now?"

"We were isolated at Mu Arae, but we had a common foe in the Malliac. People banded together and took care of each other."

He nodded. "Here, the only commonality about the enemy is that they are human, possibly former friends. It appears that everyone is adopting a 'live for today' philosophy."

"Why do you think they are so interested in *Scimitar*? Do you think it's possible that they learned about...?" Stella checked the room. "You know what."

"How? Any conventional radio signal would take decades to reach here, and nobody else can..." he lowered his voice "...do what we can. There is no chance they can know about us."

"Then what could it be?"

"I don't know. I've captained her for almost twenty-five years."

"*Scimitar* is older than that. Who commanded her before you?"

"I replaced Admiral Thomas when he was promoted, and he was her captain from *Scimitar*'s first day of service."

"So, no others than you two?"

"Nope. The old girl is pretty monogamous."

She raised an eyebrow. "That's just weird."

Pavlovich shrugged.

"It does raise an interesting possibility, though," she said. "Maybe what they are interested in is related to your predecessor? Perhaps he left something valuable hidden on board?"

"That idea occurred to me, but I can't imagine what it could be. Between routine refits, Cora's repairs, and the Glenatat augmentation, *Scimitar*'s been pretty much rebuilt more than once. Ironically, there is very little of the original ship left."

"So, what remains?"

"I dunno." He scratched his beard. "My command chair...maybe a couple of deck plates and bulkheads. Not much."

"What about the ship's computer?"

"No, the core was updated twice during refits, and with what Cora and her Glenatat robot did, it's completely replaced."

"What about the data that was on it? Any chance of hidden files?"

"No. Everything was routinely backed up to the military network whenever we made port."

"What if something were put into the computer when the ship was built? Something someone intended to hide?"

"Whatever it might be is important enough for both sides to sacrifice ships they couldn't afford to lose."

"Which makes it valuable enough to kill us for," she said.

"I'm afraid so."

"Yegor, you old dog!"

The man who advanced toward them from across the room was a head shorter than the captain and sported a middle-aged paunch. His pudgy face and curly, dark brown hair reminded Stella of a cherub.

"It's been too long," said Pavlovich as the two men embraced.

"Thirty years, isn't it?"

"Something like that. You look good, Ullie."

"Oh, bullshit. I'm at least twenty kilos heavier than when we last saw each other."

"But no grey in your hair."

"A concession to my vanity. But look at you, Yegor; still as fit and trim as you were at the academy. The salt and pepper in that rat's nest on your face even makes you appear wise."

Pavlovich stroked his beard as he turned to indicate Stella. "Ulysses Stromm, allow me to introduce you to Stella Gabriel, my first officer."

She tried to mask her discomfort. Even though she was listed as XO in the doctored crew manifest, it was the first time she heard herself referred to as such.

"A pleasure to meet you." He took a moment to examine their clothing. "Given up on wearing the uniform, Pavlovich?"

"It's been ten years, Ullie. Things wear thin, including morale. Allowing the crew to dress themselves in civvies was—"

Stromm waved a dismissive hand. "Say no more, old friend. I completely understand. We've been forced to make sartorial concessions of our own." He indicated his own modified uniform.

"So, general, is it?" said Pavlovich, pointing to the insignia at Stromm's collar.

"Less baggage than the rank of admiral carried. Besides, I haven't been on the bridge of a ship in five years. I'm mostly planet-bound these days."

Stromm invited them to join him at a table set with three place settings at the side of the room. When they were seated, the general motioned to someone who lurked near the door. Within seconds, three waiters entered, carrying covered trays.

"I hope you brought your appetites," said Stromm as he stuffed a napkin into his collar. A server placed a plate in front of each of them, filled with sumptuous-looking food.

"This looks amazing, Ullie."

"A lot better than dehydrated rations, eh?"

"We constructed a hydroponic garden a few years ago. It broke up the monotony," said Pavlovich.

"And undoubtedly prevented a mutiny or two."

"Why would you say that, General?" Stella said.

Stromm appeared surprised. "Oh, I was told your ship had been in transit since the light gates went down."

"Yes, that's right," said Pavlovich. "But *Scimitar*'s crew is close-knit and well trained."

"More like a family," Stella said before raising a fork full of meat to her mouth.

"You always managed to command loyalty from your subordinates, Yegor. Even in the academy, you had more friends willing to give you the shirt off their backs than anyone I knew."

"It came in handy for some of those string dynamics assignments." Pavlovich grinned.

"Yes, everybody fell under your spell. I forgot that about you."

"Not everyone. Not Eliza."

Stromm smiled. "She taught both of us a valuable lesson, didn't she?"

They paused, staring at each other for a few seconds before together saying, "Don't trust women!" They simultaneously broke out in raucous laughter.

Stella caught herself scowling at them and returned her attention to her meal, hoping they hadn't noticed.

"Your XO obviously does not have a high opinion of us, Yegor."

Pincered between her own embarrassment and the strong emotion she detected from Stromm, she had difficulty maintaining her composure.

"Not of you gentlemen," she said, "just the substance of your comment."

"You are well within your right to be offended, Miss Gabriel. Please accept my apology."

She forced a smile she hoped appeared sincere. "No offence is taken, General. Let's put it behind us, if you don't mind?"

"I can see why she is your number one, Pavlovich. She's probably the only one who can keep you in line."

He smiled. "That she does."

The remainder of the meal was less contentious, with the conversation drifting between discussing officers they both knew and how they'd each spent the past thirty years.

"So, Miss Gabriel—is it Commander Gabriel?"

Stella sensed a shift in the emotional tension in the room, particularly in the captain.

"Lieutenant Commander," said Pavlovich.

"Forgive me, General. Being in transit for a decade has resulted in a relaxed attitude among our crew. I can't remember the last time I was addressed by my rank." She glanced at Pavlovich.

Stromm narrowed his eyes. "I imagined adherence to command structure and discipline would have been a necessity in your situation."

"We were in it together," said the captain. "Sure, we had a few bumps in the first couple of years. When it became apparent that we were alone with no real hope of encountering anyone from home for a long time, it didn't become an issue."

Stromm raised his wine glass. "A testament to your wise crew selection, Yegor."

He acknowledged the toast. "You're generous. It is more due to my crew's determination to survive."

"Well, your accomplishment is something I never would have expected."

Pavlovich frowned. "Why is that?"

"Well, as far as I can recall, you were out of favour with the High Command ten years ago."

The room felt uncomfortably small for Stella with the sudden increase in tension.

"It is true that Thomas and I didn't agree on some issues."

"I heard it was a little more serious, but who can trust rumours?"

Though Stromm's smile appeared disarming, she detected a growing confidence in him. Her heart pounded rapidly as she tried to decouple her own emotions from the others in the room.

"It was common knowledge that your ship was a dumping ground for undesirables who pissed off Thomas. Didn't he assign you Walden Kaine's son?"

Pavlovich's face remained unreadable, but she sensed his growing panic. "Yes, Kaine was a member of my crew, but he died almost a decade ago."

"During the events at Mu Arae?" Stromm appeared satisfied, as if he'd solved a puzzle.

Silence hung in the air as Pavlovich stared at him. Stella was almost overwhelmed by the intensity of the conflicting emotions in the room.

"I was privy to the reports transmitted to Command by Doctor Ishmael Gabriel," said the general. "Some of us were aware of his research and the alien threat it uncovered. His ramblings seemed mad until your messengers arrived at Earth shortly before the network collapsed." He faced Stella. "Are you any relation to him?"

"We share a common name."

He nodded. "Some distant cousin, no doubt. Still, it is an interesting coincidence that you were both there, don't you think? What happened to the good doctor?"

"He died," she said.

Pavlovich came to her rescue. "I'm glad our message made it home. But tell me, Ullie, if you were on Earth when the gate collapsed, how do you come to be here?"

"Oh, I was here. I received an intelligence packet before it went down."

"So, they got the word out; that's a relief," said Pavlovich. His face appeared to match his words, but Stella could tell he was anxious. "At least people know of the circumstances of the collapse."

"It must have been an overwhelming decision for you. I'm grateful I am not the one who made the call to destroy the network." Stromm spread his hands.

"There was no other option."

"I'm just confused by one small detail, Yegor. If you destroyed the network to prevent the aliens from accessing it, how did you escape the system?"

Pavlovich swallowed. Stella caught a glimpse of perspiration darkening the armpits of his uniform.

"We jumped before it collapsed. Kaine volunteered to remain behind and disable the gate."

"His father would be gratified his son died a hero's death, if he could be told."

"He was an exceptional officer," said Pavlovich.

Stromm nodded, then turned to Stella. "You seem to have distinguished yourself, Lieutenant Commander. To serve as XO at such a young age—I'm surprised someone more seasoned isn't in the position."

"She's earned her rank."

"I have no doubt," said Stromm before emptying his wine glass. He wiped his mouth with the napkin and placed it neatly beside his empty plate. "Now, shall we turn the conversation to the *Scimitar*? A radiation containment failure, is it?"

Stella relaxed as she felt Pavlovich do so.

"Yes," said the captain. "Fortunately, your fleet was present when it happened. I'm anxious to return to her to oversee the decontamination and repairs."

A subtle smile turned up on Stromm's face. "We dispatched a repair ship almost as soon as we learned of the problem. It should arrive at *Scimitar* in another day or so. We'll have her repaired and back here before you know it."

Pavlovich smiled. "That *is* good news, although I wish you'd waited for me to join them. There are some unconventional modifications we've made."

"My people are very good at improvising. We've had to be, given our isolation and limited access to resources." The general placed his arms on the table and leaned forward. "*Scimitar* is far too valuable to leave exposed in orbit around Elgar. We suspect rebels are operating from one of its moons. After we get her safely into port here, she will make a crucial addition to our fleet. As will her captain and crew."

"Of course," said Pavlovich.

Stella stared at the remains of her meal, no longer hungry. Two opposing emotions dominated her senses from the room's occupants: triumph and despair. She didn't need to guess which came from whom.

A Monster on the Loose

"DESTROYED? EVERYONE?"

"Yup," said Cora, "but that isn't the worst news."

"What could be worse than finding six bombarded moons?" asked Hayden as he continued to read the report from the drone survey.

"Only one of them showed evidence of being a military target. There was debris of ships, big guns, and extensive, fortified building complexes; it was all wiped out in a massive attack from orbit."

"And the other five?"

"They were all colony moons. No military presence at all."

"The rebels concealed their base amidst a bunch of settlements?"

"No, it was isolated on a moon well out of range of the populated ones. They took great care to keep the civilian population out of the conflict."

"Then why would someone obliterate nonmilitary targets?" said Hayden. "That is a war crime."

"Indeed, it is. They were targeted for being in the general neighbourhood of a rebel base."

"Casualty estimates?"

"The records we have for this system only indicate that there were plans to establish colonies out here. If they followed through with them, there could have been six hundred thousand people between all five settlements."

"We have no way of knowing how big they were. Maybe they were scaled down from the initial plan."

"Hayden, whether the population was a million or only a few hundred, it doesn't diminish the crime. Stromm's forces targeted civilian noncombatants."

"We're sure Stromm is responsible?"

"Well, no, but the circumstances suggest it was him. If not, then it was the captain's cousin, but I have a more difficult time believing that."

"Why? I don't know Pavlovich well," said Hayden. "They might both be monsters."

"Well, I served with him for the last twelve years. I know the man, and he was raised right. He would never do such a thing, and I can't believe anyone from the same family would either."

"I'll bet the relatives of Hitler or Stalin wished people thought that way. I'll trust your judgement, Cora." His brow creased as another thought developed. "If it was Stromm, then our people are in the hands of a man capable of doing anything. They are in grave danger."

"What should we do?"

"Right now, we can't do anything. *Scimitar* is undermanned and hardly in a position to mount a rescue operation."

"What's going to happen?" she asked.

"We are going to proceed with our mission: find the erganium and get this ship's FTL back online. After that, we might have a better idea of what happened to Pavlovich and the others." Thoughts of Stella flashed across his mind, and his stomach tied into a knot.

"Perhaps I'm wrong and the villain is Malkovich, and not Stromm," said Cora. "Maybe they are in the best hands possible."

"I hope so. But you're right about one thing. There is definitely a monster on the loose in this system, and we will come up against him soon enough."

A Game of Chess

"WHAT ARE WE GOING TO do?"

"Not so loud," said Pavlovich. He appeared untroubled, his chair tilted on its back legs and his feet perched on the top of the table.

Stella was aware, however, of the emotional turmoil the captain tried to conceal. Her eyes searched the small, sparse room they were confined in.

"Are they watching us?"

"Of course. They spied on us during the trip." He lowered his feet to the floor and leaned forward. "Damn! Ten years away made me addle-brained."

"Listening in on others' conversation isn't something normal people do."

"It was common. You always had to watch what you said aboard another ship." He shook his head. "How could I have forgotten that crap?"

She placed a hand on his shoulder. "Maybe you just learned to trust people."

He patted her hand. "Yeah, well, I won't be making that mistake again." He looked up to the ceiling as if ensuring his message was clear to those who eavesdropped on them.

They fell into silence. Stella sat on the only other chair in the room on the opposite side of the table.

"What is going to happen to us?" she asked.

Pavlovich shrugged.

She sighed. "Sometimes I wish I was a telepath."

"It would be a handy skill at the moment."

His eyelids narrowed, and he studied her closely. "But you've been known to be...influential on large groups, with your own particular gift."

Stella frowned, unsure to what he referred. "You are the persuasive one. The way you convinced me—" She caught herself before she mentioned Hayden's name.

The captain smiled at her conspiratorially. "Yes, but not like you—not like at Mu Arae. You had the entire crew under your spell at one point." He raised his eyebrow slightly.

Stella realized he was attempting to speak in code, but she was at a loss as to what it might be. Then it came to her.

Pavlovich referred to a time when she had less control over her empathic ability; a time when she inadvertently incapacitated most of *Scimitar*'s crew because they all had active LINK modules in their heads.

She scowled at him. "I told you I won't do that."

He stared at her, unconvinced.

"Besides," she said, "I don't know if I could...persuade enough people for it to help us. And even if I could, what good would it do?"

"It isn't something to try at the moment, but when the opportunity presents itself, I trust you'll consider it?"

"I'll think about it."

"That's all I ask."

Another silence fell between them. Stella scrutinized Pavlovich as his wandering gaze seemed to examine every corner of the room.

"Well, I suppose there is only one thing that we can do," he said. He spoke loudly into the air. "I'll just have to inform Stromm that I know where he can find Cesar Malkovich."

"You do?" whispered Stella.

He nodded.

"But why would you do that?"

He lowered his voice. "You'll see."

She didn't have to wait long before the door to the room opened and a junior officer stepped in. As the door closed, she caught a glimpse of the armed guard who remained outside.

"Captain Pavlovich, will you please accompany me? General Stromm has some questions for you."

"What about my XO?"

"I've been sent only for you."

Pavlovich shrugged. "I'm not going anywhere without her."

"Sir, neither of you are prisoners."

"Oh, my apologies. I tend to think that way when I am locked inside a windowless room for a period. She's with me, or Stromm can come here."

The young man regarded Pavlovich for a few seconds before turning his attention to Stella. After a moment, his smile sagged, and he sighed. "Very well. Will you both come with me to see the general?"

Pavlovich's smug grin matched the satisfaction Stella read from him. "We would be delighted. Please lead on."

They followed the man through the door. Two armed soldiers fell in step behind them. The officer who led them through the labyrinthine corridors of Stromm's headquarters seemed pensive. Even without her empathic ability, Stella could tell he and the guards were nervous.

After a long walk, they passed through a security checkpoint, where they were handed over to two different men. Though not as well armed as the previous escort, they still displayed a high degree of vigilance. She noticed an increase in the tension of every person they encountered as they approached what she assumed to be Stromm's inner sanctum. She could not help but wonder what put so many on edge.

Double doors opened to a large office where Stromm and Kovacs were hunched over a table, studying something. Both men looked up, but only the general smiled. The other man maintained a stony visage. Though she tried to read him, she was surprised that she could detect no emotional leakage from the man. She'd never encountered anyone from whom she could not sense at least rudimentary emotions.

"Please, come in," said Stromm in an inviting tone. "Can I get you anything? I have some exceptional brandy, Yegor."

"Just water," said Pavlovich as he sat, uninvited, on one of the comfortable-looking chairs around the table. "We didn't get much to drink during our confinement."

Stromm seemed to be surprised. "What do you know of this, Kovacs?"

"A standard security precaution. It seemed reasonable given recent events, don't you think?"

Pavlovich arched an eyebrow. "Having troubles, Ullie?"

The general invited Stella to take a seat then assumed one of his own. Kovacs remained standing, one hand resting on the sidearm at his belt. He said, "We've had a series of incursions into our headquarters over the past few weeks. There have been a few close calls."

"That explains your security," said Pavlovich. "What happened?"

Kovacs studied him, as if weighing the wisdom of saying anything. "We recently discovered Malkovich's agent among our people."

"A sleeper?"

"Yes." Stromm rolled up his sleeve to reveal an ugly, recent scar. "My own chief of staff did this to me two months ago."

"Holy shit, Ullie. You need to give your people a pay increase."

Kovacs scowled at him. "It is hardly a laughing matter."

Pavlovich nodded. "You believed we might be agents for Malkovich?"

"You, or members of your crew."

"I take it they are all confined?"

"Until we can vet them."

"But Yegor has been outside of this system since he left Mu Arae," said Stromm to Kovacs. "It is not plausible that he is involved with the rebels."

"He is related to Malkovich. They are cousins."

"If you are going to condemn a man because of his genetics, we know from history where that goes."

Stella did not detect any of the expected emotional variance from Stromm in his defence of Pavlovich. She was convinced that they played out a well-rehearsed scene. It was no coincidence that they had been removed from that cell the moment the captain mentioned he was prepared to betray his relative.

"We may be cousins, but that doesn't mean we're friends."

"Easy words to say," said Kovacs. "Without access to your ship's comm logs, we are forced to take your word that you have not been in communication with him. That situation will soon be rectified, however. What will we discover, I wonder?"

Pavlovich crossed his arms and put his feet on the table. "I'll save you the trouble. I contacted Cesar when I entered the system, the same as I did you, Ullie."

"I knew it!" Kovacs undid the clasp of his sidearm holster.

Stromm signalled him to calm down. "Explain yourself, Yegor."

"It's simple, really. I had no idea what the situation was. To the best of my knowledge, the old government was still in place and Kwong still in charge of the fleet. I first reached out to him because, well, he may be an asshole, but he is family. He gave me his version of what happened, and, frankly, knowing him as I do, I thought it smelled hinky. So, I contacted you."

"You led us into an ambush," Kovacs said. "One that cost me three good ships."

"It seems to me that Cesar lost a few more than you. It couldn't be helped. I thought I'd let you guys demonstrate who was the stronger before I declared myself."

"You always were one to hedge your bets," said Stromm.

"The one thing that had me confused was what you boys thought so special about my ship. Why risk so many of your own for an old tub like *Scimitar*? Then you tipped me off when we met, Ullie. You and Cesar both knew about our encounter with the Glenatat."

"We suspected you had some kind of advanced weaponry; maybe something that can end this bloody war, once and for all."

"And it does."

Stella's mouth fell open. Besides her own emotional upheaval, the only other person from whom she detected a reaction was Stromm. Pavlovich appeared as calm as ever and Kovacs remained unreadable.

"You're only telling us now because our ship has almost arrived at yours," sneered Kovacs. "You are just trying to curry favour and save your ass."

"Not only mine, but my crew's, too."

Stromm smiled. "What's your play? What do you have up your sleeve, Yegor?"

He grinned. "In addition to weapons, *Scimitar* has a pretty sweet security AI. Anyone who sets foot on her decks without my authorization will be a steaming lump of protoplasm before they leave the airlock."

"So what?" said Kovacs. "We'll tow her back here."

"I'd like to see you try."

"What do you want, Yegor?" asked Stromm.

"I want my ship back, along with my people. I knew you wouldn't simply return them to me, so, I am offering to help end your little disagreement with Cesar."

"That's it?" Amusement danced in Stromm's eyes. Stella did not like what she saw.

"You could spend several months, and possibly even hack into *Scimitar*'s systems," said Pavlovich, "but I'm betting you don't have that kind of time, do you?"

Stromm and Kovacs exchanged a knowing look.

Pavlovich smiled. "Ullie, you never could play poker worth shit. Put us back on *Scimitar*. We'll use our weaponry and take out Cesar's base."

"And what do you want out of this?"

"We get the freedom to go wherever we want when this is over. I'll make you king, and you'll let us go."

"What will prevent you from turning your weapons on us?"

"Ullie, it's one vessel. A powerful one, but still a single ship. Besides, I expect you'll want to put some babysitters aboard to keep an eye on us. I understand that."

"You've given me an interesting offer," said Stromm as he signalled the guards who had remained by the door. "We will discuss it and get back to you."

Pavlovich stood, smiling confidently. "Don't take too long. I don't think Cesar is going to give you much time to dwell on it."

After their escort had returned them to the windowless room and left, Stella whispered, "Why did you tell them about the weapons? I read Stromm like a book. He didn't know anything about them until you blabbed about it."

He smiled. "I had to sell it. Now, they have no choice but to take us back to *Scimitar*, and once there, we can find out what they are really after."

"And what about the others still out there? What happens when that repair ship arrives?"

"Presumably, Stromm will signal them to hang around and wait. I just hope your boyfriend has the good sense not to blow them out of the skies. If he does, we will definitely have a problem."

The Best of Poor Choices

"THIS IS A CRAZY IDEA," said Hayden.

"It's the only one with a tactical chance," said Gunney.

The two of them were in the conference room. The central sphere that housed Cora's essence glowed and pulsed with light, as if she were thinking.

"What kind of probability are you giving it?"

"Thirty percent, tops."

"Shit!" Hayden lowered his head to the table. He hadn't caught more than three hours of sleep since the rest of the crew had departed aboard *Iliad*. "Isn't there anything else we can do?"

"Captain, our options are limited. We either follow through with this plan to distract the other ship, or..." Gunney shrugged.

"I won't fire on them. Not unless we have no other choice."

"Sir, that repair vessel will be in scanning range in seventy hours. If we don't act soon, we will lose our only window of opportunity. Then the only action remaining to us will be to destroy both ships."

"Pavlovich might be aboard it."

"That isn't possible, Hayden," said Cora's disembodied voice. "It is approaching on a completely different vector. There is no way he could have transferred to it. I think it was dispatched as soon as *Iliad* left here."

"I don't have the personnel to defend us in a boarding situation," said Gunney.

"Do we have time to adapt Glenatat technology into a security system?" asked Hayden.

"They provided external shielding and dark energy cannons; nothing else can be adapted for use inside the ship without weeks of testing," said Cora.

"Remind me to put that on the maintenance list, if we get out of this."

"Noted, Captain."

He winced internally when they addressed him by that title. This was Pavlovich's ship—it had been for decades. Perhaps, once, long ago he might have coveted a command of his own, but those days and dreams were far behind him. What he wanted was to retreat to his cabin and dig out the hidden bottle, but Gunney and Cora both depended on him to keep his head and remain sharp. He wouldn't put them in any more danger than they already were.

He sat straight. "Okay, let's go over your idea again, Gunney."

"We haven't had an opportunity to launch the shuttle because of the unpredictable search pattern the ship they left behind is using."

"Cora?"

"Their movements are random. I can't predict where they'll go next, so the chance of them spotting you are too great."

"So, what we require is some way to know where they will be?"

"Precisely why Gunney's plan creates our best opportunity."

"Okay," said Hayden, rubbing the sleep from his eyes. "Give me the details again."

"We have to time things for when Elgar is between us and the approaching repair vessel. That will be trivial. The more complex part involves the relative locations of the search ship, us, the moon we want to get to, and our target."

"And it needs to be that particular one? It's no more than a captured asteroid, isn't it?"

Cora said, "It has to be a large enough body to attract the other ship's attention when we destroy it. There are other asteroids in Elgar's orbit, but most of them are too small or in the wrong position to do any good."

"And you're sure the dark energy cannon will supply the kind of fireworks we need?"

"Given the composition of the asteroid, the explosion should be spectacular enough to get anyone's attention without leaving a detectable radiation signature."

"What is the power draw to pull this off?"

"We will tax the engines."

"Meaning?"

"We only have the opportunity for one shot," said Gunney. "After that, we'll be defenceless until we can recharge."

"During which time I have to launch the shuttle and hope the search ship doesn't notice."

"Yes."

"Well, that doesn't sound so difficult," said Hayden as he rolled his eyes.

"That is the easy part," said the cyborg. "The problem will be getting you back to *Scimitar*."

"Even if everything goes flawlessly once you land," said Cora, "the elapsed time to complete your mission will mean the approaching repair ship will be within sensor range."

"Then we must avoid being spotted by them as well. I get it."

"Captain, I won't bullshit you," said Gunney. "Like it or not, we may need to destroy one or both of those ships to get you back here."

Hayden shook his head. "Those people are not our enemy."

"If they try to board us, or open fire, they are not our friends. I will act accordingly to defend you and this ship." After a pause, he added, "Sir."

"Thank you. I appreciate your concern for *Scimitar*'s and my welfare."

The cyborg uttered a grunt and nodded.

"Hayden," said Cora, "the probability is that we will not be able to avoid a conflict."

"That may be so, but if we do end up in a fight, we will put the lives of our people in grave danger."

"I can improve our chances greatly if you let me come with you."

"I told you before, you're needed to run the ship."

"You are thinking of me as if I'm still human. I can partition my consciousness and accompany you."

"But what about *Scimitar*? Gunney and Chin can't afford for you not to be here."

"I will be here, or at least an operational clone of me will. It will lack my core personality, but that won't affect anything."

"I don't know, Cora..."

"Hayden, you need me. Besides, I promised Stella I would look after you."

"You would occupy my ship's computer, is that it?"

"Yes, and I prepared a synth for when we venture out onto the surface—for some of the heavy lifting."

He smiled. "It's a small moon, Cora. I doubt gravity will be an issue."

"You still need somebody to watch your back. What if you are injured?"

He raised his hands in surrender. "I give up. You can come." He looked to Gunney and glanced up at Cora's sphere. "How long is needed to prepare?"

"We're ready. Our positioning window will open in three hours."

Hayden sighed. "Okay, let's do this."

He hoped he wasn't leading them down the path to disaster.

"T-MINUS ONE MINUTE," came the announcement over Hayden's helmet speaker.

"You sound like you're in my head, Cora. Isn't VR supposed to be the other way around?"

"You know how it works, silly. We can chat about it later. You need to stay focused."

"Right," he said as he resumed his prelaunch check sequence. When the console in front of him lit up with green lights, he said, "Everything is good here, Bridge."

"Acknowledged," said Gunney. "Good luck, Captain."

"You're in charge now. Take care of the ship."

"Aye-aye."

The hangar bay doors slid open in silence, revealing the blue and red-banded surface of Elgar that dominated the field of view.

"Remember to park in our sensor shadow until the asteroid blows," said the gunnery officer. "Then be prepared to punch your engines on my signal. I'm guessing you will have about thirty seconds of cover from the radiation burst."

"Don't worry, I only have to make it into the planet's third ring."

"Let's hope they take the bait. You will be visible and vulnerable until you reach it. I can't defend you against any missiles they may launch your way."

"Acknowledged, Bridge. I'm launching now."

"Are you sure you don't want me to fly us, Hayden?" asked Cora. "My reaction times are much faster than yours and—"

"I prefer to pilot, if you don't mind. It gives me something to stay focused on."

"Of course, I'll just keep an eye on the ship systems."

A bead of sweat trickled down Hayden's forehead, and he needed to scratch his nose behind the closed visor.

With practised ease, his hands played over the ship's controls, and the small craft floated from the hangar. Once parked in position, he shut everything down and waited in darkness for Gunney to fire on the asteroid. The only thing he heard was his controlled deep breathing and the sound of the blood swishing in his ears.

"Hayden, are you okay? Your pulse is up thirty-five percent."

"I'm just anxious," he whispered.

"I've almost forgotten how that feels." There was a hint of regret in her words.

He wanted to tell her that he was glad for the anxiety—that it helped him remain sharp and feel alive in such situations—but he knew how insensitive that remark would be. Though Cora still sounded like the carefree girl he'd met a decade before, he had a difficult time imagining that she did not regret losing her body. He didn't believe he would have accepted the same situation with the grace she displayed.

"Get ready, Hayden. Gunney's diverted power to the weapons."

Hayden's hands hovered over the dark controls. He counted down the time. The tally ran to a minute, then another. He had trouble working up spittle to swallow.

"Cora, what's the delay?"

"Shh. Stay alert."

He frowned but managed to bite back a sharp reply.

A brilliant flare bloomed around the edges of *Scimitar*, briefly snuffing out the stars.

"That's it, Hayden. Let's go!"

But his hands were already in motion before her urging, and the thruster of his small craft fired at full burn. Instantly, he was thrown into the back of his chair with what felt like the weight of the entire ship trying to crush his ribcage. His blood pressure suddenly dropped, and his vision darkened. Within seconds, the bladders in his g-suit expanded with fluid, squeezing his leg and abdominal muscles.

His head clearing, Hayden tried to blink the flashing stars from his eyes and ignored the ringing in his ears. He struggled in vain to turn his head, but it was pinned to his seat under the g-force. Unable to lift his arms to reach the control panel, he hoped that Cora would soon shut down the engine. His attempts at speech amounted to a few weak grunts.

Finally, when he believed he'd reached his limit of endurance, the vibration stopped and the pressure that pressed down on his chest relented. A second later, the g-suit deflated, releasing his muscles from its iron grip.

After flexing his shoulders to assure himself he once more had control of his body, he said, "Did it work?"

"We are inside the third ring." Cora's voice was calm, as if nothing had just happened. From her perspective, that was true, he thought.

"Did they take the bait?"

"I don't know for sure. The same ionized particles that protect us from detection also obscure our sensors. Before we entered, they had adjusted their course toward the blast, though."

"How long do we stay here?"

"We should remain obscured until we pass into Elgar's shadow ten hours from now."

"Wow, that long."

Cora laughed. "Don't worry, Hayden. We don't need to make small talk. You should rehydrate and get some sleep. Your body needs to recover from the strain you just experienced, and you'll want to be at your best for whatever comes next."

"Are you sure you don't want me to keep you company?"

"Are you worried I can't drive? Or was there something you wanted to talk to me about? Did you want to join me in VR?"

He felt himself blush. "Ah, er, no..."

"You are so easy to tease. Relax, the ship is in good hands, and I promise to wake you if anything unexpected comes up."

He chuckled to mask his embarrassment. "Okay, you win. I'll get some shuteye."

He closed his eyes and drifted off. After what seemed like a few seconds, he was startled awake by Cora.

"Up and at 'em, sleepyhead."

"What is it? I just dozed off for a second."

She laughed. "You've been snoring for the last nine and a half hours, silly."

"What? No way." He blinked, trying to force himself to be fully alert. Through the front window loomed the night side of Elgar. "Oh. I guess I was tired."

"We will be at our course correction point in twenty minutes. You have time for some personal needs. I won't watch."

Hayden hesitated to reach for the buckle of his restraint harness, suddenly self-conscious. Realizing how foolish that was, and needing to relieve himself, he released the belt and floated through the cramped cabin to the toilet.

When he returned to the pilot chair and strapped himself back in, he looked out at the spherical shadow, barely discernible against the black of space. "Is that where we're headed to? Pomp, is it?"

"Yes. I've been scanning it as we've drifted nearer the thin edge of the ring, but I'm still getting too much interference for more than the basic thermal and radiation readings. Everything appears normal. It is a cold, dead moon."

"One with a treasure we are risking our asses to find. I'm worried about what will happen if we don't locate any erganium. We'll be stuck in this system."

"We must not fail, Hayden. I fear that our lives will be very short, otherwise. But there is some on that moon."

"How can you be so sure?"

"All the data suggest it is so, and I have faith."

"That isn't something I've had a lot of over these past few years. My father taught me not to rely on providence or the goodwill of others. If he ever possessed faith of any kind, it was only in his ability to get what he wanted."

"And how's that philosophy working out for you?"

Hayden smiled. "Perhaps not very well."

"So, can we try things my way?"

"I really have no other options, Cora. Besides, I trust you, and if you believe that this will work out, that is good enough for me."

"That sounds like a big change from how you were brought up."

He looked out the window at the slowly growing moon. "I'm not the man I used to be. Being cut off from the world I grew up in for so long... well, I don't really know who I am."

"I can tell you." Her voice was tender.

Hayden bit back the comment on the tip of his tongue. How could she believe she knew him? Cora hadn't seen him in ten years and was now more AI than person...and then there was Stella. She'd caught a glimpse of how shallow his real self was and high-tailed it. She'd wanted nothing to do with the remnant he'd become, and he couldn't really blame her. She was trying to bring them together, and he admired her for it, but her faith in him was misplaced, as was Cora's.

"How long until our course correction?" he asked.

The topic transitioned; Cora returned her attention to piloting. Was it his imagination, or did the cabin temperature seem cooler?

At the predetermined coordinates, she fired the engines and adjusted their heading to an approach vector to Pomp.

In continued silence, she manoeuvred them into orbit and then began their descent to the surface. Not until after they landed did she finally speak.

"That outcrop on the left is our best candidate. While you put on your pressure suit, I'll transfer over to the synth."

"We're going to leave the ship unguarded?"

"Who do you think might steal it?" She still sounded pissed with him. Then her voice softened. "Besides, I can partition myself again and keep watch over it while I go with you. Does that make you feel better?"

"Cora, I'm sorry for cutting off the conversation earlier."

"I understand. Don't worry about it. We can talk another time when you're ready. Right now, we have more pressing matters, don't you agree?"

He nodded and retrieved the suit from the locker.

A few minutes later, he exited, followed by a two-metre-tall humanoid robot. The only surviving, functional synth aboard *Scimitar* was a modified medical model. It was rudimentary and possessed only a basic robotic frame and featureless face. He found Cora's voice coming from it disconcerting and was grateful when, once outside, he could only hear her through his helmet receiver.

"The strongest readings are about a hundred metres away, over the top of that crater rim." The android pointed toward a nearby ridge. Without further delay, it started walking to the outcrop, striding easily across the rocky surface.

Hayden took a step and propelled forward. His toes dug into the dusty regolith, and his arms windmilled to regain his balance. Failing, he tumbled in slow motion to the ground.

"Damn it!"

"Are you all right?" asked Cora, looming over him, offering a hand.

Accepting her help, he returned to his feet and knocked the dust off.

"It's been a long time since my low-G training. I'll be fine."

After a moment examining him for damage to his suit, she turned and continued to the base of the hill. Hayden stepped cautiously, and when no further calamity befell him, repeated the process, quickly adapting to the low gravity. His confidence returned, he followed Cora to the rock face and climbed toward the nearby summit.

As he caught up with the synth, he found it kneeling beside a large boulder, motioning for him to keep low, so he ducked and joined her.

"What's wrong?"

"Something isn't right," she said.

"What is it?"

Cora's attention was not on him, instead on something in the direction from where they'd come. Hayden turned to see what had caught her interest, and his heart dropped into his stomach.

Their small ship was surrounded by a group of armed soldiers.

The troops had not yet spotted them, but it wouldn't take long for that to happen.

They were screwed.

Sacrifice

"HAYDEN, WHAT ARE WE going to do?"

It was difficult to reconcile the fear in Cora's voice with the impassive face on the synth she occupied.

"I don't think it will take them too long to figure out where we are," he said. "There are two sets of footprints to lead them here."

He returned his attention to the scene below. The squad of soldiers was still assessing their ship. There was time, but not much.

"How did they follow us?" he asked.

"I kept a close eye on our sensors; nobody followed us. This is a different group. Do you think they are who Kovacs's people are searching for?"

"Maybe Malkovich keeps a hidden base on this moon."

"And we just happened to land on top of it?" said Cora. "That isn't likely. I think they tracked us as we came in."

"Regardless of how they found us, they don't look friendly." He checked out their nearby surroundings. "How far are we from the erganium deposit?"

"Do you really think that's a priority, Hayden?"

"Just tell me. Is it close?"

"Inside the crater."

"Okay." He watched the men around their vessel. They were attempting to gain access to it.

"Do you have control of our ship from here?"

"Yes."

"If it comes down to an emergency, can you transfer back there from this body? Or the other way around?"

"If I'm within range, yes. Why?"

"I'm just assessing possibilities."

He turned again to study the activity below.

"I'm going down there, and—"

145

"Hayden! You can't."

"Cora, they are going to follow our tracks. If I go to them, it gives you the time to find the erganium."

"But you could be killed. I should be the one who goes."

"Then they'll have our ship and you. Besides, I don't know what the stuff looks like. You are our best shot. Once you locate it, call the ship to you and get yourself and the mineral back to *Scimitar*."

"No! There must be another way."

"Cora, there is no other way, at least not one that I can think of. You are the only hope for the crew. I'm expendable, but you aren't."

"I won't leave without you."

"Yes, you will, because I am ordering you."

The expressionless face of the synth did not reflect the pain in Cora's voice. "Hayden, please?"

He shook his head. "I order you to complete the mission, Chief Engineer Symes."

The android looked at him with its unblinking eyes, and for a moment he feared she would ignore him and cart him away from the soldiers.

"Yes, sir." Her voice cracked. "What will I tell Stella? The captain?"

"Tell them the truth and that I'm not going to simply roll over and surrender. I will find a way back to *Scimitar*, if I can."

"I'm holding you to that." She leaned forward and enveloped him in a hug. Unsure how to respond, he put his arms around the synth and patted it on the back.

Cora disengaged the embrace and held him by his shoulders. "Keep channel 4Z open for me to monitor you. That's far enough down the band that they shouldn't realize it's active. I will come back for you."

"Well, I was kind of hoping somebody might." He looked down toward the ship. "I have to go now."

"Be careful."

She crawled to the edge of the rim and scrambled down into the crater. Hayden inhaled deeply then climbed down to the soldiers below. As he picked his way over the rocks, he flipped through the available communications channels, searching for the one the men used.

He was halfway down the slope when he found it. He stopped and ducked behind a large boulder.

"Hello, can anybody hear me?" he said.

"Who is that?"

"Me, the guy on the hill." He poked his head up and waved his arms.

First one, then the others aimed their weapons at him.

"Don't shoot! I'm not armed!"

"Stay where you are." One of them motioned and four of them ran toward him. He watched with relief as their footprints all but obliterated his and Cora's. At least they wouldn't have reason to go looking for her. He hoped he bought her the time she needed.

They seized Hayden and forced him back to his ship. It required a few steps for him to adjust to the odd sensation of being frog-marched in low gravity. The troops who captured him wore standard UEF battle suits, with one major difference: the emblem of the United Earth Forces was absent, replaced by an unfamiliar one.

After his initial comm contact with the squad, they switched to a secondary channel to communicate, leaving Hayden in the dark about their plans for him. A quick glance assured him they had not gained access to his small ship. He wondered how long he could drag out offering up the entry codes. Every second they wasted with him was one more for Cora to complete her assignment.

A voice crackled through his helmet speaker. "Who are you?"

"Fine, thanks. How are you?"

"Not how, idiot! *Who* are you?"

He was unsure which of them spoke. All their visors were tinted, obscuring their faces.

"Oh, sorry. This channel is a little scratchy. I'm Hayden Kaine."

One of the soldiers separated himself from the three in front of him and stood directly before him, peering through Hayden's visor. "Why are you here?"

He shrugged. "I'm afraid I can't tell you."

Though he'd been prepared for rough handling, the blow from behind was unexpected. Knocked from his feet, he flew two metres from the force of the impact, ending up sprawled in a cloud of dust.

A faint hiss near where he was struck informed him that his suit was torn. He tried to locate the tear with his hand, but it was just out of his reach.

The man who hit him strode over and seized him by his elbow. Hayden kicked out, knocking the soldier's leg out from under him. Two more advanced and grabbed both of his arms, pinning him to the ground.

"My suit is leaking!"

As the soldiers struggled to hold him down, the leader approached and squatted on his haunches. "Well, that is unfortunate. Perhaps if you prove cooperative with your answers, we'll patch you up before your blood boils."

"My name is Lieutenant Hayden Kaine, first officer of the UEF cruiser *Scimitar*, serial number 034D-7688R."

"This ship isn't military," he said, indicating Hayden's craft.

"We're not from this system. We've been in subluminal transit for the past ten years."

"So, you're telling me your uniform is real; you really are UEF?"

"Yes, who else would I be with?"

"I'm asking the questions."

Hayden started to shiver as the temperature in his suit dropped with the air pressure. He tested the grip that restrained him for a moment before deciding a struggle would only use up his oxygen.

"That's better. Now, why are you here?"

"I was scouting this moon for raw materials I need for repairs."

"What kind of material?"

"Our rail gun is out of projectiles. We need tungsten and titanium for fixing structural damage."

"Why are you out of bullets?"

"Because some idiots have been shooting at us since our arrival."

"Where is your ship now?"

Hayden suddenly realized these soldiers were not Stromm's, who would know exactly where *Scimitar* was. As the escaping air continued to hiss in his ear, he decided on a wild gambit. If he was wrong, they might kill him, but it would be faster than suffocating.

"You guys are with Malkovich's forces, aren't you?"

The man who questioned him leaned menacingly over Hayden and pressed down on his chest.

"Your ship; where is it?"

"It's in orbit around the gas giant. We're playing dead, trying not to draw too much attention from the cruiser searching for you."

"Yours is the one the battle was about?"

"One and the same."

"You assholes baited us; drew us into a trap."

"Is there a question in that?"

"Smartass!"

"Listen, we can stay here and play twenty questions, but by the time you get to the interesting ones, I'll be unconscious or dead. Can we please patch up my suit?"

His interrogator hovered over him, face unreadable behind the combat visor.

"Look," said Hayden, fighting his rising panic and trying to sound conciliatory, "I promise I have a lot of stuff to tell you, but it will take more time than I have air left. I really will make the information worth your while."

"Give me one good reason why I shouldn't simply tear off your helmet now and finish you."

Hayden could no longer feel his extremities, and his chest was beginning to congest. These guys intended to kill him. He had to try something.

"Because our bosses are kin. Cousins, in fact. Let me die, and you'll piss off my captain. I guarantee that won't end well for you."

The soldier stood and studied him, clearly weighing his options and the potential costs of making a wrong decision. He hoped the man would make up his mind before it was too late.

Finally, he motioned for Hayden to be lifted to his feet. "Take him inside."

The words confused him. Had they gained access to his ship after all? Not until they marched him in the opposite direction did he realize they meant something else.

With blurring vision, he scanned the landscape ahead, seeing nothing but smaller craters and rocks peppering the regolith. For a moment, the horizon and star field above it wavered out of focus before they vanished completely, replaced by an open hatchway and an airlock suspended in space.

It took his oxygen-starved brain a few seconds to put the pieces together; he was being taken to a cloaked ship like the ones that had attacked *Scimitar*. If he had harboured any doubt before, he was now positive that he was a captive of Malkovich's troops. Things were about to get very interesting.

Very Few Secrets Remain

HAYDEN WAS SHOVED INTO the cabin of the small ship and forced onto an acceleration couch. After he was slapped in restraints and strapped in, one guard kept a weapon pointed at him while the others took off their helmets.

Finally, when everyone had assumed a station or location, the man who was the group's commander removed Hayden's helmet.

He gulped in air. Gradually, his lungs stopped burning and the sensation returned to his fingers and toes, hot, stinging pricks of pain that reminded him he still lived.

The man who stood over him was a grizzled veteran. His gaunt, lined face sported a couple of days of greying whiskers. What little hair his short, military cut revealed was salt-and-pepper. He guessed that the man was a Ranger by his manner and appearance; mid-to-late forties, he estimated. Despite the rough handling dealt him, the commander showed a degree of deference to Hayden, suggesting he was a squad sergeant or warrant officer, someone who respected an officer's rank, if not the person who carried it.

Without a word, he checked Hayden's restraints before strapping himself in for launch and giving the pilot a brisk nod. The familiar push of acceleration told Hayden they'd lifted from the surface, taking him, he knew not where.

Though the leader did not appear to be armed, the man who sat across from him cradled a flechette rifle and never took his eyes from Hayden. He tried a smile on the stone-faced soldier before averting his gaze and studying his own feet.

From the interior configuration and lack of windows, he recognized the ship as a small dropship. He'd spent time in his early days at the academy fighting nausea in them. This one smelled a lot better than those training vessels, probably since none of this bunch had vomited in it like raw cadets.

Once launched and underway, the commander retrieved two bottles of water and handed one to him before settling back into his seat. Hayden greedily gulped the lukewarm liquid, savouring the sensation as it washed over his tongue and down his parched throat.

He toyed with asking questions but reconsidered after careful thought. It was obvious from the silence that the man planned to let somebody else interrogate him at their destination. As much as he wanted to learn what these men had been through over the last decade, he didn't believe they would be in a sharing mood with a prisoner. The less he said, the less he risked giving away. He took the opportunity to work on his story for later and hoped that Malkovich didn't condone torture.

After what he estimated to be ten minutes of travel, they decelerated and descended once more. They'd never left the weak pull of gravity, so they were somewhere on the same moon.

A familiar bump informed him that they'd landed, and moments later the commander stood and released Hayden's seat harness. He was escorted through the airlock and into a hangar. Looking up, he noted the outline of a large set of doors and concluded that they were in a concealed, underground base. A firm push from behind reminded him of who his hosts were, and he curbed his curious impulses.

He was led through a warren of tunnels cut into the rock until he arrived at a small room. A table stood in the middle with uncomfortable-looking chairs on either side. To his relief, he did not see any brackets for restraint. He was instructed to sit, facing the doorway, and left alone with a single soldier guarding the exit.

It was not long before the door opened and a man not much older than himself entered. He wore an officer's uniform, though with similar modifications as the others. The rank epaulet suggested the man was a major in what would have one time been the intelligence corps. He studied Hayden for a moment before sitting in the chair opposite him and placing a data pad between them.

"You informed the sergeant that you are a United Earth Forces officer, is that correct?"

"Lieutenant Hayden Kaine—"

"A simple yes or no to my questions will suffice, Mister Kaine, or whatever your name may be."

"I *am* Hayden Kaine."

Ignoring him, the major continued. "You are from the UEF *Scimitar*?"

Hayden sat back and crossed his arms. "Yes."

"Who is your captain?"

"Yegor Pavlovich."

"Describe him."

"What?"

"Please tell me what he looks like."

"Well, he's about two metres tall, fit, weighs around a hundred kilos. Sports a big black bushy beard...well, perhaps more salt-and-pepper these days. A real grumpy son-of-a-bitch."

"How long have you served under Captain Pavlovich?"

Hayden paused. In truth, his total time spent aboard *Scimitar* had only been a few months.

"A little over ten years."

"What is your father's name?"

He frowned. "What does my father have to do with anything?"

"Please answer the question."

"Walden Kaine."

"Who issued the order assigning you to *Scimitar*?"

"Admiral Thomas. What the hell is this all about?"

They stared across the table at each other, the major's face inscrutable. Hayden was the first to break eye contact.

"Account for the whereabouts of your ship since its departure from Mu Arae."

Hayden sighed and began the well-rehearsed narrative that he and the rest of the crew had committed to memory.

The officer made a notation on the data pad. "Describe the events that unfolded upon your arrival in this system."

Perspiration ran down the small of Hayden's back. This was something that nobody had anticipated, and he had no memorized story to regurgitate.

"The captain was aware that his cousin was assigned here at the time of the network collapse. He contacted him when we got here, and a rendezvous was coordinated. Prior to the arrival of his—your ships, we were intercepted by another fleet. They captured us and engaged your forces when they arrived."

"Did your captain resist the other ships?"

"As I told the sergeant, our munitions are depleted and our primary drive is damaged, limiting the power to our lasers."

"So, you surrendered."

"They were a superior force. We didn't survive a decade in deep space to spend our lives fighting a lost cause. Of course we did."

"Where are your ship and crew now?"

"We had a radiation leak. They were evacuated to one of the other ships, and *Scimitar* was parked in orbit to await a repair vessel."

The major smiled and leaned forward.

"And how did you come to be found on this moon?"

"The captain did not wish to leave our vessel unoccupied, thus opening it up to salvage. A skeleton crew of volunteers remained behind. Since the radioactive threat is significant, we decided to try limiting our exposure. Each of us was to take a shift searching this system's moons for some of the materials we need. I was the first one."

His interrogator examined something on his pad. "Explain why the ship we found you with is not a military vessel."

"We reprovisioned before departing Mu Arae. We replaced a damaged dropship with it."

The major nodded, half attentively, as he continued to read. He looked up and smiled. "Why have you no active LINK?"

"It was defective, and I had it deactivated."

"What was your original mission to Mu Arae?"

"We were to recover a scientist and return him to the Sol system."

"Were you successful?"

Yes or no. That was all the simple question required, but Hayden had no idea which was the correct one. It was clear from the line of questioning that this man knew far more about *Scimitar*, her crew complement, and her mission than expected. The events in the last few hours prior to the battle with the Malliac were frenetic. Volunteers had been dispatched to Earth and a couple of the key systems to apprise them of the situation and warn of the impending collapse of the light gate network. Nobody was sent here, to Pictor, but if word had reached here before...

"Yes, we located Doctor Gabriel and recovered his research. The information was transmitted to Fleet Command immediately before the disaster. Unfortunately, he died a short time later." A small embellishment. No point in mentioning the encounter with the Glenatat.

The major stared at him. The seconds of silence ticked on. Hayden struggled to maintain his composure and dared not be the first to break eye contact.

Finally, the officer picked up the data pad and stood. "Thank you for your cooperation, Lieutenant Kaine. You will be provided quarters and given an opportunity to change into something more comfortable than your damaged suit. General Malkovich expects to meet with you in two hours."

He departed, leaving Hayden alone with the guard. He had no idea what had just transpired, and that worried him more than his captivity.

Malkovich

THE COLLAR CHAFED. Except for the patch on the shoulder, the uniform they gave him was standard officer's kit. It even sported a lieutenant's epaulette, prompting salutes from the armed Rangers he encountered as he was escorted through the catacombs. The only difference was the crest that replaced that of the UEF. For Hayden, that alone was enough to make him feel like a traitor.

He had discovered it laid out on the bunk when he emerged from the shower. Concerned that he was being observed, he masked his revulsion as his finger traced the outline of the unfamiliar emblem patch. His mind wandered to thoughts of his father and what his words would have been on the matter. For generations, Kaines were raised to be staunch patriots and defenders of the Confederacy. To see it fragmented must have devastated him. To know that his own son was responsible for it would have killed him.

Hayden understood and respected the Confederation; its emblems, flags, coats of arms, and insignia were all pregnant with centuries of tradition. It had all been drilled into him since he could remember. The Kaine name was forever linked to the empire, for his family had been key players in its history. To say that it all was a part of his makeup would not have been an exaggeration.

But this new flag—he had no knowledge of what it stood for. He understood the meaning and commitment associated with wearing the UEF uniform, but this abomination merely made him feel like taking another shower.

The ironic thing about his reaction was that he hadn't always felt this way. During his youth, and later after graduation from the academy, he regarded everything the Confederation represented with ambivalence. He knew his future was intricately intertwined with its institutions, and he was destined to serve—perhaps even govern one day. It was a canvas upon which his own achievements would be painted. But the ideals of patriotism that his grandfather and father shared had never been his.

Not until everything was lost.

Hayden spent ten years contemplating the consequences of his actions. He alone had brought crashing down what his family helped build. In their eyes, he would be a worse traitor than the men who wore this uniform. They only did so because they had no other hope. Perhaps a variation of this scenario was playing out in every star system that had once been a part of the great empire: billions of people forced to abandon ties to the home world for something less, merely to survive. The idea made him ill.

And yet what a decade of wandering in self-imposed exile attempted to teach him—what Stella had tried to convince him of—was that had he not acted, everything would be much worse.

Then along came Pavlovich, with his promise of a new dawn, a chance to rebuild everything and root out the evil he claimed rotted the Confederacy's core. If what he said were true, perhaps reestablishing FTL capability would be a mistake. Maybe humanity needed to take some time wandering as a diaspora in the wilderness; isolating the conspirators in different systems; letting the cancer die with them.

He wished he knew what the correct course of action was, but he had more immediate concerns to dwell on. He was still a captive among people who most likely planned to murder him—people who might do so if they learned the truth about him. Even as he was escorted to his audience with Malkovich, every soldier he encountered regarded him with suspicion. He was an outsider and not to be trusted.

Hayden was not safe—this he understood. What he couldn't understand was how his status had changed from prisoner to guest.

He replayed the interrogation in his mind for the tenth time, finding no new clue to help solve the mystery. The questioning had been targeted; the major was aware of far more than he pretended to know. Perhaps the impending meeting with the rebel leader, Malkovich, would shed some light, though he had his doubts. The man was, after all, related to Pavlovich.

He approached a metal door set into the rock of the tunnel. One of his escorts rapped on it, and seconds later, it was pulled open to admit them.

The room Hayden entered was nothing like he expected. The quarters he just came from were spartan, little more than an alcove carved into the bedrock and fitted with a bunk and a crude shower that hardly managed to drip enough cold water to get him wet. The labyrinth of corridors he traversed were functional and austere. The entire facility showed the signs of being constructed hastily to provide a hideout from Stromm's forces.

General Malkovich's office, in contrast, was expansive and panelled in dark mahogany. The stone floor of the cavern was covered by a polished hardwood beneath richly embroidered carpets. Memorabilia and what appeared to be archaeological artifacts decorated the room on occasional tables and bookshelves that lined one wall.

Behind a large desk sat a man who, under any other circumstance, could have been a beardless Yegor Pavlovich.

The man stood and walked around to greet him; right hand extended. "It is a great privilege to meet you, Lieutenant Kaine. I am Cesar Malkovich. Welcome to our humble lodgings."

He directed Hayden to be seated before resuming his own seat. Kaine's escort was dismissed with a casual wave of the hand. The men saluted and departed without a word.

"I do not believe you have been completely honest with us."

Hayden raised his eyebrows. "Oh? What gives you that impression, General?"

"My men went to recover your vessel, and it was nowhere to be found."

"Are you sure they remembered where I parked it?"

Malkovich was amused. "I can see why Yegor selected you to be his first officer. He shares that sort of humour." His expression hardened. "Please explain where your ship is."

"In all honesty, General, I have no idea where it went. It is under the control of an advanced AI, with strict security and evasion protocols."

"And where would Yegor have acquired such technology?"

Hayden smiled disarmingly. "Ten years is a long time to experiment."

"You're saying your people developed it? I am familiar with the qualifications of *Scimitar's* crew. I find your claim difficult to believe."

He shrugged. "As I said, we had a lot of free time to brush up on things. Besides, your people seem to have been industrious. The stealth technology I witnessed is impressive."

Malkovich studied him warily. "I suppose it is possible that your captain located the cynosure..."

"The what?"

The general smirked. "No, you aren't much of a liar, are you?" He shifted in his chair, placed his hands on the desk, and leaned forward. "Speaking of your commanding officer, where might I find him, were I to bother looking?"

"He and the rest of the crew were taken aboard one of Stromm's ships to the central planet."

"Yes, yes—so you explained. I presume he went willingly?"

"He thought it wise to cooperate. Especially since your fleet was destroyed."

Malkovich smiled. "There is no need to measure your words. I am aware that Yegor played both sides. He hasn't changed."

"Am I to be considered an enemy combatant, General?"

"Are you my enemy, Lieutenant? Where does your loyalty lie?"

Hayden tried to swallow the lump in his throat. "Sir, I have no quarrel with you or Stromm."

"Simply a neutral bystander, caught up in all this?" He shook his head. "Your captain's actions have revealed his loyalties. What about you? I don't believe he did you any great favours by leaving you behind."

"What are you asking?"

"I think you know."

"I prefer to hear you say it, General."

"I want your ship, Lieutenant."

"I told you, I don't know where it is."

"I mean *Scimitar*."

"What is so valuable about her? Both you and Stromm sacrificed your ships in a battle over us. It doesn't make any sense."

Malkovich grinned. "Do you know the story of the pearl of great price?"

"I'm afraid I don't."

"An ancient parable, referring to a treasure of such value that someone would sacrifice everything to possess it."

"*Scimitar*? Now you're the one who's joking."

He studied Hayden for several seconds. "I'll make you a deal, Lieutenant. Help me secure it, and you won't die horribly."

Even though he expected an ultimatum, hearing it set Hayden's pulse racing. "Actually, I'd prefer another choice, General."

"Give me access to the ship and I'll consider it."

Hayden frowned. "As much as I appreciate the opportunity to gamble with my life, sir, and at the risk of throwing that away..."

"Yes?" Malkovich appeared amused.

"*Scimitar* is just sitting up there in orbit. Except for one of Stromm's ships keeping an eye on her, she's ripe for the taking. Given your cloaking technology..."

"Don't play coy, Lieutenant Kaine. I know my cousin. He would hardly have hidden the key to the front door under the mat. Neither he, nor you, would have left his ship unguarded, and if my suspicions are correct..."

"About the cynosure?" he ventured.

He felt like he was dumped into the middle of an ocean without a life preserver. Whatever the thing was, it was incredibly important both to Stromm and Malkovich.

Pavlovich was a liar; Hayden had no doubt. It was entirely possible that he kept some dark secret, one that might more believably explain how he'd acquired faster-than-light technology and survived falling into a black hole. It was also within reason that his contemporaries were aware of it too and coveted it.

He needed to tread very carefully until he could figure it all out.

Hayden smiled and spread his hands in a gesture of helplessness. "If I betray my captain's confidence, what does that say about me? You would never be able to trust me."

"And yet you would still live."

There it was.

"Until Pavlovich found out. Either way, I'm a dead man."

He would not turn his back on what was left of the UEF by betraying his commanding officer. His father would be proud if he knew. The realization that he'd signed his own death warrant, however, squashed any pride he might have indulged in.

Malkovich stared daggers at him from across the desk. Waiting for the general's inevitable explosion of rage, Hayden thought his heart would burst from his chest.

And then the older man's expression softened. A satisfied smile spread across his face, and laughter exploded from him. "My cousin chose an exceptional executive officer. Well done, Kaine."

Hayden's mouth dropped open, and he gawked at the smiling general. "Sir?"

"Had you even hinted at the possibility of a deal to save your ass; I would have shot you myself."

He tried to swallow. "I'm glad."

Malkovich grinned. "No doubt. But I shan't keep you in suspense any longer, Lieutenant. You haven't been operating with all the necessary information. Some time ago, my intelligence forces infiltrated Stromm's headquarters. He thinks he's rooted out my people, but he hasn't a clue as to how deeply imbedded my agents are."

"I fail to see what this has to do with me or with *Scimitar*."

"Please permit me to finish?" the general said playfully.

Bristling at the mild rebuke, Hayden forced himself to appear impassive and nodded.

"I am aware of far more about you and your ship mates than you can possibly realize. My sources inform me that a certain young woman is masquerading before Stromm as my cousin's XO."

The words hit him like a punch in the gut. Too late, he realized that his reaction had betrayed his surprise.

"What bothers me is that while my dear cousin can be unconventional, I have no idea why he would require two executive officers. Can you shed any light on this situation?"

"I cannot."

"Is Miss Gabriel Yegor's first officer, or are you? I'm sure you can appreciate my consternation?"

"I do understand. I assure you, General, I am the XO of the *Scimitar*."

"And yet your name does not appear on the crew manifest, while hers' does, and listed in the same position you claim to hold. What do you expect me to believe?"

"I think your agents may have gotten bad intelligence, sir."

"Oh, I don't think so. They also inform me that you and she are...close, to use a polite term. Is that incorrect as well, Lieutenant?"

For a second time, Malkovich's comments struck Hayden dumb.

"I presume," said the general, "if this woman is no friend of yours and is in fact impersonating an officer, you would have no objections if I simply order her killed?"

"No!"

Malkovich sat back and templed his fingers, satisfied. "Now we are negotiating, Lieutenant."

Perspiration ran down Hayden's forehead. His shout had been involuntary. He'd been prepared for almost any threat against his life, but the mention of the danger to Stella made his resolve collapse like a house of cards. Confused, he searched for a response, but it was as if his thoughts were dust scattered on the wind.

"Let me help you make your decision, Lieutenant. You have been lied to. The fact that you did not know of the cynosure is proof of that."

"He kept classified information from a junior officer. That hardly constitutes a lie."

"If you knew what the secret is, you would not believe that. You would know that he not only deceived you but betrayed you."

"Those are easy words, General, but meaningless. I know my captain, and he has my trust and loyalty."

His brave response tasted like sawdust in his mouth. How well did he really know Pavlovich?

Malkovich rose and went to the sideboard. He poured two glasses of an amber fluid and returned to hand one to Kaine.

"Make yourself comfortable, son. We are going to be spending a lot of time together, I think."

Family History

"WE GREW UP TOGETHER. Yegor's parents died when he was a toddler, and mine took him in and raised him as my brother."

"Uh-huh," replied Hayden.

Malkovich's presence in the copilot's seat unnerved him, almost as much as the squad of Rangers occupying the passenger seats behind them. He stole a glance back at them in their battle suits. None of their faces were visible behind their helmet visors. To him they looked like an assembly of automatons, though there was not a synth or even a cyborg among them.

"We competed at everything, though Yegor more often emerged the victor. I can admit, and even accept it now..."

"That's all very interesting, General, but I'm trying to concentrate on piloting. I'm not yet familiar with this interface."

"You're testy, Lieutenant. I understand. You shouldn't think of this as a compromise or a betrayal. It is an opportunity to save millions of lives."

"To be completely honest, I only give a damn about a few people. Once I help you defeat your enemy, you and everyone else in this bloody system can go to hell."

Malkovich began to reply, then appeared to reconsider and leaned back in his chair to study a distant moon out the window.

After several minutes of tense silence, Hayden asked, "What happened to the colonies here?"

The older man's expression hardened, and he ground his teeth.

"Three hundred and fifty-two thousand."

"The number of colonists?"

Malkovich nodded, maintaining his grim stare out the cockpit. He turned to appraise the soldiers behind him. "We all lost someone."

"What took place here?"

"When the network collapsed, it was as if the government knew it was coming. They had everything in place and declared martial law within days of the event. I was in command of the heavy cruiser *Agamemnon*, patrolling near the light gate. The conspirators were well organized and had operatives on every ship in the system. My first officer attempted a mutiny, supported by a third of my crew. Fortunately, my Rangers remained loyal. We defeated the mutineers, but at a terrible loss of life. My vessel was damaged beyond repair, so we survivors abandoned her and made our way to the colony moons of Elgar. We had no idea if the coup had extended to the local leadership, but we had no other options."

Hayden forgot his animosity and became enraptured by the tale. "How were you greeted?"

Malkovich smiled weakly. "Kwong only had claws in the central government and the military. He ignored the civilian colonies, presuming he'd consolidate his rule over them later. It was a key mistake. The purpose for the colonies was scientific research."

"They are the source of your stealth technology?"

The general nodded. "It took some persuading, but after they saw what was taking place on Pictor Prime, the leadership decided to resist Kwong's coup. For a while, it was effective; he had too many irons in the fire to worry about some defiant scientists. Then Stromm killed him, and everything changed for the worse."

"He saw the value of the research?"

"Oh, yes. He dispatched a fleet to seize control. By this time, a sizeable but scattered resistance had grown." Malkovich laughed humourlessly. "Oh, we were so naïve. We thought a group of rebels, armed with some stealth tech and righteousness, would be sufficient."

"What did you hope to gain by defying Stromm?"

"At the time we had no idea of the reason for the light gate being shut down. Almost everyone believed it was a temporary lockout engineered by Kwong. We thought if we could engage and harass the military government—keep it preoccupied—it would only be matter of time before Earth heard about things and sent in troops to reestablish order. It was only much later that we learned of the collapse of the entire network."

Hayden swallowed nervously. "What happened?"

The general looked back again at his men. "We engaged the attacking fleet. Our stealth technology compensated for our lack of numbers, and Stromm's forces took heavy losses. When he realized we had the upper hand, Stromm changed tactics. He ordered his surviving ships to carpet-bomb every colony on every moon. He never even issued terms for surrender—just wiped out every living person."

"So instead of engaging you, he turned his weapons on the colonies?"

"It worked. We lost our resolve against an enemy who would act so capriciously. Our fleet broke up and retreated to wherever was left to go."

"How long ago was this?"

"Six years. Since then, we've played a game of cat-and-mouse, hitting them when we can and retreating to our hidden bases scattered throughout the system. Now, much of our time and efforts go to convincing Stromm's people of his ruthlessness and his atrocities."

"But both sides are running out of resources."

Malkovich nodded. "Stromm outnumbers us. Eventually, we will lose our last ships before he does. Our only hope is to cut the head off the snake while there is still time."

"You still haven't told me how *Scimitar* fits in all this."

"That old wreck is a key element in ending this conflict. Its secret will draw Stromm out into the open—expose him."

"You already attempted to assassinate him. If anything, he'll be more cautious. What do you think is so irresistible that he will risk exposing himself?"

"The cynosure. *Scimitar* holds one of the last pieces of a puzzle we thought unsolvable until your reappearance a few days ago."

"I'm calling bullshit."

Malkovich smiled patronizingly. "You're still young and surprisingly naïve."

"I'm more familiar with the political machinations within the Confederation than you can imagine, General."

"Ah, yes, your family's history. Believe me, Kaine, and I mean no disrespect to you or your father: you have no idea of what is going on."

"I'm aware of Thomas's plot and his attempts to recruit officers to him. How do I know he didn't get to you?"

"My cousin told you about that? That is only a fragment of the big picture, Kaine."

"Then why don't you enlighten me? This farce of intrigue is getting tiresome."

"I'd need the cynosure to prove my claim."

Hayden shook his head and returned his attention to the console. "That's bloody convenient, isn't it? You'd rather threaten the lives of people who might be able to help you than be forthcoming. You're full of shit, General."

Malkovich chuckled. "You sound like Yegor."

Hayden frowned at the distracting comment. "Why are you two enemies? You said earlier you were raised together."

The older man sighed and studied something outside. "It's complicated."

Hayden watched him stare out the window.

Bloody secrets every time he turned around. It seemed like everyone wanted to keep him in the dark and use him as a pawn. If there were, as Malkovich claimed, machinations behind the Confederacy, his father and grandfather had to be aware of them. They'd kept him ignorant, feeding him bits of information to motivate him to do his part. That they didn't trust him enough to tell him anything cut like a knife.

Perhaps they had waited for a time when his ambivalence would be replaced by something more mature; more malleable. Maybe if he hadn't destroyed the jump network, he would now be on Earth and steeped in whatever arcane mysteries were kept from him.

"Ah, there she is," said Malkovich.

Hayden looked up and searched the black for what had caught the man's attention. Then he saw it: a tiny white speck floating in the void.

Scimitar.

A second object came into view seconds before a proximity alert sounded on his console.

The repair ship had entered orbit of Elgar.

Things were about to get complicated.

Bringing Guests

"WHAT ARE YOU DOING?" asked Hayden.

Malkovich's attention was on the control interface as he inputted command codes. "I'm arming missiles to take out that ship."

"You can't. Stromm's patrol ship is still in the area. If that repair vessel goes up, there's no telling what kind of shitstorm will unfold."

"Well, I'm not prepared to risk Stromm gaining control of *Scimitar*. Is there anyone aboard her that can put up a resistance? An automated defence system?"

Hayden thought of Gunney and the couple of engineers and techs working with Cora and Chin. Except for the gunnery officer, there was nobody with combat training. *Scimitar*'s only defences were the Glenatat dark energy cannons but deploying those would precipitate the same crisis he wanted to prevent.

"No, but I have an idea. I need access to communications."

Malkovich eyed him.

"Look," said Hayden, "there is only one solution here, and I need to talk to *Scimitar*."

"I'm listening, Lieutenant."

"We want to avoid any kind of conflict that will scare off Stromm, am I right?"

"Yes."

"And neither of us wishes to risk *Scimitar* in a firefight. This ship we're on is undetectable, at least until you fire those missiles. We can use that advantage to board her unseen. With your Rangers, we will have the manpower to quietly overpower the repair ship's crew when they dock. We can avoid attracting unwanted attention from Stromm's patrol ship and spooking Stromm himself."

"We? It sounds like you joined us."

Hayden shrugged. "You know: the enemy of my enemy."

Malkovich appraised him. "I don't know. You have too much of your father about you; the Kaine duplicitous nature. I'm not sure I can trust you."

"I'll program a five-second delay into the comms; put a gun at my head, and if I say anything to betray you, feel free to pull the trigger. Your only other option is to reveal yourself by shooting at everybody. Given that your people shot at us once before, my gunnery officer won't hesitate to track our location and blow us out of the skies."

"So, *Scimitar* is not as wounded as you let us believe, eh?"

Hayden put on his best poker face and stared impassively back at the general.

"Very well, Kaine. We will try it your way." He unclipped his sidearm holster. "You may have your delayed communication." Reaching across the console, he released the lockout on Hayden's communications panel then drew his pistol. "But I'm keeping my missiles at the ready."

"Fair enough." Hayden set up the tight-beam transmission and programmed in the delay.

After wiping the perspiration from his hands onto his trousers, he opened the comm link.

"*Scimitar*, this is Lieutenant Kaine. Are you there, Cora?"

A few seconds later, the speaker crackled. "Thank goodness you're alive. Where are you?"

He glanced at Malkovich before replying. "Umm, it's kind of difficult to explain, but I'm tight-beaming you from about fifteen hundred kilometres off your port stern."

An even longer pause ensued. He imagined Cora examining the output from every drone and sensor sweep that ran through her systems.

"I can't verify that. You'll have to prove your identity to me."

"Quit horsing around, Kaine," said Malkovich. "It won't take her long to get a fix on the origin for your tight beam."

"Cora, do you remember the last thing I said to you before we stepped out of my shuttle? I apologized for cutting off our conversation."

Another long pause. His stomach was tied in a knot as he stared at the console, avoiding Malkovich's gaze.

"I believe I understand the situation. What are your orders?"

"I'm going to dock at port B2 in ten minutes. I have, ah, some guests with me—"

Malkovich's arm shot across the panel and terminated the connection.

"Hey!"

"What the hell kind of fool do you take me for, Kaine? Do you think I don't know a trap when I see one?"

"Listen, Malkovich. Cora is...a highly advanced security AI; She—I mean it—is really smart. It will have deduced the likelihood of my escaping in one of your stealth craft. If I don't give it the whole story, this ship will be taken out, no matter what I say."

The two men stared each other down, grim-faced.

"What are you going to tell it?"

"Something you might not be familiar with; the truth."

"I never lied to you, Kaine."

"So you claim, but you love secrets, like every other senior officer in the fleet, it would seem."

"Listen, Kaine—"

"No, *you* listen. By now the AI will have figured out our position and have weapons locked on us. If it doesn't hear from me soon...well, it has full control of our X-ray lasers."

"Lieutenant Kaine, are you still receiving?"

He glared at Malkovich. "Tick-tock, General. What's it to be? Are you willing to trust me?"

He pointed his pistol at Hayden's head. "Go on; answer. I'll judge the situation as it unfolds."

Hayden reestablished the comm signal. "Cora, I have a team of Malkovich's Rangers with me. They are not hostile and are coming to help us neutralize a boarding party from the repair ship. May we please have permission to dock?"

No response came from the speaker. After almost a minute of silence, Malkovich pressed the pistol into Hayden's temple.

"It's being thorough, General; running a voice analysis on my transmission; looking for signs of stress or anomalies in my speech patterns; considering a myriad of probable outcomes."

"It sounds like one hell of an AI."

"You have no idea."

"Lieutenant, you are cleared for docking at port B2."

"Thank you, Cora. Please clear all sections between the airlock and the bridge. Tell Gunney to stand down and be prepared to receive guests. They are friendlies. I repeat, these are allies."

"I understand, XO. I'll roll out the red carpet."

"I'll see you in a few minutes. Kaine out."

Hayden turned to face the muzzle of Malkovich's pistol. After a second, he slowly raised his hand and pushed the barrel away from him. "Are you satisfied, General?"

Malkovich smiled and holstered his gun. "You have no idea how much I am. I've been waiting a long time for this opportunity."

True Character

STELLA CURSED PAVLOVICH.

The chamber she and the remaining members of *Scimitar*'s crew were confined in was cramped, hot, and poorly ventilated. Sitting on the floor, she couldn't shift her position without bumping into the people crammed next to her. Her skin felt clammy with old perspiration, and the pungent smell of unwashed bodies filled her nostrils. None of this distressed her as much as the raw fear that assaulted her senses. Not just her own, but the collective dread of every person who shared that space with her.

The cell was only able to accommodate a third of the crew. The last time they led her down the corridor to rejoin them, she tried to reach out empathically to determine if any of the doors she passed hid those who were not accounted for. The only thing she could sense was the bored determination of her escorting guards.

After Pavlovich departed with Kovacs to return to *Scimitar*, Stromm's treatment of her and the others who remained behind changed.

No longer guests, they were now treated as enemy combatants and prisoners of war.

Individuals were plucked from the crowded chamber at irregular intervals. Like her, most came back after a few hours of intensive questioning, unharmed but drained; at least until recently.

For what she believed to be the past several hours—she'd lost all sense of time—individuals had been removed but not returned before the soldiers came to take another. The population in their oubliette grew thin, and terror ran through the group every time the door opened.

Two men, armed and wearing light combat armour, stood in the entryway, silhouetted by the bright lights of the outer corridor. A third shadow of a man Stella had become familiar with passed by them as he entered the chamber.

In a scene that had played out too many times for her to recall, his adjusting eyes scanned the dark room for his next victim. In time, his gaze fell on her, and panic gripped her heart.

Seated along the walls, the other prisoners pulled their legs to their chests to clear his path to her.

The grim-faced gaoler advanced, like a poor caricature of Moses crossing the parted sea. Standing before her, he stared down. She detected no malicious emotion or enjoyment from him, only fatigue. This was merely a routine job to which he gave no more special consideration than filling out some form for the thousandth time.

"You will come with me."

"You just brought me back a short time ago," she said, voice cracking from a parched throat.

"Get up," he said in a tone that left no room for interpretation.

Sighing, she stiffly struggled to stand and stared at the officer. "Where are we going?"

His reply was to grip her upper arm and push her toward the door.

The other prisoners avoided her gaze as she passed, as if doing so protected them from falling under the officer's notice.

She couldn't blame them. If her empathic ability had not revealed every person's raw emotions to her, she too would have tried to distance herself from events as much as possible.

Her abilities were only known to a handful of her shipmates. Hayden, Pavlovich, Cora, and Gunney all had history with her "gift." They had agreed to keep it between themselves, so none of the new crew was aware that she could read their relief at it being her who was selected in their stead.

In silence, the guards escorted her down the now familiar corridors. Not until they passed the interrogation room did their moods shift, as if they questioned something about their orders.

"Where are you taking me?" she asked.

Her escort ignored her, but she sensed their anxiety increase. Something about their assigned duties unnerved them.

They paraded her along unfamiliar corridors and down several levels to a closed door at the end of a long hallway.

With her pulse pounding in her ears, she was led in to a small, dimly lit chamber. A single chair, more like an inclined medical examination table, occupied the middle of the room. Two trolleys holding trays containing unfamiliar instruments waited on either side of it. When she spotted the restraints hanging from the table, naked panic seized her. She struggled against the hands that gripped her arms and wrestled her forward. Though significantly smaller than each of the burly men manhandling her, she gave them considerable, if not ultimately futile, difficulty.

Once she was tightly restrained and barely able to move, they left the chamber, leaving Stella alone in the dark, cold room.

A shuffled footstep from behind, out of sight, startled her. Seconds later, she was blinded by a brilliant light shone in her face. Squeezing her eyelids shut, she turned away as she heard the mysterious footfalls move in front of her. Firm hands grasped and turned her head. A restraint was attached, forcing her to face the blinding lamp.

One of the trolley's wheels squeaked as it was rolled closer. Someone fumbled with one of the instruments on it. Moments later, a pair of hands assaulted her face, prying open one eye. She shook her head, trying to protect herself. Something was affixed to her, and she found that she could no longer close her eyelid.

When they repeated the procedure on the other, Stella screamed and fought against the restraints.

"Why are you doing this?" she cried as, unable to blink, tears pooled in her eyes to eventually run down her cheeks. Panic threatened to overwhelm all her senses.

The procedure complete, she saw the silhouette of her tormenter move away and pause near the edge of her vision, as if appraising the work before vanishing into the shadows. Footfalls receded toward the door. It opened, and muffled words were exchanged.

Two sets of footsteps—or perhaps three—returned to her. Stella tried to calm herself so she could take an empathic reading of the room, but it was too difficult to override her own heightened emotions masking everything.

A shadowed head, with a halo of curls, loomed over her.

"Why are you doing this, Stromm? I answered your questions."

"You supplied answers, Miss Gabriel, but after some deeper investigation, I concluded that you are keeping things from me; things I must know."

"No," she said, her voice cracking, "I told you the truth. Don't hurt me."

A calming hand patted her shoulder. "There, there. I don't want them to harm you. You simply need to answer my questions truthfully, and you can return to your crew mates."

"What do you want to know?"

"I want you to tell me what you know about the cynosure."

"I... I've never heard of it."

"That is an unfortunate reply, my dear. This will not be pleasant for you, after all."

The Cynosure

"YOU'RE WANTED ON THE bridge."

Pavlovich looked up from his book to the ensign delivering the summons. The young man appeared annoyed.

He imagined the pipsqueak believed he had more important duties to attend to than playing messenger. Where did Kovacs find someone so young? This youngster wouldn't have popped his first zit when the light gate collapsed. He concluded that Stromm was conscripting from the general population to supplement his ranks.

He wondered what kind of training the youth, or any of his compatriots received. Then he realized that the same scenario was playing out in countless other star systems. This fellow and his peers would be the last to benefit from the academy education and experience of his superiors. Subsequent generations would progressively become less capable as a fighting force or surviving off planet. He pondered how long it would take for their descendants to forget there ever was a Confederation. How much time before space was abandoned and humans were forced to accept their isolation? Would people be able to build new civilizations on the worlds where fate had isolated them?

Maybe Stromm had the right idea. Consolidate control while the technology still worked and there were people who knew how to run it. Then there might be some hope to prevent humanity from regressing into the stone age.

"I'll be right there," he said as he laid his pad down.

Satisfied with the response, the ensign made a quick visual inspection of the room before departing without another word.

Pavlovich rose from his bunk and stretched before pulling his boots on and making the journey to *Iliad*'s bridge. He was curious why Kovacs sent a messenger. The intercom system functioned perfectly.

But then Kovacs was always an anachronism. He was one of the old-school intelligence officers, someone who didn't believe that modern surveillance technology could replace good, old-fashioned human observation.

Had he used the comm system for the summons, he wouldn't gain insight into how his guest dealt with confinement. Only an experienced observer could glean a person's psychological state by simply observing him, relaxed on the bunk, reading a trashy novel. It was subtle, spooky shit that a surveillance AI couldn't accomplish. He suspected the young man had empathic abilities akin to those of Stella.

Amused, Pavlovich nodded and smiled to himself. The ensign was no mere junior officer but an agent in an ideal position to gather valuable intelligence, unsuspected. He decided he needed to be more cautious in how he behaved around anyone on the ship.

The two Rangers guarding the entry to the bridge snapped to attention at his approach. He casually returned their salute and entered.

Standing on the threshold, he took a moment to survey the activity in the command centre. *Iliad* was one of the newest ships put into service before the collapse. State-of-the-art technology meant that a minimal crew could run her, with all operations managed via LINK. There were no control interfaces anywhere from what he could see. Every bridge officer reclined on an acceleration couch, staring blankly ahead. Occasionally, their hands would make a movement, creating an input into the virtual environment they were jacked into. He wondered if it was like the world Cora occupied aboard *Scimitar.*

"Ah, you're finally here," said Kovacs from his position on the elevated, circular platform.

Pavlovich grinned and joined him. "You asked so nicely, I couldn't refuse."

Kovacs waved an arm to activate a holographic projection. A three-dimensional view of *Scimitar* appeared, as viewed through the *Iliad*'s sensor drones.

Pavlovich's light mood was deflated by what he saw. The repair ship was docked with her, and that would generate a lot of questions about why people were discovered aboard his supposedly abandoned vessel.

"I thought you were going to wait for our arrival," he said, trying to conceal his disappointment with feigned annoyance.

"I gave the order for them to dock. I thought you were full of shit."

Pavlovich swallowed past his dry throat but said nothing, opting to study the hologram until he could think of a response.

"They boarded your ship twelve hours ago, and we haven't heard from them since."

Pavlovich's frown masked his surprise. Had Kaine and Gunney overpowered the repair crew? It was not out of the realm of possibility; most maintenance ships did not carry combat personnel and had no weaponry.

"Well, their deaths are on you. I warned Stromm about my security system."

Kovacs sneered. "Are there any other traps I should know about?"

"No, not if you just send me over to deactivate it and resume command."

Kovacs grunted. Then a smile spread across his face. "There is something I want to show you."

He strode past Pavlovich to the doorway. Turning, he said, "Are you coming?"

Overcoming his reticence, the captain replied, "Of course," and followed him into the corridor. The two Rangers guarding the entrance fell in step behind them. Their orders were apparently to protect their commanding officer. He wondered if the internal threat was so pervasive that Kovacs needed a personal guard to feel safe. If so, Stromm's grasp on power was shakier than he let on.

The group entered a lift and travelled to a part of *Iliad* he hadn't seen. That there were places on the ship he was not familiar with was not unexpected. The Lau class destroyer had been in the planning stages when he'd last shown his face at headquarters on Earth. Much of the design was novel to him. But the location they were headed to, far removed from the operations centre, coupled with the armed escort, had his imagination working overtime.

Stromm and Kovacs had spent a decade in isolation. When he considered the stealth technology, Malkovich had surprised them with on their arrival, he realized these guys might have something unexpected hidden away. He strongly doubted that his host was merely interested in showing off. There was another, more ominous purpose to this little side trip.

They exited the elevator and proceeded down a long corridor that ran the length of *Iliad*, in the core of the ship. It had a sterile feel. Pavlovich's anxiety increased markedly as they passed through a third security check before entering a laboratory. Much to his relief, the guards remained outside.

Kovacs invited him to the far end of the room, where there was another hologram display. Floating in the air were at least two dozen oddly shaped objects. Separated, they were arranged as if they were pieces of some elaborate three-dimensional puzzle not yet assembled.

"What the hell is this?"

"Don't pretend you can't guess."

Pavlovich strolled around the image, studying each unique piece, trying to visualize what they would construct when put together. "Nope, I don't have a clue."

Frowning, Kovacs waved his arm, sweeping a section of the assembly out of view. At the interior of the yet-to-be-completed structure lay a distinctively shaped void. He reached into the hologram, pulled out an almost real-looking mold of the empty space, and held it up.

"Have you ever seen anything similar to this?"

Pavlovich carefully examined the object. Compared with the other pieces that floated in the display, this one was crude and misshapen. It lacked the intricate surface detail that covered each of the others.

"You've got me, Kovacs. What is it supposed to be?"

"Think! In over a decade, you've never noticed anything like this on your ship?"

Pavlovich's eyes widened. "So, this is what Stromm is after."

Kovacs's brow furrowed and he shouted, "Don't play the fool with me, Pavlovich! I know you're aware of the cynosure."

"It's a myth; something that couldn't possibly exist."

"But you've heard of it?" His tone was more hopeful than accusatory.

"I'm sure there are a number of us who have. It was part of the story Thomas fed me when he tried to recruit me. Frankly, I'm surprised he didn't approach you, from the sounds of things."

"Oh, I joined with him, as did Stromm and Malkovich."

Pavlovich couldn't mask his reaction at the mention of his cousin.

"Does it surprise you that he was in on it with the rest of us?"

"As I said before, we're related; that doesn't mean we're alike. What is it you want from me, Kovacs?"

"Stromm was tasked by Thomas to recover and assemble the device that would reveal the cynosure. Pieces were hidden on UEF ships in thirty-two systems, including yours. He'd managed to retrieve all but two when the light gate collapsed."

Pavlovich reexamined the three-dimensional image. "You're guessing what this piece looks like. It's why there is no detail, like on the other pieces."

"With two parts missing, we can only conjecture their exact appearance, but we know this one is on your ship."

"How can you be so certain?"

"Because Thomas hid it there."

"If he told you that, then you should know where to find it."

"You knew the old fossil," said Kovacs. "He wasn't the most trusting sort. He only fed Stromm the information in drips, presumably so he wouldn't run off halfcocked and think he could build the thing himself and use it."

Pavlovich chuckled. "He knew Ullie fairly well, didn't he?"

"He hid the part on *Scimitar* when he was her commander, long before he understood its importance. It is a key functional component."

"I've commanded her for a long time and never seen anything that looks like this."

"Then we have no other choice. We'll have to tow her back to Pictor Prime and tear her apart."

Pavlovich returned his attention to the object. "Not so hasty," he said. "I have an idea."

"I hope it's a good one."

"My AI is patterned off my chief engineer. It is possible that the information we are looking for resides in that database. She knows...knew the ship better than anyone."

Kovacs appeared hopeful. "Do you think so?"

"Maybe, but I won't know until I get to *Scimitar*."

"Okay, I'll send you over with the squad of my Rangers."

"They aren't necessary."

"If you think I trust you, then you haven't been paying attention. They will ensure you don't do anything stupid."

"And what do you want me to do if I find this piece?"

"You will tell no one, for starters. Bring it here to me."

"Kovacs, we don't even know where this might be. For all I know it's a component inside one of the reactors."

"Just find it."

Pavlovich raised an eyebrow. "You haven't exactly given me a good reason to cooperate with you. I have an idea what you and Stromm stand to gain by putting this thing together. What's in it for me?"

A sly smile grew on Kovacs's face. "You are so naïve. Do you think we've been entertaining your crew with tea and crumpets while you are on this little mission? Even as we speak, everyone is being interrogated for this information. The longer you delay or try to negotiate a deal with me, more of them die."

Pavlovich lunged and seized him by the front of his uniform, slamming him into the wall. Kovacs almost seemed amused.

"Get as angry as you want, but I'm the only chance they have. Cooperate, and I'll help you."

"Why would you do this? They know nothing."

Kovacs shrugged. "One word from me and the interrogations stop."

Pavlovich pressed him harder against the bulkhead. "You set this up, you son of a bitch. Why the hell didn't you two just ask me?"

Full realization hit him like a punch to the gut. Suddenly, the enhanced security everywhere and the pervading paranoia made sense to him. "He doesn't trust you."

"No one trusts anyone. The clock is ticking. What's it to be?"

As much as he wanted to snap the other man's neck, he realized he was trapped. He released him and stepped back. "I'll do it, but you stop torturing my crew immediately."

Kovacs straightened his uniform. "You're in no position to bargain. We'll talk about that when you return with the piece, not before."

Snarling, Pavlovich turned on his heel and marched to the door.

"Where are you going?" asked Kovacs, amused.

"Tell your Rangers to meet me at the hangar in ten minutes, or I'll leave them behind."

"HAS *Iliad* done anything besides scan us?" asked Hayden.

"You mean like lock missiles?" said Cora in his earpiece. "No, but they've finally stopped trying to contact the repair ship. For the record, I still believe it was a bad idea not to reply."

"And who would we have pretended to be? Malkovich's Rangers made sure none of the crew's remains were identifiable."

"I could have cracked their security lockout, if you'd have let me keep trying," she said.

"We need your talents for other things, Cora."

"It would help if somebody could tell me what this cynosure thing is supposed to be. I have no idea where to look. I've already cleared all the high-level files in the database and am now going through the operating kernel, but without knowing what I'm looking for, it is taking a lot of time."

"That's why I want your focus there. You have to find it before Malkovich does."

"Hayden, there is a significant chance that I may not be able to locate it. We are assuming it is hidden in the computer system, but what if it isn't?"

"As you said, it would be easier if we understood what we searched for, but we don't, so..."

"Malkovich hasn't even hinted at what it is?" she asked.

"No, he prefers to keep me in the dark while he runs his own search. He spent two hours tearing the captain's quarters apart before he began to concentrate on the archived files."

"He is currently reviewing all of Pavlovich's logs and those of his predecessor."

"Do you think he realizes you're watching him?"

"Not unless he suspects I exist. We've been pretty careful about keeping me a secret from him."

Why did everything have to revolve around secrets? It seemed like they permeated his existence, and everyone he knew, including his own father, kept him ignorant of the political realities of the empire.

"We should be thankful he didn't bring any engineers with him," said Cora. "Keeping the FTL engine hidden would be a bigger challenge."

"Don't discount Malkovich's men. They've been patrolling every deck."

"Yeah, but aside from the routine peek into the engineering section, they've left Chin alone."

"I'm still concerned that his search won't remain confined to the computer," he said. "If he starts sniffing around down there, it won't take him very long to find the false wall. Speaking of that, how are things progressing with the erganium?"

Cora sighed. "That is another issue that would be easier to deal with if we didn't have unwelcome guests. The mineral I located is sufficiently pure that refining it is relatively simple. The problem is that every time one of the Rangers gets close to engineering, Chen must tear down the equipment and hide it. The process is taking longer than it needs to."

"How much more time do you need?"

"Thirty to forty-hours. It all depends on the interruptions."

"We don't have any other options. The less Malkovich knows about the FTL drive, the better."

A lengthy pause occurred before Cora announced. "Uh-ohh! We have a new problem. The *Iliad* just launched a dropship that is coming our way."

"Shit, how long until it arrives?"

"Fifty-seven minutes. Based on the comm chatter, Malkovich's people have noticed too."

Hayden rose from his bunk and grabbed his jacket. "I'm going to the bridge." He adjusted the receiver in his ear canal. "Keep me posted on everything."

"What are you going to do?"

"First? I'm going to ensure Malkovich doesn't blow that ship out of the skies. The last thing we need is to precipitate a shootout. After that, I'll be making things up as I go."

Arriving at the bridge entrance unnoticed, he paused to collect himself before he opened the hatchway and entered.

Malkovich looked up from a console. "Ah, Kaine, your timing is perfect. Stromm's ship has dispatched a boarding party."

"Really?" Hayden didn't think he fooled anyone, but continued, "Aren't they following standard procedure if they've lost communications with the repair crew?"

"Yes, but now I have a decision to make. Do I open fire?"

"What are you going to shoot at them with? I told you; we're out of ammunition, and even cloaked, your vessel can't take out two cruisers and the dropship before being targeted."

"I am perfectly aware of the tactical limitations, son. I've been doing this a lot longer than you, remember? I'm hoping you weren't bullshitting me about having a weapon. Are you sure you still want to go with that story?"

Hayden glanced over to Gunney, who sat stone-faced in his alcove. The old cyborg was hard to read. He wasn't sure if that was because the gunnery officer had a handle on his emotions or simply didn't own more than one expression. Malkovich should have been aware the only weapon *Scimitar* was supposed to have available was the X-ray laser. He couldn't want to start a firefight. Hayden wondered if he suspected the more advanced Glenatat technology existed and was attempting to force their revelation.

"General, it would be foolhardy to engage either of those ships, even if *Scimitar* possessed a full complement of ordnance. I hope you have a better plan than one which won't end well for us."

"Who do you think is aboard that craft, Lieutenant?"

Hayden regarded the growing image of the shuttle on the screen. "Tactically, it should be an armed squadron."

"Which, of course, means we'll have a messy conflict on our hands when the airlock opens. My Rangers are good, but all Stromm's men need to do is get a short message back to their mothership, and we will be scattered debris within a matter of minutes."

"You believe Stromm would do that? Destroy the ship he covets?"

"As far as he knows, he left an abandoned warship behind. If his soldiers meet resistance, he can only conclude that I have taken possession of *Scimitar*."

"Well, he wouldn't be wrong."

"You see, Mister Kaine, we are damned either way; effectively checkmated, unless you have some advantage that you've kept from me?"

Malkovich was one helluva poker player, Hayden decided. The last thing he wanted to do was to reveal *Scimitar*'s Glenatat enhancements. Their armour could easily withstand any nukes *Iliad* or her sister vessel tossed their way, and the dark energy cannon would make short work of them before either ship got a single shot off. That scenario, while much simpler, could only play out if he revealed the truth about *Scimitar* to Malkovich.

He really needed to confer with Cora. Doing so, however, risked revealing her true nature and would create an entirely new set of problems.

"As far as they are concerned," he said, "their nonresponsive crew is a huge red flag. What if they were to reestablish contact?"

"That would be a neat trick, given their present condition. What do you have in mind, Kaine?"

"Let's give them what they expected to find; an empty ship. We will transfer to the repair vessel. My AI can crack the security lockout and reply to *Iliad* from there. The comm glitch will be explained away as an effect of the radiation leak they were supposed to fix." He hoped Cora was paying attention.

"You want me to hand the ship over to Stromm? Fat chance. I'll destroy her myself first."

Hayden scowled, and his voice hardened. "Listen to the entire plan, General. You and your Rangers will return to your stealth vessel but remain docked. Stromm's men will let down their guard once they board, search and confirm she's abandoned. You then can sneak aboard and retake *Scimitar*. Your men *are* trained for that kind of thing, right?"

Malkovich frowned. "They are. What you're proposing is risky, Lieutenant."

"It's the only idea I have that will keep this ship you want so badly in one piece. Unless you have a better plan...?"

The two men stared at each other for a long time. "Very well, Kaine, I'll agree, but with one alteration. You will accompany me aboard our vessel. I want to keep an eye on you."

Welcome Home

INSIDE THE CROWDED stealth ship, Kaine and Malkovich were captivated by the image on the viewer. The screen showed a squad of soldiers pouring from an airlock. By Hayden's count, they outnumbered Malkovich's rangers two to one.

"This plan is shit," said the general. "Those are Stromm's elite personal guard—"

"Stromm has a personal guard? Isn't that a little, I don't know, pretentious, perhaps?"

Malkovich snorted. "Think what you will, Kaine, but I know those men. They won't drop their guard. Sneaking up on them just became impossible. Your plan is starting to stink."

"I'm still open to another one."

"Hmph. Is there no way we can use your ship's AI more creatively?"

In his earpiece Hayden thought he heard Cora snicker at the remark.

"I suppose I could order it to evacuate the air from the ship and shut off the artificial gravity, but those guys look equipped to handle that sort of thing."

"How about the emergency bulkhead controls? Can you override them manually?"

Hayden sat back to consider the idea. "You mean divide and conquer? Separate and isolate them from each other? I suppose that might work in the short term."

"We don't need long if we plan it right. We can keep a path clear for my men to reach the isolated sections. Then they open the doors and take them out in smaller batches."

"I thought you said these guys were elite. Besides, even if we go with that idea, we'd still need to jam their comm channels and put a damper field in place to suppress their LINKS."

"That's a piece of cake," said Cora in his ear.

Ignoring her comment, he continued. "On top of that, they have enough firepower to do real damage to my ship during the shootout."

"Well, you'd better come up with something or—"

"Wait," said Hayden, raising his hand for silence. His eyes were glued to the screen as Yegor Pavlovich emerged from the airlock, dressed in light armour but not armed.

Malkovich beamed. "Son, things just got a whole lot easier."

"What are you talking about?"

"That's my cousin. We have a man on the inside."

"I don't know. It looks to me like he's a prisoner."

"Naw, he's exactly where he means to be, just like we planned."

"The captain? I'm confused. I thought you two hated each other. Your ships attacked us—"

"Did they hit *Scimitar*?"

"Well, no, but—"

"Look, Kaine, I know of Yegor's penchant for intrigue and can understand why he might justify keeping you in the dark."

Hayden knotted his brow and fixed his full attention on Malkovich.

"Yegor contacted me as soon as you arrived in the system. I apprised him of the situation, and we worked out a little plan. We agreed he would work his way into Stromm's good graces by turning on one of my ships."

"But it was destroyed. How could—?"

"Yeah, Kovacs fired on it while you painted it with your lasers, exactly like we planned. It was all a ruse to convince him that Yegor was trustworthy."

"You sacrificed an entire crew just to get a man inside Stromm's camp?"

"Of course not. That ship was run remotely. Most of my fleet is. I told you, we're on the losing side of our conflict with Stromm, under-manned and underequipped. Those Rangers sitting behind us represent a far larger portion of my available troops than I care to admit."

"But why?"

"Why did your captain agree? Because I asked him."

He put a comforting hand on Hayden's knee. "Yegor can be a difficult man to get to know, let alone like. If you've spent as much time with him as you say, you know that he is a just man, an honourable soldier, and a loyal friend. When he learned what Stromm had become—what he is doing, he couldn't ignore the situation."

"He is working with you?"

"I've known for some time what the real impact of the light gate collapse is to Stromm. He was part of the group that Thomas recruited, the same club that Yegor turned his nose up at. Stromm oversaw collecting and assembling the device that would reveal the location of the cynosure. It is a secret with its parts hidden on dozens of ships in the fleet. Once assembled, it will point to a weapon so powerful that whomever controls it will control the galaxy. At least, that's the story that some of us have gleaned. *Scimitar* contains one of the last pieces of the puzzle to be found."

"But nobody foresaw the collapse of the network."

"No, and it sent everyone's plans into the crapper. Stromm is the only one with full knowledge of all the other parts to decipher the cynosure. When the gates collapsed, and *Scimitar* was trapped at the ends of the empire; well, let's just say that Stromm modified the agenda. He decided to make honey out of horse shit, as the expression goes, and became the ruler of this system as compensation for his loss."

"Our arrival changed all that."

"It tipped the balance more in our favour, Kaine. Stromm has been living in virtual seclusion, ever since our failed attempt on his life. We have agents in place, but nobody can get near him anymore. But now that the final piece of the puzzle has appeared, he won't be able to resist the temptation to get his hands on it."

"Why doesn't he rely on someone he trusts to retrieve it?"

Malkovich nodded. "Yes, Kovacs is in Stromm's inner circle, but that hardly means he's trusted. He'll be useful to confirm this isn't some elaborate ruse. His mission is to secure *Scimitar* and return it to Pictor Prime."

Hayden needed time to digest the information. He turned back to the monitor, which had switched to follow the squad as they advanced through the corridors. Pavlovich followed in their wake as they cleared each room on their way to whatever destination they intended; probably the bridge.

Everything was unravelling. Their original plan called for him to return on the repair ship and take *Scimitar* back to rejoin the crew. It was obvious that something had gone sideways.

Hayden shook his head, feeling like a fool. Pictor was not a random choice for their destination. Nor did he believe it was the only system with erganium for the FTL drive. They were here for the cynosure. Hayden didn't share Malkovich's admiration for his captain's nobility. Somebody like Pavlovich didn't operate like an altruistic hero. He had another yet unknown motivation for coming to this system and putting all their lives at risk. Everything the man had told him was manipulative bullshit. He regretted allowing himself to be conned.

Did Stella know? Was she a party to the duplicity, or was she just as much a pawn as Hayden? He'd have to find her to learn that, but he didn't know if she remained on *Iliad* or if she was back on Pictor Prime.

He forced his attention back to the monitor. Pavlovich was calling out as he searched.

"He's looking for me and the others," Hayden said.

"There's no audio feed; are you sure?"

He pretended to scrutinize the screen while Cora spoke quietly in his ear. "He's searching for us. I know you told me to keep a low profile until we know what's happening, but should I contact him?"

He stood. "I'm going to meet him. I have to learn what's going on."

Malkovich seized his upper arm. "What's going on is that he's led a squad of Stromm's Rangers into your ship."

"I thought you two had a plan. Are you telling me you no longer trust him? Or am I the problem?"

Their eyes locked, and they stared at each other for several breaths.

"Make a decision, General."

Malkovich seemed to deflate as he released him. "Go. You're Yegor's man, so I need to trust you."

Hayden frowned as he considered him. "I won't betray you."

The older man returned a wan smile. "It's either that or I shoot you. I guess I'll have to put my faith in you, Kaine. If my cousin made you XO, that has to count for something."

Hayden wasn't so sure.

All he knew was that he needed some answers, and he was determined to get them. He checked the sidearm strapped to his thigh, then headed for the airlock.

Hayden crept through the corridors, maintaining a cautious eye on the security feed Cora routed to his helmet's HUD.

"I can't tell if they are protecting, or guarding him," she said. "Those Rangers haven't left the cap'n's side since he came aboard."

"Let's assume the latter. We need to separate him from them. Any ideas, Cora?"

"Everything I could do to the soldiers will also hurt the cap'n," she said.

"Well, keep working on it."

After checking that the last corridor was empty, he entered the engineering section and sealed the door behind him. They had agreed that Pavlovich would, at some point, check on the FTL engine, and this was the best place to wait for him.

"He's still calling out for me," she said. "He's decided you're not aboard."

"Let's keep him in the dark for as long as possible."

"Why?"

"I have my reasons," he said before he removed his helmet. He moved to the monitoring panel. An amalgam recollection of the dozens of times he'd seen Cora at the station bubbled up, a wave of guilt and regret along with it.

"Are you okay, Hayden? Your pulse just shot up."

"I'm fine. Where is the captain right now?"

"On the forward rail gun deck. He seems to be searching for something."

"Where are the Rangers?"

"They are still with him."

"Cora, I've changed my mind. I want you to answer Pavlovich, but not in a normal way. Can you send him a text message through one of the control stations?"

"Of course. What do you want me to tell him?"

"Tell him to take a deep breath and hang on to something."

A Tight Spot

"WHAT THE HELL ARE WE looking for?"

The squad leader was in a foul mood and didn't attempt to conceal it.

"That's need-to-know, and you don't," Pavlovich snapped.

He was still trying to digest what had happened to his crew. The maintenance ship had departed, and their report suggested they'd discovered nothing unexpected, which made no sense.

He couldn't imagine under what conditions Kaine or Gunney would abandon *Scimitar*, yet there was no sign of anyone. The repair ship's crew should have discovered and reported that the radiation leak was bogus, but that hadn't happened. If nothing else, the modifications and the FTL drive should have created a cascade of questions for him to answer. None of it made sense.

Gravity, environmental—everything functioned normally. The bridge, every cabin, every station was operational, as if the people had been snatched away. Kaine's ship was still in the hangar, and all the emergency escape pods were in their cradles. Even Cora seemed to have abandoned *Scimitar*.

So far, they'd seen no signs of violence, so whatever happened didn't appear to have involved a struggle. But their search still had to take them to the engineering section, something he'd been avoiding since they'd boarded. Soon, he would have no more excuses.

"Sir," interrupted one of the rangers.

"Yes?" Pavlovich and the squad leader answered in unison. He scowled and without attempting to hide his annoyance deferred to the other man.

"What is it?" asked the grizzled sergeant.

"There is no indication that the rail guns are operational."

"They haven't fired in years," Pavlovich growled. "We have no ordnance."

The sergeant grunted, seeming to accept the explanation. "Keep alert for anything out of the ordinary." He turned to the captain. "Unless there is something more you want to tell us?"

"Like what?" He remained adversarial to conceal his growing anxiety.

"If you were to tell us what we are searching for—"

"I'm not going to repeat myself, Sergeant. You and your men aren't required for this. In fact, you are starting to interfere. Why don't you remain here and take a break while I continue my search?"

"I have my orders."

"I'm sure you do," he grumbled under his breath.

"It looks like this part of the ship isn't turning anything up. We should make our way to the engineering section."

Pavlovich frowned and tried to sound more exasperated than nervous. "As I said before, the radiation levels down there are still above acceptable..."

"And I told you that our armour is rated for it. I'm not supposed to take my eyes off you, and you have led us everywhere else on this snipe hunt. Enough is enough; we're going to engineering."

He grabbed the captain by the shoulder.

Not many were as large as Yegor Pavlovich, something he'd exploited for much of his career to avoid argument. The sergeant had at least a twenty-kilo advantage on him. The man was a literal giant, as were most of his force.

"What the hell did your mother teach you? You don't manhandle a superior officer, soldier."

The man sneered. "The only reason I haven't beaten the answer out of you so we can get back to our bunks is that Kovacs gave orders to not hurt you...unless absolutely required. Please tell me that you're going to resist and make it necessary."

Pavlovich examined the man and weighed his chances against him, deciding they were dismal if the Ranger was suited in his armour; probably not much different if he were not.

The sergeant was a career jarhead. Ten years ago, if this man had even wiped his nose improperly in the presence of an officer, he'd have been demoted to scrubbing latrines. It was clear that discipline was breaking down as a result of the civil war and the isolation.

"Sarge, I'm not your enemy. Let's finish up our search here, and then I'll happily show you the way to engineering."

Taking these apes to the beating heart of his ship was the last thing he intended. Even if these clowns didn't know what a standard engine looked like, they would take one look at the FTL drive and immediately realize something wasn't right. They'd report the anomaly to Kovacs, and within the hour *Scimitar* would have techs crawling through her. The real secret would be out, he would be screwed, and a disaster he couldn't imagine would follow.

He had no plan and delayed in the hope he might be able to think of something to overpower this group, or at least trap them in a part of the ship where they could do no harm. That had depended on Cora, but she, like the rest of his crew, was missing. He worried that the repair ship's teams may have damaged her. He wanted to rush to inspect the housing of her chamber, but that was another anomaly he'd have difficulty explaining.

"Sarge," called one of the men, "this panel just lit up."

"What does the readout say?"

"It doesn't make any sense to me."

The sergeant grunted and went to investigate, leaving Pavlovich to wonder what was amiss.

A moment later he was called over. "Could you please explain what is wrong with this interface? It is requesting an authorization code for some damned reason."

Frowning, he approached, confused. "We made several operating system customizations over the last decade." That was complete bullshit. No modifications were made to the rail gun control systems. He wondered if it was Cora trying to reach him.

He reached the panel and scowled at the two men. They took his meaning and stepped back to avoid crowding him.

The system was, indeed, asking for his access code. Not seeing any way to diagnose the issue, he entered his command ID.

The screen displayed a message: *Empty your lungs and grab something.*

Pavlovich's initial confusion was quickly replaced with realization. He adjusted his position and gripped the base of the console with one hand. With his other, he entered a response: *Ready*.

He exhaled and hung on as the outer doors opened and a hurricane rush of air roared around them.

Make Sure You Use It

A DISHEVELLED YEGOR Pavlovich entered engineering. Tracks of blood ran from both ears and his nose. His bloodshot eyes lit up at the sight of Hayden.

"Kaine! You've got a pair of balls on you! I almost got sucked out with the others. There aren't a lot of places to grab hold of in the rail gun chamber."

"I was counting on you knowing where to look for one."

Pavlovich wiggled a finger in his ear and looked about the room. "Speak up. I think I busted an eardrum with your little stunt. Are you alone? What happened to Cora?"

"I'm happy to see you safe, Cap'n."

"Cora! I'm so glad to hear your voice. You had me worried when you didn't respond."

"The XO's order, sir. Sorry."

"I can't believe he talked you into almost killing me."

"Cora didn't know what I had planned. I locked her out of that system when she watched to make sure you'd understood the message."

"I didn't know you could do that. Very sneaky, Kaine. Cora, keep a closer eye on this man in the future."

"I intend to, sir."

"Where the hell is everyone else?"

Hayden filled him in on what had happened since his departure, and Pavlovich informed him of what he'd learned.

"The entire crew?" said Hayden, stunned by the news. "Stella too?"

"I'm afraid so. I—"

Hayden's unexpected right hook sent Pavlovich sprawling to the deck.

"You son of a bitch! It's your fault they're in danger!"

The captain sat up, rubbing his jaw. "You're right, Kaine. I took a huge risk. I should have conferred with you first and—"

"This crew isn't UEF, in case you've forgotten. They're civilians you conned into joining you. You owed them a choice since you knew what you were stepping into—who Stromm is and what he's capable of. Or didn't your cousin tell you about him?"

"He did, and I knew what I was getting into. But you must understand what is at stake, Kaine."

"Then explain it to me so I can decide whether I should space you too." He pointed his sidearm at Pavlovich.

"Hayden!" said Cora. "What are you doing? This is mutiny."

"I don't believe he gives a shit about that." The captain struggled to his feet. Hayden made no move to assist him and considered hitting him again.

"There's no need for this, Kaine. You asked for an explanation, and I'm prepared to give you one. Put the gun down and let's have a chat about it over a stiff drink."

"I believe this is more motivating. Start talking."

Pavlovich stood tall and his jaw set beneath his unkempt beard. "Soldier, it's time for you to make a decision. Shoot that weapon or holster it, but don't threaten me with it unless you intend to fire it."

"I'm not a soldier anymore. None of us are. There is no more UEF; no more chain of command. The empire is shattered and anarchy reigns, so don't presume to order me around as if it means anything."

He waved the pistol. "I'm pissed enough with you to use this thing. Now talk, so I can decide whether to believe you."

The door opened, and through it poured a squad of Rangers, followed by Malkovich.

"What the hell is going on here?" yelled the general.

"Cesar!" said Pavlovich, breaking into a wide smile.

Malkovich scowled at him. "You, shut up!"

Then he turned his attention to Hayden. "Kaine, you said you needed to speak with him. What's with the gun? Lower your weapon."

"Not until I get some answers." He glared at the captain. "Honest ones."

"And how will you judge that he tells you the truth, son? Put that thing down, we're all on the same side here."

Belying his point, three Rangers trained their weapons on Kaine.

"Hayden, please do as he asks," said Cora.

Malkovich looked around for the source of the voice. "Who is that?"

"Think of Stella," she continued. "She wouldn't want this to happen."

"We'll save her, Kaine," said Pavlovich. "The others too. Listen to Cora before you get yourself killed."

Hayden took a long time to weigh their words. Finally, he nodded and holstered his weapon. "Fine."

The Rangers who had him in their sites started toward him, but a sharp command from Malkovich stopped them in their tracks. Without hesitation, they lowered their guns, bringing the standoff to an end.

The tension broken; Malkovich turned his attention to Pavlovich. Seeing them together, Hayden couldn't believe how similar the two men were. If not for the beard, it could have been a mirror image.

"Yegor, you miserable son of a bitch!"

He advanced on the captain and before anyone could react sent him to the deck with a left cross.

Dark fury filled Pavlovich's eyes as he sat up and rubbed his jaw. "This is wearing thin."

Malkovich held his head high and stared down at him.

Then a smirk turned up the corners of Pavlovich's mouth. Malkovich continued to glare at the fallen man before a smile grew on his face as well.

"You know, I believe it was my turn to hit you, Cousin."

The general shrugged. "It's been too long; I forgot."

"Bullshit." He rose and they embraced, slapping each other on the back.

Malkovich grinned. "I've been waiting to do that for years."

Pavlovich rubbed his jaw. "I didn't think I'd pissed you off that much when we last met."

"I've had a lot of years to stew over it. Sorry I punched you so hard."

The captain grinned. "No, you're not."

Malkovich returned the smile. "No, I'm not."

Kaine shook his head in disbelief, and thought, *My family is dysfunctional, but we have nothing on these two.*

"Cap'n, if you're finished, we have a crew to recover and a warship to deal with," said Cora.

"Who the hell is that?" asked Malkovich.

"I'll explain later. Let's go to the conference room to make our plans."

Pavlovich put his big arm around his cousin and gestured to the door. When everyone had exited to the corridor, the captain excused himself and signalled Hayden.

"Kaine, a word in private, if you don't mind," he said pleasantly before reentering engineering. Hayden hesitated for a moment then followed.

The door closed behind him and he approached Pavlovich, whose back was toward him.

"Yes, sir?"

Pavlovich whirled and punched him savagely in the gut. Kaine doubled over and fell to the deck. While he fought for breath, Pavlovich kneeled over him and said, "The next time you pull a weapon on someone, make sure you use it, because you usually won't get another chance."

He patted Hayden patronizingly on the cheek before he exited.

Allies

HAYDEN ENTERED THE conference room to the cousins sharing a drink and a laugh.

"Ah, Kaine, come and join us. I hope you're feeling better?"

Hayden's hand reflexively covered his stomach. His abdomen still ached from the blow. "I'll be fine, sir."

The captain seemed amused and satisfied. Malkovich regarded him with disappointment and disdain.

Feeling like a chastened child, Hayden assumed his seat at the table.

"Cora, please resume your summary."

"Yes, Cap'n. As I was saying, the erganium we recovered was of sufficient grade that it required little in the way of refinement. We completed most of the conversion process before Chin and the others were evacuated."

"Estimated time to finish it once they return?"

"About six hours."

Hayden looked quizzically at Pavlovich, not quite able to believe what he'd just heard. Noticing his incredulity, the captain said, "We've no secrets from Cesar, Kaine. We all share the same goal."

His aching midsection reminding him to be cautious, Hayden said as respectfully as he could manage, "I'm afraid I'm a little unclear on that matter, sir. What, exactly, is our goal?"

"My resources are at your disposal to help recover your shipmates, Lieutenant," said Malkovich.

"In return, we will assist the rebels to bring Stromm down and reestablish ordered governance to this system," said Pavlovich.

"And how does our FTL drive fit into this arrangement?"

"We're pooling resources. It would be pointless to conceal all our technology, since we will be dependent upon Cesar's people to fill in the positions for our missing people. We can't operate *Scimitar* in a combat scenario without a crew."

"You anticipate a conflict?"

"It may come to that, Kaine," said Malkovich. "My last reports indicated the prisoners are held in a high-security wing in the presidential palace on Pictor Prime. We won't be able to get near the place without some advanced technology."

"Right now, Cora is evaluating the possibility of adapting the rebel stealth tech to *Scimitar*," said Pavlovich. "If that doesn't prove possible, we may have to outfit Cesar's ships with Glenatat weaponry."

"That could take weeks. Our crew might be dead by then."

"Not while Kovacs believes threatening them is motivating me to cooperate."

"And how long can that lie be maintained? The bodies of his troops are floating around outside. Surely he is concerned they haven't reported in recently?"

"Cora tapped into their comm frequency and has been sending text updates back to *Iliad*. That should keep them off our back for a short time."

"To accomplish what?" said Hayden.

"We have to draw Stromm out from his fortress," said Malkovich. "Right now, he trusts Kovacs to work in his interest. That trust must be broken to compel Stromm to come and retrieve the missing component himself."

"What is this thing you two have been tearing the ship apart to locate?"

"Show him, Cora," said Pavlovich.

A hologram appeared over the table and slowly rotated in front of Hayden.

"This is the thing that Kovacs and Stromm are so hot to get their hands on," said the captain.

"What is it?"

Pavlovich shrugged. "Damned if I know. This image is a poor estimate of what it looks like, based on my description to Cora. It is a component for a much larger machine, already assembled and ready to use, once this part is located."

"What is this device Stromm is assembling?"

"Something that reveals the cynosure," said Malkovich.

"What the hell is that?" asked Hayden.

Pavlovich leaned forward, elbows on the table, like a professor about to go into a long explanation for an especially slow student. "Kaine, have you never wondered why, in the centuries since we've colonized our little corner of the galaxy, we have encountered no one else? Why does it look like we are the only ones out here?"

"That's not true. We've found ruins on a number of worlds."

"Ruins, yes, but never a living, thriving advanced civilization."

"Until we met the Glenatat," said Hayden.

"Yes, and their nemesis, the Malliac. But we were never meant to find them. It was only dumb luck and a crazy scientist that allowed you to pilot *Scimitar* through that wormhole. If not for that, the Glenatat would still be believed a dead civilization."

"What is your point?"

"There are more advanced races out there than even the Glenatat," said Malkovich. "The cynosure will point us to them."

"Like a compass?"

He chuckled. "A bit like that, but there is much, much more. The cynosure is a portal."

"Imagine a transportation network, but one not limited to jumping between receiver stations," said Pavlovich. "One that is capable of transporting, not just ships, but entire planets to anywhere across the galaxy...even to other galaxies."

"It would make our jump system seem like stone-age technology by comparison," said Malkovich.

Hayden regarded Pavlovich. "You're buying this?"

"I didn't when I first heard it. When Thomas tried to recruit me, the story sounded too fantastic. I wasn't about to drink from the crazy juice and join him. But when we encountered the Glenatat, Thomas's delusions became credible."

"They were aware of the cynosure," said Malkovich. "For some reason, they disassembled the device that points to it and hid the components around the galaxy."

"Why would they do that?"

"Who knows? Maybe you two should have asked them when you visited. Anyway, when their civilization collapsed, knowledge of it was lost until our archaeologists stumbled onto something about 180 years ago."

"Since then," said Pavlovich, "Thomas and others before him quietly recovered the missing pieces, looking forward to the day when they could assemble them."

"But the plan went awry when you destroyed the light gate network, Mister Kaine," said Malkovich. "Two ships, yours being one, were trapped at the farthest ends of the empire, and there was no way to recover them. Thomas and his conspirators' plans were dashed, and it would have ended there had *Scimitar* not shown up here."

Hayden faced Pavlovich. "You knew about this all along. We're not in this mess by accident."

Pavlovich nodded. "I knew there was something aboard *Scimitar* that Thomas wanted brought to this system. Two months before you were sent to us, I was ordered to come here for an unspecified mission. The order made no sense. I thought Thomas had finally decided to get rid of me. Naturally, I found several excuses to delay our departure. Then, when you arrived with orders that left no wiggle room about our return, I knew my days were numbered. When the network collapsed, I thought it was all finished and my worries over."

"But you discovered the FTL technology."

"It put me in a position of advantage. I reasoned that if the Glenatat and the Malliac existed, then the cynosure might also be real. If the technology exists to move entire planets out of the path of the Malliac threat, don't we have an obligation to find it?"

"Did it ever occur to you that it might lead to something far worse?" asked Hayden.

"Look around you, Kaine! We're witnessing the end of human civilization. Do you think Pictor is the only system experiencing this kind of anarchy? In another generation, there may be nobody left to save."

"And who do you imagine having control of the cynosure and all the power it points to? You?" He pointed at Malkovich. "Him?"

The cousins regarded each other as the question hung in the air.

"Gentlemen," said Cora, "we have a more pressing matter to deal with. The *Iliad* has launched missiles."

Taking Off the Gloves

PAVLOVICH STRODE ONTO the bridge, Hayden and Malkovich on his heels.

"Cora, can you shut down that damned klaxon? We're all here."

"Aye, Cap'n," she replied as the alarm ended.

Hayden rushed to the science monitoring station.

"Yegor," said Malkovich, "we still have time to escape in my ship. The missiles will not be able to detect it."

Pavlovich glared at him. "Would you abandon your command so easily, Cesar?"

His cousin raised his hands in surrender. "It is only something for you to take into consideration, Cousin."

"Captain," said Hayden, "Cora has confirmed that missiles are locked on *Scimitar* and the repair vessel with our people aboard."

"Well, that ends the debate." Pavlovich assumed the command chair. "Cora, what do we have available?"

"Three of our engines are cold, sir, including the one powering the X-ray lasers."

"We don't have enough time to bring them online," said Hayden.

"What kind of ordnance is coming our way?"

"Nukes, by the radiation readings."

"Cora, can they hurt us?"

"No, sir, our armour should protect us."

"But the repair ship hasn't any protection."

"Captain," said Hayden, "the Glenatat weapons are tied into the active engine."

"Do you know how to target them, Kaine?"

He hurried to Gunney's tactical alcove. "I guess we're going to find out. Cora, time to impact?"

"Two minutes, thirty-one seconds," she said.

Pavlovich's voice boomed. "Bring the other engines online. We aren't hiding any more."

"Way ahead of you, Cap'n, but they won't be up to power for twelve minutes."

Hayden took one last look at the interface then said, "Dark energy cannon charged and locked on the missiles. May I fire, sir?"

"Take 'em out, Kaine."

Moments later, the lighting flickered as the alien weapon drew power. Hayden's eyes remained glued to the tactical display as he watched the two approaching warheads vanish from the screen. "Enemy missiles neutralized."

"That's gonna piss off Kovacs."

Kaine moved across the bridge to the engineering panel. "Let's hope it will confuse him long enough for us to get our engines online."

"Captain," said Cora, "I'm detecting coded transmissions between *Iliad* and their other ship. Looks like it's responded and is changing course, heading this way. ETA, seventeen minutes to weapons range."

"Sounds like Kovacs called for help."

"We should retreat once your engines are hot," said Malkovich. "Poor old *Scimitar* is no match for one of those ship's rail guns, let alone two."

Pavlovich scowled at his cousin. "Careful how you speak about the old girl. She's got more fight in her than you realize."

Malkovich glared at him. "Yegor, you are out of your mind. This ship is over sixty years old and is three classes smaller than those modern warships. They have ten times your firepower and can withstand a direct hit by a nuke, if you had one. You don't stand a chance. Your only advantage is speed. Use your FTL drive and get us out of here."

Pavlovich looked up at Hayden. "What is your opinion, XO? Should we tuck our tail and run?"

"With all due respect, sir, if the general wishes to leave, his ship is still docked."

"Yeah, I kind of agree with my first officer, Cesar. Feel free to go while you can, just make sure you close the door on your way out."

Malkovich stared at Pavlovich then shot a withering look at Kaine. After a moment of consideration, he said, "Fine, I'll stay. But at least let me put my ship into the fight."

"Cora, have you accounted for the additional mass of the stealth ship attached to our hull?"

"Cap'n, you've hurt my feelings. Of course I have. It's no problem."

"Sorry, I didn't mean to offend you."

The general smiled and said, "Human merged with machine, you say? Impressive."

Pavlovich returned the smile. "If you're staying, we need you to do something useful. Do you remember how to fly?"

Malkovich glanced at the helm station. "I think I can recall a thing or two about how these old ships function..." He became more sober. "I can drive her where you tell me to go, but with only three of us, we don't have much chance to engage Kovacs."

"Cora will run engineering and keep the weapons hot. She's got most of the ship on automation. Right girl?"

"Cap'n, I have a handle on all systems at the moment and can keep things humming as long as everything holds together. But we really need the crew. My temporary network is mostly bailing wire and spit. If a key connection blows, I don't know if I can restore things. The general might be right."

"Bullshit. Helmsman, bring us about and put us on an intercept course to meet the approaching ship...does she have a name, Cora?"

"*Deimos*, Cap'n."

"Hmm, that's a tad aggressive. Target her, Kaine; full power."

"Sir?"

Annoyed, Pavlovich turned to Hayden. "That means turn the dial to maximum, XO. Cesar isn't often correct about a lot of things, but he is right about our ability to take on two ships in our present condition. The sooner we remove one from the board, the easier this will become."

"But there must be two hundred crewmen on that vessel..."

"Kaine, we don't have time for a philosophical argument. Take out that ship."

Frowning, Hayden lifted his chin. "Cora, what is your assessment of our defences? How much can we take?"

Pavlovich scowled at his XO as she replied, "The captain and the general are correct. Even our enhanced armour won't survive a combined attack from them."

"It's them or us, Kaine. What's it going to be?"

He jumped to his feet. "We can outrun them."

"I'm afraid it is too late for that," said Cora. "*Iliad* has changed course to cover our only potential escape vector. Our other engines won't come online before we are in weapons range of both ships. We won't be able to build enough acceleration to take us out of danger."

"It's do or die, son, and I don't plan on dying."

Hayden noticed Pavlovich's hand over his holstered sidearm. After their earlier altercation, he had no doubt that his captain would use it.

He returned to his place in the tactical alcove. "I am targeting *Deimos* with the dark energy cannon; full power."

The words tasted like bile. He couldn't get the image out of his mind of the floating armada of dead Malliac ships. How many of them had died on that day ten years ago? They were monsters, true, and needed to be stopped, but the crew aboard *Deimos* were not warrior aliens. They were men and women, just like him, trapped in a place they never intended to live for the rest of their lives; caught up in a conflict between two megalomaniacs, all because of his fateful decision on that day. Now they would die by his hand.

The light he dreaded seeing flashed on his panel. With a heavy heart, his hand rose to the interface. "Cannon charged. Target locked."

He hesitated, until he heard Pavlovich shift in the command chair. Pressing the button, he said, "Firing."

Despite his misgivings and shame, he couldn't avoid watching the tactical display. Morbid fascination demanded he observe what the weapon could do against a human vessel.

What he witnessed tore at his heart with icy claws.

Undetectable by any human instrumentation, the dark energy beam struck *Deimos* with unimaginable fury.

Its bow crumpled as if piloted into an invisible wall. The vessel's spine buckled while explosions blew her hull apart from within. Advancing from the impact point, a rippling distortion wave seemed to devour what remained undamaged. As the fury washed toward the stern, the hull plating vaporized, exposing the skeletal support structure beneath.

Brief flashes of light popped in the wake of the destructive tide, like a trail of sparks. The phenomenon confused Hayden, until with sickened understanding, he realized they were human bodies, incinerated by the terrible energy that consumed the ship.

"Holy shit," said Malkovich, his eyes glued to the viewer. Hayden looked at the captain, whose attention was also riveted to what unfolded. The shock on his face was unmistakable.

The dark energy cannon, like the armour that protected *Scimitar*, was gifted to them by the Glenatat to confront the Malliac. He'd only seen it employed on that one day that they met them in battle.

Even in that situation, a much lower charge level was used that permitted rapid firing of the weapon in combat. None of them had any concept of what the cannon was capable of at full power.

Cora broke the shared trance. "*Iliad* has fired her main rail gun. Impact in five seconds."

There was only enough time for Hayden and the others to brace themselves.

Iliad

HAYDEN FLOATED IN DEATHLY silence, confused about where he was. He opened his eyes to blackness and panicked.

Weightless, he flailed about until his hand struck something, sending a jolt of pain along his arm. His aching head and body convinced him he still lived.

Where was he?

The last thing he remembered was...*Iliad*!

As the understanding of the situation sank in, he groped about for a handhold and tried to shut out the images that flashed across his mind.

All he could see was repeated replay of *Deimos'* crew being atomized.

How many had he killed?

After finding the back of his chair, he paused to slow his breathing and calm his racing heart. Swallowing around the lump in his throat, Hayden quietly spoke into his headset.

"Cora, are you okay?"

"I'm still here."

"Do you have control of anything?"

There was a brief pause before she replied. "I can't get access to anything. You're still breathing, so we're lucky the environmental systems aren't compromised, because there would be nothing I could do if they were."

"What is still operating?"

"I can't say. Hayden, I'm blind and helpless."

"What the hell did they hit us with?"

"The sensor logs are offline, but before the lights and gravity went out, a rail gun projectile slammed into us. It exploded with a quantum level distortion."

"Quantum fusion? How is that possible?"

"You saw Malkovich's stealth ships. These boys have had time to tinker with things."

"I suppose so...why were we hurt?"

"Hard to say. There are a couple of microfissures in our hull. It may have been a lucky shot."

"Why didn't the Glenatat armour hold up?"

"You're still breathing, aren't you? The numbers I crunched as the rail gun hit us told me that thing was travelling with enough relativistic mass to cut us in half. The armour is why we're still talking."

"Can you tell me anything about the state of the ship?"

"We're still in one piece, but that shot took out all my automations. I have very restricted diagnostics; basically, I can tell you some of what's wrong and deduce the rest, but I can't do a darned thing to fix any of it."

Blind and crippled, they were a great big target for *Iliad* to finish off. The only reason they yet lived was because Stromm wanted *Scimitar*.

"Okay, let's take it one step at a time. Engines?"

"Offline."

"Weapons?"

"Do you really need to ask? Everything runs off the engines."

Hayden's mind whirled, running through the list of every system. As his eyes adjusted to the darkness, the few remaining lights on the control panel glowed like red and green stars against the void. An idea struck him.

Pavlovich and his cousin were arguing somewhere in the dark, and it was apparent from their conversation that neither of them was injured.

"Can I still fire the cannon from my station?" he asked Cora.

"You should be able to, but there is no way to energize it."

"Maybe there doesn't need to be. How much recharge time elapsed before everything went down?"

"A little over thirty seconds, but that is only enough for five percent after our full power discharge."

"Do you still have access to the external sensor net? Can you tell me what *Iliad* is doing?"

"I'm blind, Hayden. Even communications are down if you wanted to surrender."

"That's not exactly what I have in mind." He filled her in on his forming plan.

"Yes, that is possible, but you would have to time everything perfectly. If they take a second shot at us, we won't survive."

"Kovacs needs this ship intact. He'll verify that we're disabled before he sends over boarding parties."

Pavlovich's voice boomed from the dark. "Kaine, who the hell are you talking to?"

Looking in the direction of the captain's voice, Hayden's adapting eyes made out a silhouette against the few, still active control panels on the bridge. Then a patch of brightness lit up the far side of the room when Malkovich turned on a torch retrieved from the emergency locker.

"Cora and I have a plan, sir."

"So does Cesar. He's going to order his ship to launch and take a run at *Iliad*."

"No! There is a better way. We have a partial charge on the energy cannon— enough, I think, to disable her, or give her a very bloody nose."

"I'm all for hammering Kovacs with everything we can," said Pavlovich, "but you're forgetting we are dead in space. There is no way to point our cannon."

"Yes, I think there is. We can use Malkovich's ship's engines to provide manoeuvring thrust for *Scimitar*."

The cousins looked remarkably similar as they considered the plan.

"I don't see why that couldn't work," said Malkovich, "but are you sure your weapon will do any good?"

Hayden swallowed hard. The truth was, he had no idea what it could do at such a diminished setting. All he knew was that there would be only one shot, and he had to make it count.

And there were other concerns eating at him. Stella and the rest of the crew were not aboard *Iliad*, but they were still on Pictor Prime. If he didn't do enough damage to her, there was a very good chance Kovacs could send a message to Stromm, endangering their lives further.

"It will be enough," he said, sounding more confident than he felt.

"Well, do it," said Pavlovich. "Cesar, you should go to your ship now before Kovacs gets trigger happy again. If this doesn't work, you may be able to fire a couple of shots before he detects you."

Hayden watched Malkovich move toward the door carrying the flashlight. Suddenly, he realized a problem he hadn't considered. "Communications are down. We will need to coordinate somehow."

Malkovich grabbed at the door and stopped himself from drifting through it. In the dim light, he appeared like a ghostly, floating spectre. He pointed at the viewer that displayed a jittery image of the star field. "Keep your eyes on that screen. I'll turn us slowly to make it appear that we are still adrift. When Kovacs's ship comes up on your targeting scanner, you'll have your shot."

"We only have enough juice for one," said Hayden.

"Then make it count," said Malkovich before he pushed off and floated out, unencumbered by artificial gravity.

Hayden made a quick estimate of how long it would take him to get to his ship. Glad that the general had taken the flashlight, he pulled himself back to the gunnery alcove and strapped himself in the chair.

He took the opportunity to adjust and confirm that the targeting imager was still active. He tried to breathe away his anxiety when a thought undid it all.

Activating his earpiece, he spoke softly. "Cora, you still have time; hop in one of the synths and board Malkovich's ship. There's nothing you can do while we're in this condition. You may as well be safe in case this doesn't work."

"Tsk, Lieutenant, you should know that I will never abandon you or the cap'n."

He cut his reply short when he heard Pavlovich approach the alcove.

"How confident are you that we can damage Kovacs, Kaine?"

All Hayden could think of were the countless dead of the destroyed ship. He pulled himself together and swallowed the dry lump in his throat.

"You saw what it did to *Deimos*."

"I had no idea it would destroy it. We've never fired at full power. I just wanted to make sure we disabled them or at least make them reconsider taking us on."

"I'm pretty sure we've given Kovacs second thoughts about a lot of things, especially when his rail gun didn't cut us in half," said Hayden. "He has seen most of what *Scimitar* is capable of. We can't let him gain control of this ship."

Pavlovich nodded. "Letting him and Stromm have access to such powerful weapons would be a disaster; giving them faster-than-light capability as well would be unforgivable. With our technology and the things the cynosure might unveil, they would go on a rampage of conquest that hasn't been seen since the Spanish armada sailed Earth's seas."

"Well, at five percent power, I can't tell you if the weapon will have any effect on them. If it doesn't work, we can't prevent it."

"Yes, we can," said Pavlovich. He pulled a small device from his pocket.

"What's that?"

"This is a detonator. A long time ago, I fitted the FTL drive with a failsafe to ensure it never fell into the wrong hands. One press of this button, power source or not, it will self-destruct. *Scimitar* and anything within ten thousand metres will become dust."

Hayden's throat was too parched for him to swallow. "I didn't realize I'd signed on for a suicide mission."

"Kaine, don't paint me as a heartless monster. I wasn't going to let my cousin launch his ship without taking you and Cora along to safety."

"That's comforting, except that we're still here."

"Yeah, I know. I guess we'd better hope your plan works, for all our sakes, eh?"

"You are such an asshole, Pavlovich, playing with people's lives—"

The captain touched him on the shoulder and pointed at the monitor. "Save your self-righteous indignation for later, Kaine. We're coming around on *Iliad*."

Hayden watched the rotating star field slowly reveal the approaching warship. Overcoming his anger, he leaned over the control panel and made sure everything was ready for him to fire. He stared at the red light that identified the firing button.

So much power. So many already dead by his hand.

"Malkovich made good time," Pavlovich said. "We must not have been too far off target. Man, that ship is big. How close is she?"

Pulled from his maudlin thoughts, Hayden focused on the little his instruments could tell him.

At five percent, he hoped the cannon would be enough to disable *Iliad*, but there was no way to be sure. It had to work. If it failed, Malkovich would unleash his nukes, ensuring *Iliad*'s destruction. This was the only way to stop the bloodshed. He had to try.

"I have no way to tell her range, sir. Sensors are offline."

"You mean to tell me you have no targeting control at all? Shit." Silence fell between them as they watched the screen fill.

"You can't miss something that big, Kaine. Push the button."

"I'm waiting for their engine section to come into position."

"Don't get fancy with our only shot. Fire!"

"In a second..." Hayden's hand was poised over the activator. He felt Pavlovich's hot breath on his neck as the big man hovered over his shoulder.

"Shoot the damned cannon. Now!"

Hayden risked a glance at the captain. Beads of sweat, nowhere to go without the pull of gravity, accumulated in a sheen on his forehead.

Returning his attention to the target, his finger twitched as he forced himself to wait for the optimal moment. Then, when his desired target lined up on the screen's crosshairs, he activated the weapon.

For a brief instant, nothing seemed to happen.

Then, evidence of their desperate discharge unfolded before them.

Iliad shuddered as a front of distortion rippled across the targeted section. The ship's entire structure convulsed. The gigantic vessel sharply altered course, as if swatted by an invisible hand.

Lights along its hull winked out, and small explosions from overloaded energy conduits burst in a path of brilliant flares that raced outward from the engineering section.

"That was five percent?" said Pavlovich, shocked.

Iliad rotated slowly, dark and lifeless. Shortly, multiple small flashes erupted along the ruins of her hull as dozens of emergency escape pods launched, carrying survivors to relative safety.

Hayden wondered where they would go. Maybe to one of Elgar's moons, but with the colony destroyed, he doubted any of the surviving rebel bases would welcome them with open arms.

Cora announced over the speaker, "I restored the secondary comm network and managed to tie into the systems aboard the general's ship. He is in communication with *Iliad.*"

"Let me hear it."

The speakers buzzed and crackled.

"—don't know why you're being so stubborn, Kovacs. Do you need more shit kicked out of you?"

"Malkovich, I would never yield to you, even if it were my only chance of survival."

The general chuckled. "I *am* your last *hope.* Surrender, before I start taking pot-shots at your escaping crew."

"What the hell is he saying?" said Pavlovich. "Cora, patch me in this conversation."

"Working on it, Cap'n."

"You do that, Malkovich. It will only be a matter of time before my signal reaches the fleet on its way from Pictor Prime. When it does, every one of the prisoners will be killed, just like your wife and two sons."

A long pause ensued before Malkovich replied, "They died when you pigs destroyed the colony."

"Oh, no, my old friend, they were very much alive, along with a hundred others. Stromm had them executed when your agent made an attempt on his life, and he'll have no problem doing the same to his current prisoners if anything happens to me."

"Is Kovacs out of his mind? Cora, I need to cut in on this communication, now!"

"I'm sorry, sir, I need more time."

He pushed himself toward the door. "Keep trying. Shut it down if you can. I'm going to Malkovich to talk sense into him."

"Captain, wait," she said. "The general's ship has fired on *Iliad*."

"No!" said both men, almost in unison. Pavlovich stared at the image on the viewer while Hayden watched the events unfold on his targeting monitor.

Bright engine flares from three missiles painted a path to the drifting wreck. Seconds later, they impacted the forward section of the ship, erupting in a cascade of blinding flashes of nuclear fury. An expanding sphere of brilliant energy engulfed the escape pods in the blink of an eye.

Scimitar's bridge was silent as a tomb as the reality of what had just happened settled on them.

Iliad, battered and scorched, hurtled away from them with nobody left alive on her decks.

Remorse

SEVEN HUNDRED AND TWENTY-six were confirmed dead.

Every part of Hayden's body was numb. His eyes felt swollen to three times their size from his tears.

None of those victims would ever return to their families. There weren't even bodies to bury.

Before *Scimitar*'s arrival, the biggest tragedy of those people's lives was their sudden, unimaginable isolation from the empire. Hayden had visited doom on them twice in their lifetimes. Now he could harm them no further.

He rubbed at the tip of his finger, trying to forget what it felt like to push the firing button that snuffed out so much life.

So many souls torn from their bodies...if there was such a thing as an immortal soul. He hoped so. If they had none, then his sin was compounded beyond his ability to comprehend.

Or endure.

He stiffened and listened as someone called his name.

It was Pavlovich. He'd finally made his way to the forward cargo hold, where Hayden hid.

Power and gravity were still out. Malkovich had put out a call to his people, but they wouldn't arrive for several hours. *Scimitar*'s skeleton crew had returned some time ago—he didn't know exactly when—and started with repairs.

After the immensity of what happened sank in, Pavlovich rushed from the bridge to confront his cousin, leaving Hayden alone in the darkness to face the full weight of his own guilt.

At one time he'd naïvely believed he'd grappled with that beast over the previous decade, and while not able to defeat it, they'd arrived at an impasse. This day he realized that demon had been merely the warm-up act.

The number of people who'd died by his hand was impossible for him to wrap his head around. With a simple, deliberate contraction of one of the weakest muscles in his body, he'd replaced the Malliac as the great threat. When they killed, it was still because of their species' struggle to survive. They consumed worlds, and lives were lost in the process.

He shook his head to clear the images of flames and bodies that flashed across his mind's eye.

Weeks before, he had set ablaze a building because it was to his advantage to do so. He made a decision to send a squad of soldiers to an icy death in the cold vacuum of space. Not an hour ago, he'd once more visited doom on someone who stood in his way.

Pavlovich tried to argue that it was kill or be killed, but that wasn't necessarily true. *Scimitar* had withstood the fury of an alien armada. There was no conceivable way in Hayden's mind that *Deimos* presented a significant threat to them.

He'd allowed himself to be cowed into agreeing with Pavlovich and his cousin that shooting first was their best course of action.

Not satisfied with having atomized one ship, he came up with the way to kill yet another one. The captain gave the order, but Hayden acted as the executioner.

All for what?

Was his life worth so much more than those just snuffed out?

He could try to mollify himself by arguing it was Malkovich who had wiped out the crew of the *Iliad*, but he was cognizant of his role in the atrocity.

Time and again, history showed that evil was rarely the product of a single person or act. Others had to cooperate to propagate it.

He was complicit in it all—a mass murderer.

It didn't seem to bother Pavlovich, who continued to call into the dark in search of him. Concern touched his voice, like a man looking for his lost pet. An obedient dog who would kill on command.

He raised his hands to his temples and pressed, as if to crush his skull. Better to die by his own hand than take another life. Hayden Kaine was a proven danger to society.

Perhaps it was best that he was cut off from his one-time destiny. Had he achieved his family's goals and risen to power; he could only imagine what the resulting body count would be like. Here, he was isolated, contained. He would do no more harm.

Coward, he thought, *if you really wanted to keep everyone safe, you'd put a mauler to your head and pull the trigger.*

Sobs burst from him. He wept like a small child.

Tears fell for the dead; for all the lives he'd destroyed; for what he did to drive Stella away. He grieved for Katie and his father and all who'd been hurt or disappointed through being associated with him.

"Kaine! What the hell is going on?"

Pavlovich hovered over him, shining a light in Hayden's eyes. He couldn't see the captain's face, but his tone was one of concern, not admonition.

Warm arms wrapped about him and pulled him close. A fatherly hand cradled the back of his head and guided his face into a sympathetic shoulder.

He guided Hayden back to the corridor.

"Come on, lad. We have something more important than this ship to fix."

It was pitch black. Hayden floated.

Was he dead? Had he worked up the courage and done it?

He recalled being discovered but nothing after that.

Suddenly, an unseen force seized and aggressively threw his back against something.

Unhurt and heart racing, he looked up at a dark figure, barely discernible, looming over him.

"Sorry about that, son," said Pavlovich, "the gravity came back on before I was ready. Luckily, I'd gotten you over your bunk."

Hayden's hand brushed against the coarse fabric of a blanket beneath him. "What's happening? Where am I?"

The room was lit by the torch lying on the floor where it fell, and he could barely make out any details to identify where he was.

"Don't lose your shit. You were exhausted and were asleep as I brought you to your quarters."

"Sleep...?" Confused, he sat up. "I remember you finding me, but then...."

"You were pretty distraught when I found you. I called a medic, and he gave you something to calm you down."

"You sedated me? Was I that far gone?" He felt his cheeks warming. Pavlovich graciously pretended to ignore Hayden's growing embarrassment.

"Take it easy. It was a mild dosage, but you might be confused for a bit until it wears off."

He dropped his head to his pillow and stared at the shadows on the ceiling. Slowly, the memory of the battle wormed itself back into his awareness. His breathing grew shallow, and his heart raced as if it wanted to burst from his chest. The dark room contracted, threatening to envelope him.

He rolled to face the wall and hide. Aching fingers clutched the pillow to his face, and he heard someone crying. It took him several seconds to realize it was him.

Pavlovich spoke, so quietly that Hayden was forced to stop weeping to hear him.

"I remember what I was like after my first battle. I went AWOL for three weeks. Spent most of that time getting hammered in a bar, just trying to forget. Luckily, my commanding officer understood and didn't put anything on my record."

"What happened?"

"You ever hear about Centauri 1061?"

"I remember reading about it at the academy. You were involved in that?"

"I was not much older than you were when I met you; a year after graduation and serving as a comms officer aboard the *Kirchoff*. We were sent to assist in a military action against a separatist faction that had seized control of the Ymir colonial government. Our intelligence was incomplete. The two fleet vessels we'd come to support had been commandeered by rebel forces. Our task force was woefully unprepared and took heavy damage as soon as we popped through the jump-gate.

"Half of our bridge crew was killed, including our XO and tactical officer. Captain Arno was a wily veteran, though. He managed to pull us out of the fire to regroup at a defensible position with the remnant of our ships. I was ordered to man the weapons as the rebels pursued to finish us off."

Hayden nodded, recalling the history class that studied the battle. "The Arno Manoeuvre."

"That's what they ended up calling it. It is a pretty sterile description of a bloody devastating tactic."

"Seventeen hundred casualties."

"One thousand, seven hundred and thirty-one dead," said Pavlovich, shaking his head. "Eleven hundred and sixty-eight were on the rebel ships. To this day I don't know how many of those deaths I am personally responsible for."

Hayden could barely make out the captain's wan face in the gloom. "When does the pain go away?"

"It doesn't, not really, but it does fade with time." He put a gentle hand on Hayden's shoulder. "But something inside of you needs to change, or the guilt will take its toll, and one more precious life will be added to the body count. Yours."

"You're saying I shouldn't care? Maybe it is possible for you to get over your culpability. I have done far worse than you. I didn't simply take all those lives from those men and women today, or those Rangers I blew into space. That was just the crowning insult to the injury I visited on them and billions of others."

"Stella told me about the burden you insist on piling upon yourself. That's nuts, Kaine, carrying that magnitude of guilt, when the notion is complete bullshit."

"She and you don't understand. I was raised with the belief that I would one day become responsible for all the lives in the Confederation. It never struck me, the magnitude of that delusion, until I destroyed the jump network. Nobody can possibly be ready for that kind of power. An isolated decision, and hundreds, thousands, maybe millions are affected. It is more than any person should be held accountable for."

"Well, I'm glad to hear you've seen the truth of that..."

"Yes, but that belief in my destiny was a core to my upbringing. When I brought down the network, I truly thought I'd be capable of making just such a decision; that all the manipulation and brainwashing my family had perpetuated for generations had culminated in me. I was the one destined to assume that role, when all along, it was an impossible fantasy."

"So, you change and learn to live within your capabilities and deal with the situations life puts in front of you. Everyone has to do the same thing, Kaine."

Tears ran down Hayden's cheeks. "What became apparent to me was that my entire life is a lie. My existence was scripted and controlled. My decisions were choreographed under the generational delusion that I was prepared for something that couldn't possibly be prepared for. Being marooned in the Mu Arae system forced me to examine my own abilities and resources for the first time in my life.

"At first, it was liberating. But as time wore on, I noticed a pattern. No matter what decisions I made, they were never good ones. I learned that I do not have the capacity to make the right choices. Everything I touch seems to end up for the worse. I realized I needed guidance; somebody to watch me and make sure I didn't mess things up. I tried to rely on Stella that way but only drove her off. When you came along, I joined you out of hope you would provide that. All that ended up happening was that I became a mass murderer."

Pavlovich studied him for a long interval. "I'm not a shrink, Kaine, so my assessment really isn't worth much, but you're bloody crazy. I've never heard anything so...so narcissistic in my entire life. Your family really did a number on you. I would feel sorry for you if it weren't so pathetic, and if that self-delusion didn't negatively impact so many people.

"Shitty things happen. Occasionally, that is all some people have. For all I know, you might be one of those unlucky bastards who nothing good happens to, but I don't think so.

"Life is like poker, and you have to play the hand you're dealt. Making calls in situations that you know are impossible can stink. You have to make the call anyway, because even a small chance of things working out is better than what will happen if you do nothing. You're a grown man, Kaine. I shouldn't have to tell you this, but your daddy did you a disservice, and now the rest of us need to pull together to fix the damage he did.

"So, here's the lesson: get over yourself. People depend on you; I do, and Stella does. Right now, she's in a situation that only we can get her out of. She's there because of my poor decision, and I accept that. But that isn't going to prevent me from trying to help her. It shouldn't stop you."

Hayden was empty. He'd never unburdened himself of everything like that to anyone. He wasn't really thinking about what to expect from the captain. He didn't believe it would be pointless reassurance, but neither did he anticipate a mirror pushed in his face to show the ugliness he always knew was inside of him. Pavlovich had disassembled him the way Cora used to take apart engines and laid all the pieces before him, challenging him to put himself back together.

He wished he had ended his life before Pavlovich discovered him. "Please leave," he said.

The big man rose and stared down at Kaine. There wasn't anger or disappointment in his eyes. There did not seem to be compassion. He had the appearance of a man who watched a sick pet, hoping it would pull through, but prepared to move on quickly regardless of what happened.

"You don't want to hear this, but it has to be said. We need you, Kaine. Stella needs you. If you give up on yourself, then...."

He turned and left.

Who Are You Going to Become?

HAYDEN THOUGHT HE WAS going to die, and for the first time in days he wished he had followed through on his thoughts of suicide.

As he lay on his bunk, the pounding on the door of his quarters exacerbated the throbbing in his head. It felt like a mountain was pressed down on his skull.

"Go away!" he shouted. The effort sent a fresh stab of pain across the back of his eyes. Even in the darkness, it was painful to open them.

Everything hurt.

Pavlovich's muffled voice called from the other side of the door. "C'mon, Kaine, answer the door."

He reached around for his pillow. Unable to locate it, he pulled the top of the blanket over his ears.

Pavlovich remained undeterred and maintained his incessant pounding.

"I should have shot him when I had the chance," Hayden muttered, sitting up and pausing on the edge of the bunk. All he could see in his mind's eye were the drifting bodies of the Rangers he'd ejected into space; the hundreds of people who were incinerated at his pressing of a button; Stella and the crew under threat, if they weren't already dead.

A wave of nausea surged. Locating his lost pillow on the floor, he pressed it to his mouth as he fought to keep from vomiting. When he'd brought his stomach under control, he rose and shuffled across the room to deal with Pavlovich.

Fumbling in the dark, he located the door and opened it.

The blast of light from the corridor hit him like a blow to the face. Covering his eyes with his forearm, he staggered back into the gloom and allowed the captain to enter.

"My God, Kaine. It smells like a frat-house in here."

"What the hell do you want, Pavlovich?" Not waiting for an answer, he retreated to the bunk and collapsed on it.

"Well, among other things, you've been missing for the past two days. When Cora couldn't raise you, I came to see if you're still alive."

"And what conclusion have you come to?"

"The jury is still out."

He heard Pavlovich fumble for something before the cabin lights brightened.

"Oh, God! Are you trying to blind me?"

"Quit your whining. They're only on at one-quarter brightness."

Still shielding his eyes, Hayden felt Pavlovich's bulk sit on the end of his cot.

"What's going on, Kaine?"

He snorted. "It isn't obvious?"

"Where'd you find the booze? I thought I ran a dry ship."

With an annoyed sigh, he accepted that Pavlovich had no intention of leaving him alone. "I brought my own, okay?"

"Is there anything left? I could use a drink right now."

Risking the pain of the light, he peeked out from under his arm and stared at his captain. He rummaged about under the blanket and produced an empty bottle. "Nope, sorry."

Pavlovich studied him, shaking his big head in silent admonishment. It reminded him of his childhood, when his father expressed disappointment at something he'd done, or failed to do. Now, as then, he told himself he didn't care what anyone thought of him.

He covered his face with the pillow and pressed his lips together.

"What would your woman think of you now?" said Pavlovich.

Hayden pulled it tightly to his face to hide the tears he couldn't control. "We killed her—Malkovich did. He's murdered them all."

"I don't believe that. Kovacs was only blustering."

"You can't know that for certain."

"No, son, I can't. But Stromm wouldn't dare eliminate his only remaining bargaining chip. He wants this ship, and he isn't foolish enough to squander any leverage in a fit of anger, despite what Kovacs claimed."

Hayden removed the pillow from his face and pulled himself to a sitting position. He released a heavy sigh. "If I hadn't destroyed the light gate network, none of this would be happening."

"No, just something far worse, like a Malliac invasion of the Confederation. We, not you alone, took down the network. It wasn't your sole decision. As I recall, I had significant input into the matter."

"But you didn't set the bomb, I did. I was the only one who could have stopped it and—"

"Shut the hell up, Kaine. My God, this martyr complex you have is tiresome. Despite what you want to believe, you are not the sole architect of the fall of the empire. Get over yourself. I'm confident that is what Stella would tell you if she was here."

"But she's not, is she? She is a prisoner of a megalomaniac, thanks to you."

"I admit that things could have gone better."

"The truth, Pavlovich. Why are we here in this system?"

The captain lowered his head to stare at the deck. "You aren't the only delusional one, Kaine. Ten years ago, when I woke up to the realization that I'd passed through a black hole and emerged from the other side, unscathed...I don't know...I guess I reassessed my significance."

"What do you mean?"

He lifted his head and regarded Hayden with a sad look on his face. "I'd survived the unsurvivable: victory over insurmountable odds against the Malliac fleet; crossing a singularity; rescuing Cora when she was beyond saving and discovering a hidden FTL technology...it was as if the cosmos was trying to tell me something...that I'd lived for a reason."

"I'd never thought of your situation like that."

"Nobody is just handed that kind of luck. It couldn't have been random. Then I remembered the threat of Thomas and his cabal...how powerless I was to oppose him. Despite what you may believe of me, Kaine, I am a patriot. The idea of a den of vipers like that seizing control of the empire sickened me. But the possibility of them somehow gaining access to the cynosure...that was something I couldn't allow; not if the universe chose to keep me alive and hand me the tools to prevent it."

Hayden shook his head. "We are quite the pair. A false martyr and a delusional messiah."

"I'm not sure I agree with you. I never used to believe myself destined for anything, but when I look at how everything has unfolded up to now, I am willing to consider it a possibility."

A bark of hoarse laughter burst from Hayden. "Don't talk to me about destiny. I was raised with the belief that Kaines are destined to rule the Confederation. My family worked for generations to make that happen, and I was intended to become the realization of their ambition. But I never bought in to it. I am no leader. I never wanted to be in politics, or enter the academy, for that matter."

"And yet here we are. Despite our best efforts to run away, fate has found us. The two of us can reset the course of history. Maybe it's time we stop deluding ourselves and accept the plan that appears to be unfolding before us."

"You sound dangerously crazy, Pavlovich. You know that, right?"

The captain shrugged. "It gets me up in the morning. How about you, Kaine? Are you going to spend the rest of your life wallowing in self-pity, running away from who you are meant to be?"

Hayden's eyes fell on the empty bottle on his mattress. "I don't know if I buy in to your fantasy about fate, but you are right about one thing; circumstances have given us tools to make a difference, if we choose to use them wisely. Stella is a prisoner, and I have no intention of letting her die if I can prevent it. Let's start with that and see where things take us."

Stella

STELLA HUDDLED IN THE corner of the cell she shared with a dozen prisoners. None of them had the strength or desire for any level of physical exertion. Extreme hunger and dehydration had finally worn the last of them down. She had no direct evidence, but she feared the small group of people with her were the sole survivors of *Scimitar*'s crew.

It was all her fault. This was the consequence for underestimating Ulysses Stromm.

She'd foolishly persuaded Pavlovich that she could play Stromm to give him the time he needed. Instead, he and his chief of security had masterfully manipulated her.

According to the plan, she was to string them along, biding for time until Pavlovich's expected return with the ship. The hope was that the crew would be released to his custody after the captain proved himself a trustworthy ally. Stella played her part, stalling, deflecting, and misdirecting the questions put to her.

Neither she nor Pavlovich considered their captors' fanatical obsession with the thing they called the cynosure. By the time she realized the true danger she was in, she was trapped.

She closed her eyes and shuddered. Even the fragments of recollection her mind had failed to block were enough to provoke an anxiety attack.

She didn't recall much of the torture, but the emotional scars were unhealed. Too late, Stella had realized why she couldn't read Kovacs when they first met. He too was an empath, and a much more adept and practiced one than she. He'd gathered and trained others like him to act as his special interrogators.

Alternating between psychotropic drugs, physical pain, and empathic torment, they wore her defences down until she spilled her guts. She couldn't remember what she divulged; all she could recall was not being able to get the words out fast enough.

Even then, they were not satisfied that she was broken. After giving her enough time to recover, they repeated the sessions, determined that she still concealed things, convinced that her empathic abilities gave her a strength to resist that she did not have.

The torture itself seemed pointless. They asked the same questions, always revolving around something called a cynosure. Through it all, she never got the impression they knew what the object they sought was. Naturally, that made interrogation a difficult process, and it was all somewhat senseless, but that was not enough to deter them.

She was so out of it through most of it that she couldn't be sure of her recollections, but she believed Stromm enjoyed hurting her too much to stop.

Then it suddenly ended.

She sighed and cast her gaze about the small chamber.

So few of them.

Every member of *Scimitar*'s crew had experienced a similar torture, though none but her was subjected to it repeatedly.

Initially, during her recovery intervals, when she thought she still had the strength, she reached out empathically to the other victims, hoping to soothe them. What she found within each was a devastated emotional landscape. Kovacs had torn them to shreds. What was left they now protected under a numbness that she could not penetrate. She feared many of them would never recover.

At some point—she had no idea how long ago—they were herded onto a ship. Whatever the reason, Stella understood their situation had not improved.

Stromm was somewhere aboard. She sensed him more than once. She could never mistake his unique coldness for anyone else.

She closed her eyes and thought of Hayden. She wanted to locate him, if only to assure herself he was safe. In the rare moments, when circumstances permitted her to sense him, he was anxious and fearful. She wished she could reach across the expanse that separated them and tell him she was alive.

There were times in the past—happier times—when he joked that he could feel her presence too. He teased her, of course. It was his way of telling her how close he felt to her during those years together, but they both knew the empathic flow could only be one way.

She regretted her abilities weren't more advanced, as they were in Kovacs and his people. With early training, she might have developed the ability not only to detect emotion, but also to project it in a precisely controlled manner.

If only things had been different.

If only she had been trained to control her gift, she would be able to do more than eavesdrop on Hayden's emotions from afar. She could tell him she was safe; maybe even where she was.

And yet...

Growing up marooned in the Mu Arae system with her father, they were cut off from any of the institutions that would have nurtured her gift. Survival was the most pressing need, and she learned how to detect danger and hide from the Malliac out of naked necessity.

The truth was, she *could* project. But instead of using it like a scalpel, as Kovacs did, she'd only ever employed it as a blunt weapon to strike back at the aliens who hunted her, harming anyone else who was nearby as well.

Before she encountered him, Stella had no idea her ability could be used in any other way.

Perhaps there was a way to use it; establish real communication with Hayden; tell him she was safe, tell him where she was so that he could come and rescue her.

She resolved that she had to make an effort. She hadn't a clue what that should comprise of or if it would even work.

She closed her eyes and leaned against the wall, letting the coolness of the bulkhead spread across her shoulders. Struggling to calm her excitement with the idea, she compelled herself to relax and still her chaotic thoughts.

Stella fought down her rising anxiety and moved toward the nothingness, as her father had taught her in her meditation lessons while growing up.

Her mind stilled, and gradually, all physical sensation dissolved away, leaving only a lightness, as if she were a cloud.

Her eyes shot open, and she jerked upright as she realized she was falling asleep.

Though exhausted and in desperate need of sleep, she could not afford to indulge in that blissful oblivion.

She needed to be awake so she could know that her connection with Hayden, should it arise, was real and not a dream or a hallucination.

Trying again, Stella breathed deeply, listening to her heartbeat slow, while guiding her thoughts to stay on point and not wander.

Eventually an image emerged, as if from a fog. Hayden's handsome face materialized before her imagination. Accompanying it was a familiar sensation she'd not experienced for a very long time.

Her heart skipped a joyful beat as she realized she was in contact with him, at least emotionally. More importantly, he sensed her. She knew that as surely as she knew herself.

She experienced his confusion and his relief when he comprehended what was happening. It was as if they embraced across whatever distance separated them, and they drew a peace from each other they had not shared in years.

Hayden knew she was alive and would come for her.

Hostages

HAYDEN ENTERED THE bridge to a bustle of activity. During the days since the battle, the repair ship with Gunney, Chin, and the others had returned. In addition, Malkovich's people had responded to his call, and now dozens of strangers scurried about *Scimitar*, repairing and readying her for what lay ahead.

"Ah, there you are," said Malkovich. "Your captain is getting the FTL drive online with Cora. My engineers have just reported that battle damage is repaired. When my remaining stealth ships arrive, we will be able to take on Stromm."

"Are we in a hurry to do that?"

"I received word from my agents. He has departed Pictor Prime with most of his fleet. Sixteen warships are on a hard burn to bring them here."

"So, the planet is relatively unguarded. We can slip around them and rescue the prisoners—"

"No, we can't. Stromm's taken them aboard his ships. I think he got word about what happened to Kovacs and intends to use them as human shields."

Hayden's mouth dropped open. "That renders our weapon useless."

"Yegor and I are working on a battle plan to best employ my stealth vessels and *Scimitar*'s dark energy cannon."

"We are still going to engage them? Even if our people are with them?"

"Of course. What did you think would happen?"

"I don't know. Maybe retreat to one of your bases and regroup?"

"That only postpones the inevitable. Stromm knows that if he has your girlfriend and your crew, *Scimitar* is trapped in this system—you'll never leave without them, FTL drive or not. He will chase you down—chase us all. I can't paint a pretty picture, Kaine. He will begin to execute them until our resolve breaks, and we give him what he wants."

Hayden recalled Kovacs' boast that Malkovich's family had survived the attack on their colony and were executed as prisoners. He could only imagine what a shock it must have been for him to hear that. Or perhaps did he disregard the claim, considering it a lie?

Stromm had control of the board. Checkmate was inevitable, and it was only a matter of how many moves it required to end things. There was no way to win, except by throwing themselves at Stromm's feet and praying he would be more merciful than Malkovich suggested. Check and mate.

"There has to be another way."

Malkovich put a large hand on Hayden's shoulder. "I'm afraid there isn't, son."

Hayden gruffly shrugged away the patronizing hand. "I can't accept that."

"That is up to you, but you will soon realize there is no way to save the lives of your friends—not without surrendering this vessel. I will not permit that. The rest of my fleet arrives within the hour, and I have no reservations about having them turn their weapons on *Scimitar* if necessary. Your shielding and weaponry are both formidable, but Kovacs demonstrated that this ship can be destroyed. It must not fall into Stromm's hands."

Everyone's attention was on the hologram floating above the conference room table. It showed a scaled model of the solar system, with bright sprites indicating the locations of Stromm's ships and their own.

Pavlovich said, "Twelve hours ago, we received a message from Stromm. He confirmed that our people are aboard his fleet and warned us to maintain our position or he will begin executing them. Immediately following the transmission, they made a hot burn and are pulling some hard G's to get here in a hurry."

"They'll have to use almost as much fuel again to decelerate," said Cora. "At those consumption rates, most of his ships won't be able to return to the inner system."

"After losing *Iliad* and *Deimos*, I don't believe he expects many of them to survive anyway," said Malkovich.

"Why would he sacrifice them to save a few days space travel?" asked Hayden. "Especially if there is a risk that we will change position once he's committed to a deceleration curve. We could leave them stranded and helpless."

"The prize is worth the price. Besides, he's desperate," said Pavlovich. "It's why he threatens to kill our people."

"What a bastard," said Hayden. "Is there anything he isn't capable of?"

Arms crossed over his chest; Malkovich grunted.

"So, when he arrives, we will be faced with a decision," said the captain. "One: we can surrender—"

"Do that and my ships have orders to turn *Scimitar* into a dust cloud," said his cousin.

"...which is clearly not an idea worth spending any time discussing." Pavlovich held up two fingers. "Two: we engage them. With our combined strength, we will win that engagement—"

"But a lot of our people will die, either in the battle or executed by Stromm," said Hayden.

"...making it an impossible option. Which leaves us with Kaine's plan, which, as crazy as it sounds, may be the only solution."

"Well, since nobody can dream up anything better, why don't we go over it anyway?" said Malkovich.

Hayden stood and tried to appear more confident than he was, but the time for doubts was long past. Stella depended on him, as did the others. There was no way he would let her down.

"It calls for the general's fleet to turn off their stealth cloaks."

"You're asking a lot of my commanders, Kaine. None of my ships can match the firepower of more than a few of Stromm's."

"There won't be any shooting if everyone sticks to the script. May I continue?"

Malkovich leaned back in his chair and invited him to do so with a wave of his arm.

"Your ship currently attached to our docking port will remain cloaked. I will lead a team of Rangers on a boarding party and sneak on to Stromm's flagship to locate and free the hostages."

"Okay," said Malkovich, "I'm going to stop you there. The first problem with your plan is that we have no way to know if any of them are aboard, or if they are held on another, or on several ships as my spies told me is the case. Second, even if they are all together and you get lucky in picking the correct one, how will you board it without detection?"

"I'm counting on some help from the inside," said Hayden.

Malkovich scowled at him.

"Kaine's girlfriend has empathic ability," said Pavlovich. "They are connected, somehow...nobody seems to know how that works. The point is, she will lead him to her."

"If she can detect him across space, and if she still lives."

"She's alive."

Malkovich raised his hands in surrender. "Okay, I'll have to take your word for it. What are we supposed to be doing while you are on your rescue mission?"

"You will have to stall for time. I'm sure Stromm doesn't expect you to give up the missing piece of the cynosure without some negotiation. Drag the discussion out for as long as you can."

Pavlovich said, "That shouldn't be too difficult. I have no idea where the hell it is on the ship."

"You will keep the FTL engine primed. The moment we return with our people, Malkovich's ships cloak and we all bug out of here."

"Do you understand that if any part of this harebrained plan fails—and it will fail, we'll have a shooting match on our hands?" said Malkovich. "This idea can come apart in so many ways that I can't begin to count them."

"Listen, General," said Hayden, "I know it sounds insane and doesn't have a high probability of success, but it is the only way I can think of that gives the hostages any degree of a chance. Without it, they have none. You've wanted to take on Stromm's fleet from the start. If it goes sideways, you will get the firefight you want. All I ask is for the opportunity to try to save our people."

Malkovich turned to his cousin. "And you're okay with this?"

"Not really, but I agree with Kaine that I can't abandon my crew without trying to rescue them. What kind of captain would I be if I did?"

"That's the difference between us, Yegor. You are too sentimental." After a moment of consideration, he threw his hands in the air. "Fine, let's do this your way. But I'm keeping my weapons hot, and I will only decloak a few ships. I can't afford to expose all of their positions."

"Fair enough, Cousin."

"Captain, I want to take Cora along in an avatar. She will come in handy to get us aboard the ship."

Pavlovich looked upward. "How about it, Cora? Are you up for a road trip?"

"If it keeps them safe, then yes."

He turned to Kaine. "There you have it. For better or worse, you've got your shot."

Preparing for Battle

HAYDEN COULD NOT RECALL ever seeing Gunney smile. But when the gunnery officer got his hands on ordnance salvaged from the wreckage of the *Iliad*, it seemed to have made his year.

"I feel a lot better having the rail gun available," he said.

"We didn't do too badly using just the Glenatat weapon," Hayden replied.

"Yeah, but I prefer the solid impact that a projectile can deliver. There's nothing like ballistics to make up for the shortcomings of energy weapons."

Hayden couldn't really argue with him. Gunney had logged almost forty years in the UEF. He did not know how much combat the old cyborg had seen over that time, but he was sure it had been extensive.

They would need all his experience and more for what was coming. The dreadnought that approached dwarfed the flotilla of other vessels accompanying it. It was a monster, designed to lay entire planets to waste. He wasn't sure how their armour would stand up to what Stromm could throw at them. Considering the damage that *Iliad*'s rail gun did to *Scimitar*, Hayden had to admit that having access to one again made him more secure. He only wished they had some of those quantum projectiles used against them.

The dark energy cannon would not defend them against a barrage from multiple ships. One lucky hit or a coordinated salvo might destroy *Scimitar*. He could only hope that the situation didn't come to that. Then it might be a case of who could get the first shot off, and their own fleet was sorely outnumbered.

Hayden's inspection tour took him to engineering as his final stop. As he entered, he saw Pavlovich in a discussion with Chin beside the interface for the FTL drive. When the captain spotted him, he ended the conversation and approached.

"How is everything shaping up, Kaine?"

"We've taken on as much salvage as possible. It was only a fraction of what Cora identified, but we have no more room."

"She must have been like a kid in a candy store."

"It was hard to tell. The synth she occupied wasn't very expressive. But from the sound of her voice, she was delighted."

"Is there any change in the status of Stromm's fleet?"

"Half an hour ago, they were still on full burn. They will be decelerating soon. I expect their arrival between three and five hours from now."

"I guess it all depends on how aggressive a deceleration curve he wants to pull."

"I think he'll leave it to the last possible second."

"Which means he'll be on our doorstep sooner than later," said Pavlovich. "Will we be ready?"

"I think so. Gunney has the armoury stocked, all our engines are running at maximum efficiency, and the FTL drive is operational. With our damage now repaired, we are as prepared as we ever will be."

"Nobody is ever prepared for combat, Kaine. No plan survives first contact with the enemy."

Hayden frowned. "I can't get used to the idea of doing battle against UEF ships. There's something wrong about it."

"You still live in your family's fantasy world about a happy and united empire. Trust me, it has never been like that. With the collapse of the network, I think you will find similar scenarios like this unfolding in most systems."

"So, you think there are more men like them?"

Pavlovich huffed. "Far more than you realize."

"It makes me wonder why it might be worth saving, if that is so."

"It's about time you came to that realization, son. The Confederation was dying. Thomas, Stromm, and the others are all just a symptom of the rot."

"Do you think my father knew that?"

"He would have been a naïve fool not to realize it. Your father is no fool."

Hayden did not try to mask his surprise. "You know him?"

"We met shortly after I became a captain. It was on one of my furloughs, when I used to take them. I returned to Earth and was introduced to him at some fancy function that the woman I was dating dragged me to. He impressed me with his sharp mind. So, when I learned that Thomas was sending you to me, I had a good idea of what to expect."

"And did I meet your expectations?"

He smiled. "I am not sure yet."

Cora's voice over the speaker interrupted them. "Cap'n, some of the approaching ships have begun their deceleration burn."

"So it begins," said Pavlovich. "Cora, what is the count and the timing for their arrivals?"

"It looks like it's mostly the smaller vessels slowing down first."

"They won't arrive here until after the dreadnought does," said Hayden. "That doesn't make sense."

"It does if Stromm knows about our alien weapon. I might have let something slip when I was with him. Maybe he thinks his flagship can take hits from us and drain our power. Then the latecomers can clean up. It's not a terrible plan when I consider it."

"That, of course, only works if his assumption that he can survive our weapons bears out," said Kaine. "After what it did to Kovacs', it might be a tactical error."

"But he can't know that. He'll have to assume the worst with none of his ships answering. In my mind, this can only mean he's going to come in with guns blazing."

"Like you said, he doesn't know what happened. For all he knows, we are damaged too, which would not have been a bad guess a few days ago," said Hayden. "I think we have to be ready for damn near anything from him. I'm worried that we may be running with the wrong plan. It was crazy enough when we assumed we knew what Stromm would do. Now, however..."

"Take my advice, son, don't second-guess yourself once you commit to a course of action. Adapt, yes, but the minute you begin to doubt, the mission is doomed to fail."

"Are you speaking from experience, Captain?"

"I have more failed plans behind me than you can imagine." He lifted his head to speak. "Cora, what is the absolute minimum time to expect Stromm's dreadnought to arrive?"

"Based on the specs I have on file for that ship, the latest he can put off his deceleration is coming up fast. But there's a lot of error in my estimate."

"What about the other ones that have not begun decelerating yet?"

"They have to start their burn sooner, which means the fleet's arrival will be staggered. Wait a minute, the dreadnought just fired braking engines. Some of the support ships are still burning hot, but they'll have to put on the brakes soon."

"Best time estimate to first arrivals, Cora?" said Kaine.

"My computations say that they'll get here in forty minutes. Stromm's flagship looks like it will arrive about fifteen minutes later. The last wave will be coming in an hour after that. But it's just a guess right now."

"He's going to let his first pass soften us up before his arrival," said Hayden.

"We should prepare for our guests," said Pavlovich. "You had better get your team ready to go."

"My place is here during the battle."

"You're assuming there will be one. I am still betting that he intends to intimidate us first. Scare us into surrendering. He can't use the hostages as leverage over us if they all die in combat, and I don't think he wants to risk damaging his prize."

"I hope you're right."

"So do I, Kaine. So do I."

A Rescue Mission

HAYDEN WAS KNOCKED off balance as he made his way to the bridge. When the battle began, he was aboard the stealth ship with the squad of Rangers, waiting to deploy the moment the dreadnought appeared. He couldn't raise Pavlovich, and the fighting sounded heavy. Something had gone terribly wrong, and he needed to learn first-hand what happened.

He spoke into his headset. "Cora, what's our status?"

After an unusual delay, she responded. "I'm a little preoccupied, Hayden."

"I can't raise anyone on the bridge. What's going on?"

"Some of the internal comm channels went down. Everyone is fine."

Scimitar jerked again. He fell forward, slamming his shoulder into a bulkhead.

"How are we holding up?"

"Our armour is solid. They're firing missiles without nukes. So far no one's used a rail gun. I don't think they're trying to hurt us."

As if to belie her comment, the bulkheads rattled again as *Scimitar* was struck by another projectile.

"Well, it feels like it from where I am."

"I think they're testing us. Seeing how much we can take."

"Who started shooting first?"

"They did, the moment they arrived. Malkovich's ships returned fire, and then all hell broke loose. I'm sorry, Hayden, I can't speak any more. My attention is required elsewhere."

Disturbed by what he had heard, he picked up his pace.

When he entered the command centre, what he saw was strangely familiar. Every station was manned, something he hadn't seen for over ten years.

"Kaine, what are you doing here?" said Pavlovich. "You're supposed to be prepping for the launch."

"Is there going to be a mission? Why is there a shooting match going on?"

"We have a good idea what Stromm's plan is, or at least we think so. He sent in this first wave to test our defences. He hopes to soften us up and make us more agreeable to surrender when the dreadnought arrives"

Hayden noticed Gunney scowling.

"Have you returned fire?"

"No," said Pavlovich, "I don't want to tip our hand too soon. Malkovich's ships are carrying the battle at the moment."

"I've lost one vessel so far," said the general. He occupied a station from which he directed fleet operations. "But we've taken out five of theirs. We are drawing a lot of the fire away from *Scimitar*. Cousin, I am going to need to put my ships in stealth mode. I don't want to lose any more before Stromm gets here."

Pavlovich acknowledged him with a wave of his hand. "Do what's necessary. Kaine, haul your ass back down to your ship and be ready to launch as soon as Stromm's flagship shows up."

As he spoke, one of Malkovich's officers called out, "The bulk of the fleet is now in visual range; arrival pending in six minutes. They have launched missiles. They're registering hot."

"Nukes? He's not pissing around."

"They may not all be aimed at this ship, Yegor. I would appreciate it if you took them off the board."

"You read my mind, Cousin. Gunney, you're up."

"It's bloody well about time," said the cyborg as he turned back to his station.

"Use only one percent juice. Don't overdo it. We don't want to tip our hand just yet."

"Understood, Cap'n. Targets locked; firing."

The lights on the bridge dimmed slightly as the energy cannon drew the required power. Hayden watched the tactical schematic. One moment the blips representing the nuclear missiles were there, the next they were gone. For being such a powerful weapon, he thought the entire operation was anticlimactic.

"Targets neutralized, sir."

"That's got to shake him up a bit," said Pavlovich. "Now what will you do, Stromm?"

As if in answer to the question, the other ships ceased shooting.

"Captain, we are receiving a message."

"Let's hear it."

"Pavlovich, I knew I couldn't trust you. Where is Kovacs?"

"He pissed me off. You should withdraw your fleet or you're going to find out first-hand what happened to him."

"You are not the only one with surprises. Tell Malkovich to pay attention."

All eyes turned to the general.

"What is he talking about?" asked Pavlovich.

A worried-looking Malkovich shook his head. "I have no idea."

Gunney shouted, "Multiple rail gun launches from the dreadnought."

"What are they targeting? Are they shooting at us?"

"That would be crazy," said Malkovich, "he needs this ship."

"Then what the hell?"

"Impacts registered," announced the tactical officer. "They're hitting the stealth ships."

"Impossible!" shouted Malkovich. Yet even has he spoke, one by one every marker on the display that denoted one, cloaked or not, vanished.

"How did he do that?" asked Hayden.

"He discovered a way to see them," said Pavlovich.

The image of the massive dreadnought grew and filled the screen.

"Tell Malkovich that I said hello," said Stromm over the still open channel.

The captain made a slashing motion at his throat to signal that communications were to be ended.

"How did he do that, Cousin?"

"The only possible way he could detect them is from their transponder codes."

"Where would he get those?" said Hayden.

"From your spy?" said Pavlovich. "Did he torture the information out of him?"

Dark fury grew on the general's face. "I'm betrayed. He had a suicide pill in case of capture."

"Is every ship destroyed?" asked Hayden.

"Yes," said Cora. All except for the one attached to our docking port."

"Why didn't they target that one? Is its transponder active?"

"Yes, but being so close to *Scimitar*, it may have gone unnoticed."

"We are being hailed again, sir."

Pavlovich nodded and sat back in his chair to listen.

"Did Malkovich like my surprise, or was he on one of those ships?"

"I got your message, Stromm, you bastard."

"Good. Now I have one for you Yegor. Surrender your ship, or every member of your crew in my custody will die."

Hayden dashed toward the communications console and shoved the ensign sitting there aside. After shutting down the comm link, he said, "Cora, shut off that transponder now."

"What are you thinking, Kaine?"

"As long as they can't see it, we still have a chance to pull off our plan. The hostages are on Stromm's ship."

"How can you be so certain?" said Malkovich.

"Because..." he hesitated. "Because I can sense Stella on that dreadnought. I have somehow been linked with her for the past few days. The...signal...grew stronger as it approached. She's aboard it. I know it."

"Son, there are a dozen ships out there. She could be on any one of them."

"There is only one way to find out for sure, General. I need to get close to that ship."

"Your people are about as dead as they can be. I know that man, and he's a butcher. He knows about the connection between you two and has kept your girlfriend alive to make us think there is still a crew to save."

Hayden turned to his captain, desperation in his voice. "You have to let me try, sir. There's no way he could know that."

Pavlovich looked to Malkovich. "What would you have me do, Cousin, surely not surrender?"

The general rose and advanced toward him. "You have the means to destroy him and every other vessel in his fleet. Use it. Wipe that monster from existence. There is no way you can permit him to gain the power of this ship. Your people are dead, there is no other choice."

Pavlovich stared at his cousin for several heartbeats then addressed Hayden. "I will buy you the time I can, but I can't guarantee it won't come down to shooting. If it does, I have no intention of losing. Do I make myself clear?"

"Absolutely, sir."

Hayden glanced at Malkovich, who was clearly enraged by Pavlovich's decision. Then he ran from the bridge. There wasn't much time, let alone hope. But he intended to try or die in the attempt.

Reunited

AS KAINE CLOSED THE docking hatch, a metallic hand grasped the door and pulled it open.

"Cora, what are you doing?"

The same synth she had occupied during their trip to the moon stepped aboard.

"You're not going anywhere without me."

"You're needed here. We can't go into battle without you."

"*Scimitar* is in good hands with Chin and the engineers that Malkovich brought over. Besides I'm partitioned and can keep an eye on both you and her."

Hayden arched an eyebrow, unsure of how truthful she was being. The synth's impassive, featureless face offered him no indication.

He moved aside and allowed her to enter. Cora stepped by him and assumed a seat among the squad of Rangers. Taking one last quizzical look at her, Hayden shrugged and closed the hatch.

Within a minute, they were launched and en route to Stromm's ship. The silence in the cabin was deafening, and under other circumstances he would've been tempted to make small talk with someone. A quick glance back at the grim-faced Rangers revealed a battle-hardened group of men and women ready for anything.

Hayden settled into the pilot seat and had a moment's anxiousness when he realized he wasn't sure he had any chance of zeroing in on Stella's location. He was certain all previous contact with her had been initiated from her side. The fact that he could not detect her sent a shot of panic through him. What if Malkovich was correct, and Stromm had already executed the prisoners?

Pushing the thought from his head, he focused on the controls and tried to calm his mind, searching for that feeling that was Stella.

As the flagship grew larger in the front window, he thought he felt something. Closing his eyes, he concentrated. Lurking beneath all his anxiety and fear for her, he found Stella's familiar spirit. He had no other word to describe what he sensed. Two sets of emotions occupied him: his own chaotic and undisciplined self and her natural calmness. It was as if she was a beacon in the darkness, guiding him to her. He had no way to know if this was indeed the case, but the idea comforted him.

"Do you sense her?" asked Cora.

"Yes, I think so. It's growing stronger as we approach that ship."

Hayden took the moment just to study the details on the surface of the dreadnought. New fears bubbled up in him. "I sure hope this stealth shield is working."

"The transponder is inactive. There is no way for them to track us."

"I suppose so..." He realized that because of his worry, he'd lost the trace to Stella. He had to refocus and try to pick up the breadcrumbs that she laid out for him to follow. He wished he shared her empathic abilities. Then the onus would not be on her alone.

He scanned the other ship's hull for an access port. Torn between wanting to act quickly and being certain, he contemplated circling the giant vessel to see if Stella's signal grew any stronger somewhere else.

"Hayden, I lost contact with *Scimitar.*"

He examined the sensor readout. It had not moved.

"What could be the problem?"

"I don't know, but I am no longer connected to any of her systems, and I can't even talk to her."

Something had happened aboard the ship, but they were in no position to deal with it. Deciding there was not time to survey the dreadnought any further, he selected a docking port and set his course to it. Once attached, he turned to Cora.

"Can you disable or interfere with their internal sensors? It would be helpful if we avoid any resistance for as long as possible."

"Why do you think I came along? I just need access to the terminal in the airlock."

The android rose and moved past the still seated Rangers, now all geared up and awaiting the order to deploy.

"Got it," she said. "I have inserted a decoy signal into their grid in this section. They won't detect us, but I can't do more than that without raising an alarm or attracting attention."

"Thanks, Cora, this will be fine."

At Hayden's command, the Rangers moved through the hatch as a disciplined unit. Hayden put on his own battle helmet and picked a weapon from the storage rack. The team had rehearsed several times, and he knew his role was not as a combatant. As desperate as he was to rush inside, gun at the ready, hurrying to where he thought he might find Stella, he deferred to the plan and his training.

The hatch opened, and the advance guard first checked then exited. Moments later, he received the "all clear" signal.

Methodically, the rescue team advanced through surprisingly empty corridors, with Hayden in the lead. He had no way to know where to go except by following the strength of his connection to Stella.

"I think we're getting closer, but I have no idea how close."

He glanced at the schematic in his heads up display, hoping the information was up to date. But what bothered him more was the absence of any crew along the route. He was worried about a trap.

"Where is everyone?"

"Give me a second," said Cora, "I am accessing the ship's duty roster."

Hayden thought that a curious thing for her to do, but before he could say anything, she said, "Multiple stations on this ship are not occupied. I don't think Stromm has enough people to staff something this size."

As they approached the next junction, he spotted two armed guards at a door down the hallway. They saw him and raised their weapons. Before they could act, the Ranger who acted as Hayden's bodyguard took them both out with precise shots.

"I jammed them," said Cora. "They didn't get any signals out."

"Let's hope they were guarding our people."

In silence the group advanced to the door, stepping over the bodies. Without prompting, the synth proceeded to the door control and seconds later opened it.

The advance guard rushed in, Hayden and the others hanging back. His jaw was clenched tight as he waited for a firefight to break out.

Instead, the "all clear" signal came. He hurried into the room to a disheartening scene. Lying about on the floor where a dozen or so people he barely recognized as his missing crewmates. They were in rough shape, looking like they hadn't eaten in weeks. Many of them appeared to have been abused. An overwhelming panic rose up inside him as he frantically searched for Stella.

"Hayden! Is that you?"

Realizing he still wore a helmet, he removed it as he looked for the source of the voice. Turning around he saw a sight that both delighted and horrified him.

She struggled to her feet, steadying herself against the wall. She looked like a starved waif; her small frame had lost more weight then she could afford.

Hayden rushed forward and enfolded her in his arms, afraid she would break if he squeezed too hard. She hugged his neck and with surprising strength pulled him close.

"I knew you would come."

"Stella, what has happened to you? Where are the others?"

She disengaged from him long enough to survey the room. "We are all that is left. Stromm murdered the rest. He is searching for something aboard *Scimitar*. He's mad."

"Everything is all right now. We are here to get you all out."

"Give me a moment," she said as she shut her eyes to concentrate. "I have spent all my energy trying to reach you. I didn't pay attention to anything else. But I can't sense anyone nearby. I must be in worse shape than I thought."

"We encountered no one on our way here. Cora thinks the ship is undermanned. That should work in our favour to escape."

"Cora is here?" She looked at the Rangers. The synth stepped forward; hand raised in greeting.

"Hello, Stella. It is good to see you safe."

"Cora?"

"It's her. I'll explain later. Right now, we need to get everyone off this ship."

She nodded as Hayden went to help the survivors to their feet.

"The going will be slow. None of these people can move quickly in their current state," said Cora.

"We will form a phalanx around them and work our way back."

She went to speak with the squad commander and make arrangements.

After a couple of minutes, they exited the cell and retraced their steps. Weapons raised, the point soldiers carefully approached every corner and cleared it. The going was agonizingly slow, with Hayden having to assist in carrying Anderson, the navigator he'd met a few weeks before. Aside from the advance and rear guard, the remaining Rangers each supported a survivor.

When they were within a dozen metres of the docking hatch, shots rang out. A Ranger fell back, mortally wounded. Seconds later, a withering barrage of weapons fire pinned them, shielded only by the corner.

"They're on to us," said Hayden as he lowered Anderson to the floor so he could reach his weapon.

More gunfire erupted behind him, and he realized that they were trapped.

Shielding survivors with their armoured bodies, the Rangers returned fire, taking down several of the attackers who tried to advance on them. Outnumbered, Malkovich's troops began to fall, one by one, as the overwhelming forces pressed their attack from both sides.

"We won't last long, sir," said the group subcommander. He was bleeding from a wound in his abdomen. The squad leader was dead at his feet. "We're the only ones left. We need to make a push for the hatch, or we won't get out of here alive."

"That's suicide,"

"So is staying here."

Hayden nodded and turned to inform Stella.

Tears in her eyes, she pushed herself to her knees. Her hand covered a red stain on her leg where she had been hit. She looked at him and shook her head, as if acknowledging they were finished. Closing her eyes, her brow furrowed in concentration.

Moments later, the Ranger screamed in pain, dropped his weapons, and clutched at his head as he fell to the floor. Confused, Hayden looked about but could see no new attackers. Strangely the gunfire had ceased. After a moment, with no further shots being sent at them, he peeked around the corner. And was shocked by what he saw.

Their assailants lay unmoving. Turning about, he saw the same thing behind them.

Stunned, he looked at Cora. "What happened?"

"I don't know, they all screamed out and collapsed."

Stella struggled to her feet and limped to Hayden's side. She wrapped her arms around his shoulders and burst into tears as he embraced her.

"They are dead. I killed them," she said between sobs.

"What do you mean?"

"They died way the Malliac did ten years ago. This was why the captain wanted me along. I was afraid of something just like this."

He searched for the words to comfort her. Her story seemed too fantastic to believe, yet something had felled all the soldiers. Only those with no cortical implant, like *Scimitar*'s crew and himself, were not hurt. Now he understood why Pavlovich had insisted his new recruits remove their implants.

Without warning, the deck shook violently. Hayden tried to stand, only to be knocked back down by another shaking of the ship.

"The dreadnought is being attacked," said Cora.

"Are you connected with *Scimitar* again? Tell them we're still aboard."

"No, I can't contact them. But it's the only explanation for what is happening."

"This is crazy, Pavlovich would not open fire if he thought we were here. If he cuts loose with the dark energy cannon..."

"Then it won't matter if we make it to the stealth ship," she said.

True Colours

WITH THE COMMUNICATION with Stromm on hold, Pavlovich took the opportunity to gather his composure and assess the bridge crew. Given that they were all Malkovich's people, none of them were familiar to him.

There was an understandable tension among them, but he had been involved in far too many combat situations over his long career, and something didn't feel right. He knew what the mood should be during a standoff like this, and the current reading he got from them was different.

Something else was going on. He felt like that person who walks into a room full of strangers only to realize they all share a secret that he is not party to.

He smiled and shook his head. He had spent too much time in the company of an empath. He was starting to believe he could read people's feelings and moods like she could. That was dangerous territory. Casual, paranoid fantasies were distracting and potentially fatal. He needed to focus on the situation and rely on his hard-earned experience.

Glancing up at the viewer, he said to Gunney, "Is anything happening out there?"

"No changes, sir. Their rail gun doors are open, and they have missile locks on us, but nothing else is going on."

Pavlovich signalled for the communications to be reopened. "Sorry about that, Stromm. We are still having some system glitches. But that doesn't extend to my weapons. How about you surrender your prisoners and we discuss what you want with my ship?"

"You won't open fire as long as I have them as my guests. The way I see it, Yegor, you really don't have any other options. Why don't you do the reasonable thing and just turn *Scimitar* over to me?"

Pavlovich glanced at his cousin, who scowled back at him. "I'm afraid some of us strongly object to that, so the answer is no."

"Tell Malkovich that if he surrenders, I will let his people live."

"Tell him he can stuff that up his ass."

Pavlovich frowned at him and shook his head. "He declines your offer, Stromm."

"I heard his response. You were always a reasonable man, Yegor. I will give you sixty minutes to reconsider before I begin executing people. Perhaps I will start with your XO, Miss Gabriel."

"He has terminated the transmission, Captain," reported the communications officer.

Malkovich growled, "You had better not be seriously considering..."

Pavlovich ignored his comment. "Why an hour, Cousin? Why would he not kill the prisoners immediately?"

"Because he is a sadist who wants to enjoy torturing you as much as your people. He has no intention of letting them live."

"Do you think he suspects we have some kind of plan?"

"How could he? I told you, he's a bastard and he's going to play this out for his own enjoyment."

Pavlovich frowned and called to Gunney, "How long until the remainder of Stromm's fleet arrives?"

"Twenty-one minutes, sir."

Pavlovich considered the information for a moment, and then his eyes widened with realization. "He doesn't think he can beat us with his current firepower. He doesn't have a clue of what we can do. All he knows for certain is that he has two missing warships."

"Then demonstrate it. Now, while he doesn't expect you to."

"My people and your Rangers are over there. I won't do anything until I hear from them."

Malkovich's scowl deepened. "You always were a soft-headed fool." He looked up to the tactical station and nodded briskly. One of his men drew his pistol and pointed it at Gunney's head. Three other members of the bridge crew rose, drawing weapons. They all aimed them at Pavlovich.

The captain considered all the firearms directed at him. "Do you really want to do it this way, Cousin?"

"Do you know how many years I waited for this opportunity? With a single shot from this ship I can take out that dreadnought and end the blight that is Ulysses Stromm. His remaining fleet won't stand a chance and will surrender once they see the power of this vessel. Don't look so shocked, Cousin. You would do the same in my place."

"I really don't think so."

Mindful of the guns, he stood slowly and moved away from the command chair.

Malkovich approached and sat in it while his men held Pavlovich by the arms.

"What now, Cesar? Are you going to throw me out an airlock?"

"Yegor, we are still family. In time you will see that I am right. Your people, if not dead already, will soon be at the hands of that monster. His reign of terror is over. Give me the codes to activate the dark energy weapon."

Pavlovich straightened his back and crossed his arms.

Malkovich sighed. "Please don't do it this way." He signalled his officer, who pressed a pistol muzzle into the back of Gunney's head.

"Don't you do it, Cap'n," said the cyborg. "The Confederation is finished, and my best days are behind me. Let me give my life for something worth dyin' for."

Pavlovich considered Gunney for a moment then returned his attention to Malkovich. "You're not Stromm, Cousin. There is no need for this."

The general frowned then nodded to his man.

A deafening shot rang out.

Gunney's lifeless body fell to the deck, his brains splattered on the bulkhead.

Desperate Deal

"YOU BASTARD! WHY DID you do that?"

"Because you did not take me seriously. Give me the codes."

"Go to hell."

Malkovich leaned forward and flipped a switch on the chair. "Lindsey, did you put it in place?"

"Yes, General, we've isolated the artificial intelligence from the rest of the ship and attached the device to its core. Awaiting your instructions."

Pavlovich frowned. "What have you done?"

"A bomb is strapped to the central processor of your ship's AI. I have less of a problem destroying the machine than shooting a man in cold blood, even one who didn't mind giving his life."

Pavlovich's brain was awhirl. "Cora? Are you still there?"

"I'm here, Cap'n. They isolated me from *Scimitar*'s systems, but I can hear everything. Don't you dare give in to his threats, not while Hayden and the others are still over there."

Malkovich shook his head. "I tried to be reasonable, Cousin, but you leave me no other choice."

He flipped the comm switch at his elbow. "Lindsey; do it."

"*No!*" Pavlovich lunged at him, but the guards restrained him.

Amused, the general said, "Well? What are the codes?"

"I'll kill you before this is over."

"I have no doubt that you want to. We are no longer children, competing for mere bragging rights. I mean to have my victory over Stromm. Give me what I want, and I will spare your life and your AI."

Pavlovich glared at him, his nostrils flaring with each rapid breath. He looked at Gunney's crumpled body on the bloodstained deck, then checked the other faces in the room. Everyone shared the look of grim determination of their leader. He fought to hold back the tide of guilt and grief that threatened to overwhelm him.

"All right, I'll give them to you."

If they were not already dead, Kaine, Stella, and the others soon would be. He was sick to his stomach. They'd entrusted their lives to his care, and because of that ill-considered decision, they would die. But Cora was someone he could still save.

The guards frog-marched him to the tactical alcove. When he arrived at Gunney, he knelt and closed the cyborg's good eye. Recalling a prayer for the dead he'd learned as a child, he recited it in his mind.

"You are stalling, Cousin. Get on with it."

Pavlovich stared at Malkovich through slitted eyelids. Every second he delayed gave Kaine more time to get off the dreadnought. It was all he could do. There was no way to know if any of the boarding party had survived. He couldn't gamble Cora's existence on those who might already be dead. There was no way he could win—have it all. He had to choose what he deemed the better of two evils.

The routine pops and pings from the instrumentation and muted voices were the only sounds on the bridge. Pavlovich rose and shifted uneasily on his feet, hoping with each passing second that Kaine would contact them and declare that he was clear.

Sitting at the station, he examined the interface, desperate for some inspiration—something he could do to save the day.

"I'm not patient, Yegor. Input the codes now, or I will kill your AI and give the test to my code breakers."

Pavlovich's shoulders slumped. His hand slowly rose to the panel, and he entered the authorization. "The weapon is at your command." The words tasted like bile. Hands pulled him to his feet, and one of Malkovich's officers took his place.

The general regarded his cousin, as if disappointed in him, and shook his head. "It didn't have to be this way, Yegor." He returned his attention to his tactical officer. "Set the cannon at five percent and fire."

Bolts of dark energy stretched out from *Scimitar* and struck the massive vessel on its bow. The impact site flexed and distended like a trampoline before the nose of the dreadnought exploded in a burst of light and flame. When the flare died down, ten percent of the ship was in ruins, but the remainder appeared untouched.

Flares sprouted along the flank of Stromm's vessel.

"They've launched missiles!"

"Brace for impact," ordered Malkovich. Seconds later, three nuclear warheads impacted in rapid succession on *Scimitar*'s armoured hull. Everyone not strapped in at their station was thrown to the deck.

Pavlovich picked himself from the floor and fearfully checked the condition of the bridge.

Alarms blared, and the crew appeared shaken, but aside from a bruise on his hip from the fall, he could detect no damage.

"Tactical, return fire," shouted Malkovich. "Increase power output to one hundred percent."

"General, the EMP of the incoming missiles discharged the emitters. The weapon is offline until the capacitor relays recharge."

"How long?"

"One or two minutes, I think."

"Damn it! Let them have a rail gun salvo. Target their gun ports."

Moments later, the deck plates rumbled as *Scimitar*'s replenished rail guns released their ordnance at Stromm's vessel.

Explosions bloomed on the dreadnought's hull. Despite the destructive payload unleashed by *Scimitar*, only fifteen percent of the monstrous ship's hull showed any degree of damage after the barrage. Pavlovich began to doubt that even his Glenatat enhancements had a chance against the planet-killer.

"Tactical, where is my cannon?"

"We have thirty percent, sir."

"That will have to do. Let 'em have it."

Pavlovich ground his teeth. That amount of energy should be overkill. He'd expected their original burst to finish Stromm, but the ship had surprised him with its capacity to take a punch.

After a brief interval, the new gunnery officer announced that the cannon was ready.

"Target Stromm's vessel, midship, and fire."

Moments later, the lights dimmed as the weapon drew power. Pavlovich turned to the holographic viewer to watch events unfold.

The middle of the massive vessel rippled, like a pond reflection marred by a stone cast into it. The distortion collapsed inward, then exploded out from the impact site, sending a tidal wave of destruction along the structure of the ship. The mighty vessel seemed to tear itself apart in the wake of the passing energy. It was as if a giant pair of hands had ripped it in two and set each half aflame. Countless explosions erupted from within, rending it into pieces. After thirty seconds, nothing remained but a dispersing cloud of fragments.

A cheer went up from the crew. Though Pavlovich was relieved to survive the battle, the idea of his cousin having access to such destructive power gave him no cause to join in the celebration.

Beaming with renewed confidence, Malkovich called his people back to the present. "When the weapon is recharged, target all of Stromm's fleet and program a firing solution to take them all out."

"Cousin, you won your war," said Pavlovich. "Allow them to surrender to you."

"What, and give them an opportunity to bide their time before they challenge me again? I can't permit that. I intend to make a definitive statement here and now to dissuade any who think to oppose me when we take this power to the rest of the empire."

Moments later, the lights on the bridge flickered, as if someone played with the switch. One by one, each ship in Stromm's armada met a similar fate as the dreadnought.

Pavlovich didn't attempt to conceal his disgust at the orgy of destruction. "Your point is made! You don't need to destroy all of the ships."

"They made their choices when they sided with the tyrant. Now, payment is due for the innocent lives they have taken."

Helpless, Pavlovich watched as ship after ship rippled then burst apart like soap bubbles, until none remained.

"I'm not sure who the actual tyrant is."

Malkovich sneered. "I'm afraid you must bear your share of responsibility for this, Yegor. If you had chosen to live up to your responsibility—sacrificed yourself, perhaps we might not have been able to crack your encryption. But I knew you were weak; you haven't changed since we were children. I don't know why I'm disappointed in you; I suppose I expected decades in the wilderness to toughen you up. I'm almost sorry I was wrong."

"If you call compassion weakness..."

Malkovich laughed coarsely. "It doesn't matter. Stromm is dead, and his tyranny is over. Now we can rebuild everything." He focused intently on Pavlovich. "There is only one last thing to accomplish. Give me the cynosure, and I will let you and your AI girlfriend live. Perhaps I will have my scientists find a way to replicate the process you used to turn her into a machine. You can join her in her virtual world, permanently. Maybe, for the first time in your life, you could be happy, Cousin."

"You murdered thousands with this ship. There is no way in hell I will enable you."

"Then I will return us to Pictor Prime and have it disassembled. Every component will be examined and dissected. It may take years, but I will find it. You, however, and your girlfriend, will not survive to see it happen."

He indicated Pavlovich to the armed soldier who had shot Gunney. The man drew his pistol.

"*Stop!* I'll help you," said a voice over the speaker.

"Cora, no!"

"Shut up, Cap'n! I'm saving your life."

He was speechless. She had never spoken to him like that.

"I will tell you exactly where the part you are looking for is hidden, but I have terms."

Amused, Malkovich said, "What are they?"

"You allow me to transfer into a synth body and give us a ship. You let us go our own way."

"And you won't do anything to sabotage *Scimitar* before you leave? That is hard to believe."

"Your team can do a complete review of all the systems. I'll even teach them how to use the FTL drive."

"Cora, please don't..."

"Why are you doing this?" asked Malkovich.

"Because you murdered everyone else I've ever loved. If I can save my captain, I don't care much what happens in the rest of the universe."

He smiled at Pavlovich. "I will admit, Cousin, your ability to command such loyalty is inspirational."

"Do we have a deal?" asked Cora.

Malkovich stroked his chin in thought. "Yes, we do."

Try Not to Kill Everyone

"DID YOU SEE THAT?" said Stella.

Hayden shook his head as he studied the screen. "That could have been us."

"Pavlovich cut that too close."

"I'm still locked out of *Scimitar*," said Cora from the pilot station. "They had no way to know we are alive or our whereabouts."

Stella returned her gaze to the cloud of drifting debris that now occupied where the dreadnought had been. "Why did he fire if he didn't know we were clear?"

"He wouldn't have," said Hayden as he continued to study the screen. Ship after ship of Stromm's armada distorted like in a carnival mirror before being consumed by a wave of dark energy. "Something must have gone terribly wrong aboard *Scimitar*."

"You don't think Pavlovich is in charge anymore?" asked Stella.

"He'd better not be, or I'll kill him for sure this time."

"You believe Malkovich has seized control?" said Cora. "That would explain a great deal."

"Shhh," hissed Hayden, glancing back at the survivors. "Not so loud."

"What are we going to do?" she asked, hushed.

Kaine checked again if anyone had overheard them. Seeing no reaction from anyone, he motioned for Cora and Stella to move closer.

"Our transponder is still inactive, and the ship is in stealth mode. *Scimitar* can't track us."

"What are you proposing?" asked Stella.

"We can redock with her without being noticed. Cora, can you deactivate the sensors on the airlock like you did on the dreadnought?"

"Yes, but if there has been a mutiny, what can the two of us do?"

"Three," said Stella, frowning.

Hayden gently held her shoulders and searched her eyes. "You're wounded and half starved, just like the others. None of you is in condition to help."

"If you get aboard, what then? You two can't take on all of Malkovich's men alone. You need me."

He raised an eyebrow. "Will your help take the form of what happened back there on Stromm's ship?"

She blanched. "That was...impulsive—reactive. Nobody will get hurt this time."

"We've seen the result of you using your ability in that way. You can't control it, and I know the price you pay when you push your gift..."

"It's not a gift," she said, "but I'm prepared to use it again if I have to protect you."

He studied the earnestness in her eyes. If he had learned anything about himself, he understood that he had no right to decide anything for her. "We will try not to let it come to that." He turned to Cora. "We need to know the situation on *Scimitar*. Then we can come up with a plan."

"We have a problem finding that out. They have somehow isolated my partition's access to ship's functions. I'm totally blind from here."

"Is there anything you can do?" asked Stella.

"There are back doors in place. If I can reach a service node aboard *Scimitar*, I can get into the system and regain control, unless they modified all the security codes."

Hayden drew and checked his sidearm. "I'll cover you as best as I can. How close is it to the airlock?"

"Ten metres down the corridor."

"I can help," said Stella. "I can still sense people's emotions. I can warn you if someone is near; if they suspect we are there."

"Can you do it from inside this ship?"

Annoyed, she said, "I can read people, but I have no way to tell you if I'm stuck in here. If I use a comm link, they might pick it up."

"She has a point, Hayden."

He looked back at the surviving crew, huddled beneath blankets, blank stares on their faces. Even wounded, Stella was in better shape than any of them. He marvelled at her strength and immediately pushed from his mind any of the imagined horrors Stromm might have visited upon her. There would be plenty of time to deal with that later, he hoped.

"I'm betting that they won't pay attention to the docking ports if they think we died aboard Stromm's ship," he said. He paused to consider the situation and the few options available to them.

Seeing no alternative, he sighed and said, "All right, you should come with us." He handed her his pistol. "Use this before you turn to your ability. We don't want to kill everyone who has a LINK..."

She snatched the gun from him and checked its settings. "I know what I'm capable of. I told Pavlovich I would never use it to help him." She looked into his eyes. "But I will not hesitate if it will save you."

"We will be docking in five minutes," said Cora.

Hayden enfolded Stella in his arms, and they clung tightly to each other. One way or another, everything would change for them once they docked with *Scimitar*. He had a difficult time imagining any way things could end well.

Show Me

"KEEP MOVING," SAID Malkovich, brandishing his pistol.

"Is that thing really necessary, Cousin?" Pavlovich looked past him at the armed soldiers who followed them. "Ten Rangers can surely protect you?"

"Shut up. We're almost there."

He ground his teeth and turned to continue walking. "What assurances do I have that you will honour our deal?"

"You have none. But you don't have any choice if you want your girlfriend to live."

"She isn't my—she's young enough to be my—"

"A niece? Just like the multitude of nieces Thomas used to parade around at functions back on Earth. I never understood the motivation for such euphemism. If a woman is a lover, one should have the balls to say so, don't you agree?"

"What happened to you? You were never like this when we grew up together."

"Maybe I was but didn't realize it about myself. It took Stromm murdering my family, friends, colleagues, men and women who entrusted me with their lives. Events like that have a way of bringing out our true self."

"Cesar, it was a tragedy, but you aren't the only one whose life was ruined by him."

"This has nothing to do with the dead. They are gone. The empire is gone. All that remains is ashes and ruin. You saw what unfolded here at Pictor. Can you imagine any scenario better than this taking place anywhere in the Confederation? Something has to be done."

"What you seek to do with the cynosure won't bring any of them back. It will only cost millions more lives in the end."

"People die every day. I am looking at the survival of the human species. Isolated as we now are, thanks to Kaine, we will wipe ourselves out. Every world is a prison supplied with modern weapons. Nobody will survive unless we reunite under a common banner. Humanity needs to expand; we need an outlet for our innate aggression and our innovative ability to kill each other. Only access to the technology the cynosure promises will save us. There is no other way."

"It's possible there is."

"You were always the idealist, letting your self-righteousness shut you out of opportunity. Your folly exiled you to the farthest reaches of the empire, and for what? So you could thumb your nose at Thomas, Stromm, and the others? Tell me, exactly how did that work out for you?"

"At least I know who I am. I can fall asleep at night."

"I sleep just fine. Keep moving, we're almost there."

They continued in silence until they reached their goal. Standing outside of the entrance to the rail gun bay, Pavlovich hesitated.

"This is one of the last places I would have looked," said Malkovich. "If this is some kind of trick—"

"This place is a coincidence. If this is where Cora says the thing is, then it's here."

"The truth will come out soon enough." The general addressed the armed men behind them. "Keep a sharp eye. I don't exactly trust that the captain has our best interest at heart."

"I have no tricks up my sleeve. Even I am not stupid enough to think the same trick will work a second time."

Malkovich nodded to the door, and Pavlovich entered the access code to unlock and open it. He led the entourage into the bay, admitting a low whistle. "I haven't been in here since it was refurbished. You guys did a nice job."

A gun pressed into his back. "Quit stalling. Turn on the comm so your girlfriend can tell us where it's hidden."

Pavlovich went to the control panel and was confused by what he saw.

"What's the problem, Yegor?"

Before he could answer, the door they had entered through slammed shut with a loud metallic bang.

Startled, everyone turned to see what had happened. As they did so, Pavlovich seized Malkovich's wrist and attempted to wrestle the pistol from his hand.

Out of the corner of his eye, he saw one of the Rangers notice their struggle. The man raised his weapon.

"Now would be a good time!" yelled Pavlovich.

A second later, the Ranger went down in a spray of blood.

Then all hell broke loose.

KAINE WASTED NO ADDITIONAL time selecting a second target. He still held the element of surprise for a few more seconds before Malkovich's men realized what was happening.

One more fell to Hayden's fire. The remaining Rangers scattered about the bay, seeking whatever shelter they could, most of them ending up under the acceleration ramp structure.

He spoke into his helmet mic. "Cora! Stella! Keep them pinned. I'm going to help the captain."

Pavlovich and Malkovich struggled in a wrestling match. The dropped pistol lay on the deck, kicked about by scuffing feet. They were matched, and it was apparent to Hayden that they were old sparring partners, each responding to the other's moves from long familiarity.

Yet there was an obvious difference in their objectives. Pavlovich sought to subdue with different holds, countered by his experienced opponent. Malkovich's efforts had more lethal intent. Multiple deep scratches marred Pavlovich's face. The two were engaged in a confrontation that the captain did not seem committed to win at the required price.

Their desperate struggle kicked the fallen pistol across the floor and out of reach. Seeing his opportunity, Hayden sprang toward the struggling men, determined to break up the conflict by knocking them both off their feet.

Searing pain exploded in his shoulder as a bullet tore through it.

He dropped and rolled for the nearest cover beneath a control console as multiple projectiles ricocheted around him.

A panicked search found the two men still locked in mortal combat. The only reason Pavlovich hadn't been gunned down by one of the Rangers was that the constantly moving pair offered no clear target. That would not last for long.

He shouted into his mic, "I need some covering fire!"

"We have most of them pinned down, but one or two have moved, and I can't see them," responded Cora.

Hayden searched for the locations where the women were hidden. He spotted a Ranger moving in the shadows, creeping up on their position.

"Stella, to your left!"

Too late, she turned to see the soldier who stalked her. One quick burst from his weapon, and she dropped to the floor.

"*No!*" He rose to his knees, prompting another spray of fire in his direction. Bullets whizzed about him, two striking home in his hip and elbow. His gun went one way while he dove back to his shelter.

"Hayden!" called Cora. "Are you okay?"

Pushing the pain down, he replied, "Never mind me. Stella's been hit!"

"I can't get to her. The Rangers are no longer pinned, they're com—"

Weapons fire erupted near Cora's position. He turned in time to watch her being riddled with bullets from multiple directions, each shot jerking her body in a macabre death dance.

Catching himself, he bit down on his tongue to avoid giving away his location.

"Kaine!"

He followed the voice to find Malkovich, breathing hard and pointing his recovered pistol at the kneeling Pavlovich. Blood trailed down his captain's face from scratches, and one of his arms hung limp and useless at his side, while the other was weakly raised in surrender.

"Stand down if you want your captain to live."

He cast his gaze about, searching for his dropped weapon, but it was nowhere in sight. The surviving Rangers emerged from their cover locations; guns directed at him. All he could see of Stella was her limp hand peeking out from behind a strut support. Two short paces away from her, Cora's android body lay motionless.

Gulping air to control his grief, he called out. "I surrender. Don't shoot."

Pulling off his helmet, he let it fall to the floor. Raising his remaining good arm over his head, he struggled to stand. He wanted to die with some dignity but was forced to appear weak by leaning against the console for support.

"I'll give you an 'A' for effort, Kaine. I had no idea you survived the destruction of the dreadnought. I'm not sure how you managed to slip away from my Rangers to set up this ambush, but it was well played."

"So now what happens?"

"Now? I think it should be obvious."

At a nod from him, Malkovich's troops approached to take him into custody.

"Don't worry about me, Kaine," said Pavlovich. "This isn't the worst situation you've put me in." He quickly glanced at the control panel Hayden leaned against.

Confused, Hayden weighed the captain's odd words for a moment before his meaning dawned on him.

Shifting his position, his injured arm draped across the interface. Using his body to shield his actions, he felt out the keypad and entered a sequence from memory.

He caught Pavlovich's eyes with his own and nodded. Kaine pressed the final number in the sequence and emptied his lungs.

A klaxon screamed, and red lights set into the ceiling flashed in time with it. Confused, Malkovich and his men looked about for the cause of the alert. Then, with no further warning, the outer rail gun doors slid open. The air in the chamber raced with hurricane force to escape into space.

Hayden leaned over and gripped the console, hoping his good arm had the required strength.

The Rangers were blown off their feet by the decompression wind. One by one, their screams of terror were cut short as they were pushed out into the void.

Hayden searched for Pavlovich.

The captain lay on the deck, one hand gripping a strut. Malkovich clung to his leg and threatened to pull him loose. Appearing like he wanted to save his foe, Pavlovich tried to reach down to help his cousin.

Malkovich's grasp slipped. With a faint scream in the thinning air, he too was dragged across the deck and flung out into the icy grip of space.

Eardrums burst and bleeding, lungs burning and vision fading, Hayden pulled himself up the console. His hands freezing, he located the button to close the doors and repressurize the bay.

As the sound of the pumps grew loud enough to overcome the ringing in his ears, he remembered Stella and Cora. Through bleary eyes, he looked for them, praying they had not been blown out with the others.

Not far from where they fell, he saw them. Cora's android arms were wrapped around Stella's legs, and her own feet were wedged between two exposed conduit pipes.

His joy at the sight of them was soon replaced by the recollection of them being shot. Hayden dropped from the panel and limped to the women.

Reaching Stella first, he searched for any sign that she lived. When he discovered her pulse, he hugged her briefly before checking on Cora.

"I'm still here, Lieutenant," she said weakly. "This synth is toast, but I'll be fine once I upload back to the ship."

Tears in his eyes, he hugged the android and whispered his thanks.

A loud groan came from Pavlovich. Hayden looked back to see him on his back, arms and legs outstretched, one hand still gripping the strut that saved his life.

"I mean it this time, Kaine. I never want to do that again."

Goodbye

IN SILENCE, HAYDEN and Stella, their wounds treated, surveyed the bodies arrayed before them. Arranged in tidy rows, each draped with a UEF flag, were sixteen men and women who had died during the previous twenty hours.

The remains of hundreds of others still floated, unretrievable, amid the drifting debris of the massacre.

Pavlovich kneeled over Gunney. Hayden was surprised at how peaceful the old cyborg appeared in death. It was as if the warrior had finally found a home for himself in its embrace.

Next to him lay Cesar Malkovich. Hayden had taken the initiative to recover all the bodies he could locate with his small ship. The generals had been among the first he sought out. He felt it was the least he could do for Pavlovich.

The captain had betrayed no outward sign of regret, but Hayden knew from Stella how much the man was affected by the loss of so many, including his cousin.

Standing at respectful attention were the remains of *Scimitar*'s crew and Malkovich's rebels.

With the death of Malkovich, the soldiers under his command had no leader. The general had, for some unfathomable reason, made no provision for his passing. All his lieutenants had been on the ships of his destroyed fleet. Hayden wasn't sure if the oversight was due to arrogance on Malkovich's part or a delusion that *Scimitar* would make him invincible.

His highest-ranking officer still alive had immediately ordered her troops to surrender. Perhaps she'd heard reports of what Stella did aboard the dreadnought, or maybe she'd had enough of war and wished to wash her hands of a bloody conflict that had lasted for years.

Pavlovich moved from Gunney's body to that of his cousin. Hayden thought he saw a slight smile peek out from beneath the bushy beard, even as tears ran unchecked down his cheek. He allowed the captain a moment to grieve in private and say his final goodbyes. Then he moved closer and placed a supportive hand on the big man's shoulder.

"He hated losing," said Pavlovich. "Even when we were children, he would sulk for days after I gave him a beating."

"You fought often?"

He looked up, eyes glistening. "Most of the time we were fast friends, getting into mischief together. It wasn't until we got older that we began to butt heads. I eventually stopped going to visit him, because every time I did it ended in a disagreement or an all-out donnybrook."

"Do you know what changed between you?"

Pavlovich let out a mirthless chuckle. "I did; I joined the academy, and that immediately put pressure on him to keep up. The experience was harder on him than me. He watched me advance and outpace him at everything. I really wanted it, while he was there to prove he was still my equal. He resented me for that."

He placed a fatherly hand on Hayden's shoulder. "Everyone has regrets and wants to make amends for past failings. When we came here, I wanted to reconcile with Cesar."

He sighed and took another lingering look at Malkovich's corpse before he led Hayden back to where Stella and the rest of the crew waited.

After the funeral rites were performed and the bodies committed to space, Pavlovich invited Hayden and Stella to join him in the conference room with Cora.

He placed an unopened bottle of single malt whisky on the table and pushed it toward Kaine.

Surprised, Hayden looked to Stella before, embarrassed, he smiled and slid it back to the captain.

Pavlovich grunted. "It looks like I'm commanding a ship full of teetotallers."

He pulled the cork and poured himself a healthy portion. After savouring the amber fluid, he looked back up at the others, and his expression softened. "Of course, I am assuming you all wish to stay."

"What happens next, if we do?" asked Stella. "Do you still intend to make your fortune with the FTL? If you do, I am out."

Hayden smiled at her. "I'm afraid I'm with her."

She returned his smile and squeezed his hand.

"Hmph. How about you, Cora?"

"I'm undecided, sir. I'm part of *Scimitar*, and I don't think that can ever change, but..."

"But you enjoyed having a body again and are thinking you might be able to go with Kaine and Stella. Am I right?"

"I'm sorry, but yes."

He nodded and leaned forward to put down his empty glass. "I'm not surprised. To answer you, Stella, I no longer have any commercial plans for the FTL tech. Kaine was right."

"I was? What about?"

"You asked a question along the lines of: What if the rest of the empire has degenerated into something like this system...or worse? I've been thinking a lot about that."

"And what have you concluded?" asked Stella.

The captain smiled as he shifted in his chair. He extracted something from his back pocket and put it on the table.

"What's that?" asked Hayden as he inspected the object.

"Cora?" said Pavlovich.

"It appears to be the missing component from the cynosure device, if your description of it to me was accurate."

"That it is."

Stella picked it up. "Did you always know where it was hidden?"

Pavlovich poured himself another drink. "No, I never had a clue of where to look."

"Then where did you find it?" asked Hayden.

"I found it inside my command chair on the bridge."

"What the hell made you think to look there?"

"Well, the idea came to me when I was on Kovacs's ship. I remembered joking that one of the few remaining parts of *Scimitar* that was factory-installed is my chair. While everything was being put back together after our encounter with Kovacs, I disassembled it and found this."

"You had it all this time and didn't say anything?"

He shrugged.

"So now what?" said Stella. "Do you intend to recover the device and complete it? Now, instead of growing obscenely wealthy, you've changed your mind and want to rule over everything?"

Pavlovich frowned. "That was Cesar's plan, not mine."

Hayden studied the captain's expression. There was something mischievous about it. He turned to Stella and raised a questioning eyebrow.

"Oh, he's definitely enjoying this," she said.

Pavlovich grinned and placed his meaty palms on the table. "Okay, full disclosure time. Let me make my pitch before you all decide I'm a power-hungry megalomaniac like everyone else we've come across. Agreed?"

Both Hayden and Stella nodded.

"Cora, how about you?"

"I'm not going anywhere just yet, Cap'n."

"Good." He downed the remains of his second drink. "I think we are all in agreement that the Malliac are the most significant threat the human race has ever faced, particularly since we are now without any form of FTL capability?"

"We sent our messengers to Earth a decade ago," said Stella. "They've had time to prepare. Look at some of the innovative technology that was developed here."

Hayden's cheeks warmed as his anger rose. "This system was warned. Instead of uniting and preparing for invasion, they chose to play king of the hill."

"I agree with Kaine. I think what we've encountered here is likely replaying itself across the remnant of the Confederacy. While our people have been fighting like starving dogs over scraps, the Malliac have advanced. Who knows how many of our outer colonies they have already overrun?"

"We four in this room have the unique perspective of having faced them," said Cora. "We know first-hand how formidable they are and how vulnerable humanity is to them, but to everyone else, they are just a story."

Pavlovich nodded. "And as time passes without incident or reminder, the sense of danger fades, and other, more immediate concerns take priority."

"What are you proposing?" said Hayden.

"If our species is to be saved, what's left of the empire is not capable of doing it. The cynosure must be located, and who or whatever it points at will have the means to defend humanity. That is our only shot, and we are the only ones who can make it happen."

"Us?" said Stella. "In case you didn't notice, this ship lacks a full crew. I have serious doubts that most of those remaining will have much stomach for more adventures under your command. I'm not sure I do."

"Besides," said Cora, "there is still one other missing component before the cynosure can be accessed."

"How about you, Kaine? Do you agree with the ladies?"

Hayden looked to Stella, feeling himself blush. "I'd like to hear the plan, although they raise some important impediments."

Pavlovich grinned, seeming satisfied. "Kovacs told me where the last component is. Now that we have refined erganium, it is within easy reach. As far as the crew," he shrugged, "I threw out some feelers among Cesar's people, and I believe some can be persuaded to join in a fight for something more significant than revenge."

He turned to face Hayden directly, a twinkle in his eye. "Of course, the chances of that would increase dramatically if the pitch comes from the Hero of Mu Arae."

Hayden pushed back in his chair, shocked. "Me? What are you...?"

"You know, Kaine, for a man raised to be a politician, you know squat about the concept of spin. The people in this room are the only ones who are aware of how things really went down, and your recollection is negatively distorted. With the right presentation, you can end up looking like a damned messiah to everyone else. At least, that's how I described you to the prospective recruits. It's going over very well, by the way."

Hayden shook his head. "You are certifiable."

"But I am not wrong. What do you say, Kaine? Do you want a shot at redeeming yourself?"

The captain offered him the chance he'd dreamed of for years, though not to undo what had happened—he now accepted its necessity. Rather, Pavlovich presented Hayden with the opportunity to change how he perceived himself, perhaps even to redeem his own soul.

Butterflies fluttered in his guts as he looked to Stella. She smiled and nodded, giving him the answer he needed.

"I'm in."

• • • •

Hayden Kaine stood on the bridge of *Scimitar*, watching the striped surface of the gas giant Elgar fade into the distance.

The recruits had integrated well with the remaining old crew, and two weeks of shakedown and training were now complete. The ship was en route to the outer system to make its FTL jump.

Stella sat in her acceleration couch, chatting with one of the new bridge officers.

Hayden glanced to the tactical officer's alcove. He was finally used to seeing it occupied by the young woman who'd been appointed gunnery officer. Over time, he believed he would stop thinking of it as Gunney's spot, though he knew he would never forget the old cyborg.

At the sound of thumping, he turned to watch Pavlovich fiddling with his command chair.

"Is something wrong, Captain?"

"What?" He looked up. "Oh, this damned thing doesn't feel right. And it squeaks when I move."

Hayden grinned. "Maybe we can get one of Cora's new engineering techs to take a look at it, though I'm not sure it is the thing that is squeaking."

"Hardy-har. Make ready to activate the FTL drive, XO."

"Aye-aye, sir."

Hayden took one final look at the receding solar system. He hoped the next one they visited had fared better over the past decade.

One thing he knew for certain was that the Malliac were on their way, and he intended to be there to greet them.

Free book offer

FREE EBOOK OFFER!

As a way of saying thank you for purchasing this novel, I want to offer you a free ebook.

To claim your free story please join my reader list by going to **https://www.prudenauthor.com/Kaine1-free-offer**

About the Author

D.M.(DOUG) PRUDEN WORKED for 35 years in the petroleum industry as a geophysicist. For most of his life he has been plagued with stories banging around inside his head that demanded to be let out into the world. He currently spends his time as an empty nester in Calgary, Alberta, Canada with his long suffering wife of many years. When he isn't writing science fiction stories, he likes to spend his time playing with his grandchildren and working on improving his golf handicap.

Don't miss out!

Visit the website below and you can sign up to receive emails whenever D.M. Pruden publishes a new book. There's no charge and no obligation.

https://books2read.com/r/B-A-MNWD-IALX

Connecting independent readers to independent writers.

Did you love *Kaine's Retribution*? Then you should read *Kaine's Reparation*[1] by D.M. Pruden!

[2]

He only wanted to save humanity...

They are coming and scattered humanity has no defence...

Human civilization is in chaos. With the collapse of the interstellar jump network, the empire has no defence against the approaching Malliac horde.

Hayden Kaine and the crew of the Scimitar discover an alien relic that offers one final hope.

---

1. https://books2read.com/u/3nKrGo

2. https://books2read.com/u/3nKrGo

Faced with a terrible dilemma, they risk everything in a last-ditch effort to prevent the extinction of the human race. But when everything goes horribly wrong, the existence of the universe itself may be the price to pay for meddling with technology beyond their understanding.

Read more at www.prudenauthor.com.

Also by D.M. Pruden

Future Vistas
Future Vistas Vol 1

Mars Ascendant
The Ares Weapon
Mother of Mars
Child of Mars
Legacy of Mars
Mars Ascendant Box Set: Books 1-4

Requiem's Run
Armstrong Station
Phobos Station
Rhea's Vault
Ganymede Station
The Jovian Collective

Shattered Empire

Kaine's Sanction
Kaine's Retribution
Kaine's Reparation
Shattered Empire Omnibus: Books 1-3

Standalone
Throwing Stones

Watch for more at www.prudenauthor.com.